# WISE ONE

# WISE ONE

## ROGER ELWOOD

**MOODY PRESS**
CHICAGO

*To my beloved parents*

# Acknowledgments

Over the past three and a half years, the Lord has brought me in contact with many brothers and sisters in Christ. This has been a tremendous blessing to me, since writing is basically a profession of isolation, one individual alone with a typewriter or a computer or a pen and a pad of paper, if you will.

Fellowship becomes even more blessed after a writer spends months writing a book. It's as though the Lord is saying, "Your batteries need some recharging."

I met Jim Bell and Duncan Jaenicke at the Christian Booksellers Association International Convention in Denver, Colorado, just a single year before *Wise One* was written. I was impressed with their friendliness, their integrity, their dedication to the cause of Christ—two editorial partners who actually couldn't be more different in personality: Jim, a quiet, scholarly sort, someone I liked immediately; Duncan, a gregarious chap with whom I could trade puns and feel very much at ease. I also had occasion to talk with Greg Thornton, manager of Moody Press, and began to feel that the Lord had indeed guided me not only into an editorial relationship but also into a kind of family, and that now I, an only child, had three brothers.

# Introduction

One of the better known biblical anecdotes involving Christ in action, so to speak, managed to escape even the massacring hand of overrated filmmaker Martin Scorcese in *The Last Temptation of Christ*. It was a rare accurate and respectful moment in an otherwise near-blasphemous hodgepodge.

The casting out of the money changers from the Temple.

Christ witnessed what had happened to the once-holy atmosphere of that place of worship.

It had been transformed into one in which carnality held if not center place, then at least a highly influential place in the scheme of things. Here is where we see the scriptural predecessor of today's "buy a blessing" trend, whatever the guise of such heresy.

He was enraged, as could be expected. So He physically overturned the tables of money, chased the greedy entrepreneurs outside, and declared in righteous anger, "My Father's house shall not be made a den of thieves!"

. . . *a den of thieves.*

The sacrifice of livestock in sanctified rites dating back many hundreds of years had been prostituted into a money-making business.

9

A necessity in the then valid form of worship, certain livestock, especially lambs, were raised by their owners specifically to be brought to the Temple as an act of obedience to Almighty God. In that way, the roadblock man's sin nature had erected between man and God could be removed. People who had no such animals could buy them directly outside the Temple—but at a scandalous price. That is what caused Christ's rage.

All of that has changed, of course.

The death of Christ in His bodily form at Calvary ended the need for any other sacrifice to be continued for the rest of mankind's finite history. There is no necessity whatever for any of us to have to pay anything to *purchase* salvation. God did *all* of that in our stead.

*Wise One* deals with this "den of thieves" syndrome in some of its manifestations today, the selling not of lambs, for example, but of the Lamb Himself, the commercialization of salvation, including one of the most alarming deviations of all: the virulent cult of personality.

It is sad indeed when a less than scrupulous TV preacher, speaking about "seed faith," is taken so seriously by his viewing audience that it amounts to their swallowing his every word—hook, line, and sinker—*whether or not he is offering Christ-centered truths or cleverly disguised seduction from the Arch Deceiver.*

We are admonished by Scripture to cast out error wherever and whenever we see it in the church.

Admittedly we may be accused of being judgmental, but then so was our Lord when, in addition to the episode at the Temple, He confronted the theological arrogance of the Pharisees and Sadducees, saying that that they were "like whitewashed tombs which indeed appear beautiful outwardly, but inside are full of dead men's bones and all uncleaness" (Matthew 23:27).

Error, heresy, and the like can be subtle, indeed is most effective when it is precisely that, as subtlety can creep into any church, any denomination, any group step-by-step until those within have lived with error so long they do not necessarily recognize it. Cancer undetected can kill a human body, and so it is with the church today, not just a cancer but rather *cancers*.

*Wise One* was written with this sort of battle in mind, a battle that must involve vigilance, a battle against just merely letting the Lord handle it, which is surely a form of satanic deception in itself, this notion that we, as Christians, can turn everything over to the Lord and then simply step aside.

But there is another battle to which I hope this book alerts its readers: the intentions of the Islamic fundamentalist movement.

Nearly all of the individuals with whom I have spoken about this aspect of *Wise One* have been quite startled about the violent core of the movement. Oh, yes, that's true of a few fanatics perhaps, they say, but surely the average Muslim, especially those being interviewed on television and pleading for tolerance, eschews that sort of thing and is really quite mild-mannered, humble.

Not so.

Any *good* Muslim, any Muslim who reads the *Qur'ān* on a regular basis, who cares about his or her religion, *must* adopt a violent and debased reaction to infidels or face the judgment of Allah as evidenced through the Messenger, the Prophet Muhammad.

You see, the Muslim holy book is very clear in this matter of the treatment of anyone who does not declare himself or herself a true believer of Islam. Unlike the necessity of blood sacrifice contained in the Old Testament, unlike the necessity of Christ's atonement on the cross of calvary, there is no *redemptive* aspect of the Islamic call for the shedding of infidel blood. It is a precept of their faith that is out-and-out a rite of vengeance, nothing more.

Nor can any Muslim successfully deny that this is so. If they read the *Qur'ān*, if they hold the Messenger in an almost-worshipful reverence, if they want to avoid the same fate that would then be visited upon them by their in-that-case more devout Muslim comrades, they cannot avoid doing what has been commanded.

11

This central command is crucial to one of the more important dimensions of the plot of *Wise One*, so I won't tell you what it is. When you come upon it within the following pages, you will indeed see why "being too hard on the Muslims" is far less likely than the tendency to be too *easy* on them in this age of lack of convictions often masquerading as humanistic tolerance both within and outside the Body of Christ.

# Prologue

The old man was feeling somewhat ill.

He did not become so very often, in spite of his age, since his spartan lifestyle produced such vigorous good health that it was impossible for anyone inclined toward casual guessing games to determine just how old he was, his stamina masking the number of his years.

Yet when he did come down with something that he could not treat on his own, he would reluctantly leave the mountains and enter the small village not far away, and seek help from a friendly doctor, but stay no more than necessary, and then return to his fortress-like haven.

Even so small a parcel of civilization as was found in that Middle Eastern vicinity made him uncomfortable. He preferred the solitude of his mountains, where his companions were birds and bears and other such creatures, none of them asking more of him than he was willing to give, which was quite contrary to the traits he had detected in so many human beings over the years.

But on a certain day in the final decade of that final century of mankind, he lingered a bit with his friend the doctor, after consuming the medicine that was prescribed, and then just before leaving, he spoke of a sudden impulse, or so it seemed—though with utter gentleness—about the beating of angel wings.

The doctor scratched his head, surprised both by the duration of the old man's visit and how he had chosen to end it, words that were strange indeed but which filled the room around them with a sense of the greatest possible joy.

The doctor, hardly young himself, but his mind filled with the most exhilarating images, suddenly started dancing, forgetting his temporary puzzlement and submitting to the exaltation that seemed to be so transcendent.

The old man from the mountains took out a hand-tooled piccolo from one pocket in his rough-hewn animal-skin garb and starting playing a tune, and a lively ditty it was.

In a matter of minutes, many citizens from that town heard the sounds coming from the doctor's place of business and decided to investigate. They found the doctor and the old mountain man dancing as though they were young and lithe.

"Come, look," the word spread as a collective call, people from all over that village gathering in front.

And then the men, the doctor and the one from the mountains, emerged outside finally, and both were laughing.

"What is going on?" asked the village's constable, thinking them both perhaps to be intoxicated.

"My friend here has been singing about angels," replied the doctor in an effervescent manner.

"And what about angels?" the old constable, a gruff and burly individual who would retire a few years later, asked.

"They will protect us," the doctor told him. "They will protect us from various evils."

"To which particular evils do you refer?" the other inquired. "There are a great many today in this world of ours. I see them even in this village, though nothing here could possibly approach what I have heard about elsewhere in the land, and abroad, ah, yes, in the so-called Christian land of America."

The rest of the villagers present shouted their own resolute agreement to that statement.

They all turned to the old mountain man, who had stood without speaking while others rambled on. For some moments he continued to be silent. Many of those present started murmuring, restlessness setting in, none of them interested in wasting any more time.

Abruptly the air seemed to turn colder.

"The temperature drops," someone shouted. "Let's forget about this nonsense and go on our separate ways."

The old man reacted then, snorting with contempt.

"You want everything on the spot," he said, with a sneer in his voice, "and yet you claim to be unlike so many other villages and towns and cities in this world at present, untainted by many of the excesses of modern civilization."

"That is true," the doctor said, "that is very true. But what is wrong with such a claim?"

The mountain man fell silent again.

Even the doctor lost patience this time, though.

"You act as though you are toying with us," he said. "Why do you treat the entire village in this manner?"

His expression grew stern.

"Please stop, mountain man. Please accord us the respect that we surely deserve."

The old man nodded as he finally spoke, "Evil itself."

"Yes—," the doctor said expectantly.

"Evil itself, not evils, as you said a moment ago."

"That sounds like idle talk, sir," the constable interjected. "I don't wish to be offensive, but you will have to explain yourself."

The old man's face grew quite serious then, a deep frown on his forehead. He said nothing for yet another moment but when he did, there was no mistaking the words or their meaning.

"Satan himself will try to destroy this village," he told not just the constable but the rest as well, speaking as though to every man, woman, and child. "He will attack most severely. The angels will protect you, since they will be sent by God Himself, but this will happen only if you rededicate yourselves to the Savior."

A shout of indignation arose from the crowd.

"How dare you mock us in this manner?" various ones shouted. "We have been Christians for a very long time, for decades in fact, and often in the face of persecution from the Muslims."

And it was the constable who said, "How can you expect us to heed your words when you sneak down from the mountains and stand there in judgment over the hundreds of us, one man we see so rarely and who smells like a billy goat?"

The old man put his piccolo back in a side pocket of the sheepskin jacket he wore, sighed with great weariness, and then pushed past everyone, as he headed toward his mountain home.

"Wait!"

One voice shouted after him.

He turned and saw the doctor running toward him.

"I will follow you, sir," he said emphatically. "I believe the message you have given us."

"Then let it be now," the old man said simply.

"Now?" the other hesitated. "Not tomorrow, sir? There is much to prepare, as you must surely know, despite your time alone in those distant mountains. You ask me to abandon everything for the unknown future you seem to be offering —and yet I do not have time to settle my affairs, to get my wife and family ready?"

"It is a test," the old man added.

"But I believe in Christ as my Savior."

"Yet can you say that He is your Lord as well?"

"Yes, I surely can. They were right when they spoke of the history of our dedication, even in the toughest times that have occurred."

"But the best of times, my friend?" the old one asked.

The doctor scratched his head.

"You speak in riddles," he replied. "You mask your meaning and I fail to understand what—"

The old one smiled.

"You love Christ with all your mind, all your heart, yea, the totality of your being?"

"I do," said the doctor.

"Then give your life into His promised care and trust Him with this very moment."

"I trust Him, yes, but you I hardly know."

16

The doctor's expression darkened, and a noticeable chill touched his spine.

"Who *are* you?" he asked, a sharp edge to the tone of his voice. "With all of your talk of angels, and your pleasant music, you try to lull us into believing that you are some kind of—."

The doctor's eyes widened.

"*Look!*" he shouted. "Look at the sky!"

The earlier sudden chill had deepened, now joined by clouds that had appeared, it seemed, out of nowhere, so thick, so dark that, in just a short while, they formed a layer through which the sun could not penetrate even though it was then the middle of that afternoon.

In the distance could be heard thunder loud enough that it seemed the ground was being convulsed by an earthquake.

"He is a devil," one villager cried. "He has come from the pit of hell to delude and seduce us!"

None disagreed. All shouted their affirmation, even the kindly doctor, who backed away from the mountain man.

"But I have foretold victory," the mountain man reminded them. "Why do you speak and act as though you have only defeat ahead of you? If Christ be for you, if angels guard your path, pray tell whatever is there to fear?"

"Your true face has appeared in front of us," someone said with a deep and cold tone. "And we shall turn from it as Scripture has admonished us to do."

"If that be so, and if I come from Lucifer, the evil lord of darkness, instead of blessed Jesus, the Prince of Peace, why must you flee my presence? Do not the Scriptures say that you should stand firm and resist Satan, and he will flee from you—not as you are doing now, which is the opposite course of action?"

None listened.

They immediately felt threatened, rather than reassured, and all of the people who had come out quickly retreated.

The old man from the mountains watched them go, his heart burning with great sorrow.

"So foolish," he whispered, "so very foolish."

Most of those who were able to do so almost ran to their respective homes, though they did their best to appear to be only walking, with no sense of gathering panic, but it was, of course, a foolish charade, and an unsuccessful one at that.

Ultimately, all locked their doors, only to shiver in fear at what might be trying to get inside and do them harm. Many prayed, but some did not, sitting instead with more physical manifestations of protection, such as guns or knives or other weapons, ready to do battle.

None of this was necessary. But they had fallen prey to the weaknesses of their sin nature, allowing their fears to gain control even of their faith. They were reacting in the only way they knew how, reacting according to the circumstances of the moment, without comprehending any of what the old mountain man had offered, the future he prophesied, not that of an imminent tomorrow, nor next week, not the following month nor the year after that one, but one much further ahead in time, beyond a decade, to be sure.

"Yet angels *shall* protect you," the mountain man whispered in melancholy repetition to the emptiness around him, adding ever so slowly words that were spoken with great solemnity, "if only you will let them."

*He saw then events still future as their images rose up clearly in that special and wondrous mind of his, blessed and cursed as it was with its singular gift, manifested in that isolated Middle Eastern village but, also, in other times, other places, over a long and strange odyssey that threatened more than once to wear him out before his mission was completed.*

*What he wanted to prepare them for, only to be rejected by the villagers, was the tragedy that would eventually befall the whole region, if the people allowed themselves to—*

"So many never listen," he said in frustration. "So many seem to throw my words of warning away as though these are nothing more than useless garbage. *Why will you not pay heed, my brothers and sisters?*"

The old one pulled his coat a bit more tightly around himself, then turned, with regret, and walked out of the village, back toward his mountain home where even the beasts did not fear him, accepting him for what he was.

In the meantime, the storm ended without ever having begun. The clouds dissipated, the air warmed, and it seemed that the stranger would never again come to their village.

For a long time the villagers chattered on about the meaning of it all, but eventually they became bored and relegated the old man and his prophesy to some back and dusty corner of occasional recollection, consequently deciding among themselves to disregard the cryptic ruminations delivered to them with such prudence, and simply go about their lives, they thought, as always had been so for them in the remote place in which they had lived for generations—but this was not to be, as it turned out, this was not to be at all.

*If anyone teaches otherwise and does not consent to wholesome words, . . . he is proud, knowing nothing, but is obsessed with disputes and arguments over words, . . . useless wranglings of men of corrupt minds and destitute of the truth, who suppose that godliness is a means of gain. From such withdraw yourself. But godliness with contentment is great gain. For we brought nothing into this world, and it is certain we can carry nothing out. And having food and clothing, with these we shall be content. But those who desire to be rich fall into temptation and a snare, and into many foolish and harmful lusts which drown men in destruction and perdition.*

1 Timothy 6:5-9

# =1=

$\mathbf{N}$ews *of what had happened in a certain Middle Eastern lo-cale, in an area long known for its lack of oil, unlike its prosperous neighbors who had a surfeit of this invaluable commodity, reached the worldwide media, and was played up in quite a major way.*

*Skepticism, though, was quite obvious.*

*"Oil is found everywhere else in that part of the globe," intoned one sardonic TV commentator. "Why not there? So what's the big deal? I can't imagine why my colleagues are making so much of this. It's not even a huge find, in fact, but rather small by comparison."*

*That newsman missed the point because he conveniently left out the circumstances. For anyone paying attention, though, and willing to put aside their normal view of reality, there was a story-within-a-story that certainly did prove to be just as interesting . . .*

Constable Fahid Bashir looked out the window at the people walking by his office, thinking how greatly the passage of just a year or so was affecting the whole lot of them.

All it took was a few strangers with glorified shovels.

Bashir sighed audibly, and with regret.

*We weren't poor as such, oh, perhaps we were precisely that by European or American or other standards,* he thought, then paused, analyzing that statement, and realizing its fundamental dishonesty.

*Nonsense! We also didn't have the immense wealth enjoyed by others in the Middle East. We seemed to have been left behind in so many ways. If we weren't poor in the sense of being beggars, then we were so close to it that the differences were of little consequence. Oh, yes, we had never starved, but that was about it. We were caught between two wealthy camps, with no one to take us into one or the other.*

He had traveled to at least two other regions where the circumstances were far more severe, two pockets of abysmal poverty, one a refugee camp near Amman, Jordan, the second a bleak institution for the insane in a certain so-called former Iron Curtain country.

*We were kings compared to them,* Bashir recalled. *We had so much, so very much.*

At the camp refugees from the then-current Middle Eastern upheaval—was it because of Iraq or a once-again savage Iran or the deposing of Mubarak of Egypt?—were huddled together in a camp that seemed little better, in some respects, than Auschwitz or Dachau or Mauthausen, excrement actually in piles several inches high that were so frequent it was difficult to avoid them as he walked through the camp.

The odor . . .

It was probable that Bashir would never be able to forget that collective merging of smells, from human waste, from sweat, from loathsome diseases too awful to contemplate as they made wrecks, literal wrecks of their hapless victims.

Some people had been dead for hours, and still their bodies remained where they dropped.

"My husband, my husband," said an elderly woman who rushed up to him, he guessed, probably because he was clean-shaven, and his clothes weren't dirty rags, which did set him apart from everyone else in that awful place. "He is gone. He is gone, and he begins to stink, and . . . and I don't know what to do with him. Sir, what can you do, please, what *can* you do to help us?"

Bashir turned to the government-appointed guide with him, and demanded that the woman's dilemma be looked into without delay.

"There are far too many like her," the guide told him in a tone that was well-nigh matter-of-fact. "You must understand that we cannot possibly get to all of them, I'm afraid."

"But you *cannot* turn your back on her," Bashir pleaded. "She is not an animal—she is a human being who should not be treated like so much trash."

"I am afraid that, to our leaders, she is *less* than trash. Trash at least can be recycled into energy."

Those last eight words summed up everything as far as Bashir was concerned. He left the camp immediately after what the guide had told him, left it with the little man running after him, pleading with him not to leave just yet, telling him frantically, "They will be displeased, sir, they will be very displeased."

Bashir stopped in his tracks, turned, and looked at the guide with unmasked contempt.

"God in heaven is displeased!" he said. "And *He* will deal with them. When they stand before His holy presence, they will have a great deal to answer for, I can promise you that!"

"You become upset over these—these derelicts?" the guide commented, scratching his head over the apparent depth of Bashir's emotions. "I do not understand why you, an intelligent man—"

Bashir spat on the ground in front of his feet and walked off.

*I had no idea I would see you again,* he thought. *I wanted to wipe you out of my head forever.*

But he did, in the institution for the insane situated in central Romania where he had been sent as part of a small group by an international rights organization to which he belonged.

The man had been reduced to an animalistic level, wallowing in urine and screaming obscenities at anyone who happened to look into the bare room he shared with ten other men.

In no way would Bashir have known who he was if the man had not somehow recognized *him*.

23

"You!"

Even so simple a word was hardly discernible, due to the man's pathetically slurred speech.

"He's had several strokes," Bashir was told by a doctor who was in charge of taking the group through the institution. "He's in very bad shape. We feel he has very little time left."

The man was at the door now, and reached out one crippled, twisted hand toward the bars.

"You knew . . . what would happen . . . to us," he said.

Bashir tried to protest.

"I am not a prophet. I just—"

"Say . . . what you . . . will," the man interrupted. "You knew of God, and God gave you the wisdom . . . to . . . to . . . say . . . those words."

Bashir saw an opportunity for an act that human nature alone would never have enabled him to do.

"Get him out of there," he demanded.

"It is not possible," the doctor stated.

"It *is* possible if you consider that this group and I will be going on to London from here, and that we will have the international media hanging on *every* word we decide to utter."

The doctor reconsidered in an instant.

Bashir's former guide from the refugee camp was brought out of that dreary room and given better quarters after he was washed clean and disinfected.

Less than two hours later, he suffered a massive coronary and died within minutes thereafter. Shortly before this happened, he had reached out and grabbed Bashir's hand and begged him for a reason, a reason he would be showing such kindness.

"I am so contemptible," he said, his voice hoarse.

"No one is beyond forgiveness," Bashir told the man.

"My leaders are . . . They sent me . . . away . . . I became . . . ill and could not function for them, and so they packed me . . . into . . . a . . . truck, and sent me off."

The doctor with them became nervous then.

"Leave him alone, sir," the doctor said. "He is crazy. He imagines things in a crazy world of his own making."

"No!" the man shouted, his voice abruptly much clearer, his head up straight, a curious dignity about him. "I am cruel perhaps. I am an adulterer, yes, I have committed many, many crimes. But I am *not* crazy in the way that you now seem to be suggesting."

He looked at Bashir.

"We were sent here as human guinea pigs. The world learned little from those years with Hitler. There are many Hitlers alive today, in Romania, and Hungary, and the Middle East."

His sudden strength and control were rapidly dissipating. He fell back against the bed on which he had been placed.

"Demand to visit Ward 607," he whispered to Bashir. "You will see the truth of what I am telling you."

Within minutes he was dead.

All the members of that group, a dozen men and women, were united behind Bashir as he inquired about Ward 607, expecting the doctor to offer any kind of excuse to keep them from it.

He bowed his head, sobs wrenching his body.

"Protect me, please, after I do so," he begged. "They will not be pleased with me. They will try to—."

Bashir and the others assured him that he would be safe. They would take him to London with them if necessary.

And so he asked that they follow him, and this they all did, to an isolated and terrifying Ward 607.

Moans.

It seemed that these came from every room, or people issuing low screams, or mumbling incoherently.

There were no lights in the corridors, and though it was noontime, no windows to let in any from the outside.

*Yea, though I walk through the valley of the shadow . . .*

Never before in his life had those words been so real to him, heard more often than not as he passed by a group of worshiping Christians gathered in the village square, Muslims like himself walking by and sneering.

*I spat more than once in their direction,* he confessed to himself, the memory making him flinch.

*Yea, though I walk . . .*

How real it seemed, in that cold institution, that dreary building of rejects shunned by a ruler who must have given Satan great pleasure, men and women naked, screaming, begging.

*. . . through the valley of the shadow.*

That was what he felt the moment he entered.

"Dismal," said another male member of the group.

"More than that," his female companion commented, "much more."

*. . . of death.*

Death was present in every corridor, in every room, it seemed, death of a sort, a hint of the real thing perhaps, even on the faces of the living patients, weary faces, with deep, dark circles under bloodshot eyes, skin pale, often blotched, lips thin, with spittle running out from the edges, bodies bony, some shivering fearfully in dirty corners, others—.

*That one, that one for whom death would come soon, life not possible any longer in that twisted body, the legs bent backward at birth and now jutting upward, immovable, frozen by neglect.*

Bashir immediately turned away. He didn't *want* to do so, and truly, that sight alone, as pitiable as it was, would not have reduced his strength to shameful mush—but it was more indeed, more in that single devastating moment, the eyes, for sure, the eyes—they seemed to lock in on his own, bloodshot eyes through which there was what appeared to be a stark and yet imagined glimpse into that man's dark and tormented soul.

To call it merely a ward was a misnomer; it was in fact more than that—rather, an entire section of the institution.

"Birkenau was not much worse," a Jewish member of the group commented. "Yes, that camp, as the others, was an image of hell, but this place in its own way must come directly from the mind of Satan itself!"

*Women who had been forced to have abortions because of the need to conduct "scientific" experiments on their babies . . . men who had been tortured because the regime suspected them of being*

26

*traitors, tortured in the most heinous ways that could be conjured up by those whose sole responsibility was devising the methods as well as the devices . . .*

Other odors.

Disgusting by themselves but when mixed together into a nauseous common pool, the effect was nearly overpowering, not only for Bashir but for several other members of the team who had begun to blanch within seconds of his own similar reaction.

*Some of the odors were the same as moments earlier, but this time the sweet smell of spilled blood intermixed with them, along with nameless chemicals and other "medicines," few of which had been present previously.*

"You must leave now," the doctor said. "No one knows that you have seen this except me. Please hurry!"

"You are going with us," Bashir told him emphatically. "We will *not* leave unless you go with us."

The doctor was stricken with panic.

"No, I cannot," he said. "They will track me down. No one can hide from these—these monsters."

"Nonsense," Bashir tried to reassure him. "The British and the Americans are really very good at that sort of thing. You can begin a new life, you really can, far away from anything that resembles—"

Bashir's eyes widened in horror, and those with him reacted similarly, as, in one instant, the doctor whipped out a revolver and shot himself in the head before anyone could stop him.

"No escape—," he said seconds before he died, falling forward that short distance into Bashir's arms.

# =2=

Those memories would never leave him, Bashir suspected, or even be dulled by any of the encroachments of age. Someday he might forget his name or the day of the week or whether he had had lunch, or forget a variety of other matters, but not that camp and not that hospital and not that guide or that doctor.

*Forgiveness* . . .

The guide, whose name he never learned, seemed aghast that he had shown forgiveness. An opportunity for saying something profound to this man had been presented, and yet nothing came of it, stymied by—.

*In such later days, I haven't done very well at what should have been a passion for me,* he admitted to himself, and never with more regret than in the present circumstances. *I was willing to die for my faith when I first embraced it, given a crisis situation, but I was, I am, so inept at witnessing for it.*

And never before, he perceived, was a deep down revival more necessary, not aimed at a reluctant group of unbelievers, not that at all, but rather to shake up once-vibrant Christians, men and women who had started out their spiritually reborn lives with such compelling fire, willing to take on the world at large and win countless souls for Christ. But with only themselves as sources of counsel, and a paucity of visitors over the years presenting no overwhelming mission field, that earlier fervor had lessened until it had become a withered series of remembered moments in days when challenges brought out heady goals they were dedicated to putting at the feet of their Savior, their Lord.

No more.

Shriveled, gone, long before the recent discovery of oil, before it was decided among themselves that *every* citizen would share equally in the revenue, a "pot" of billions of dollars giving each one extraordinary wealth.

Bashir saw frenzy in the little village where he had been born, where he had spent all of his childhood as well as his adult life.

The frenzy of greed.

Making it all somehow quite understandable, and, therefore, all the more dangerous, was the relative deprivation under which they had lived for so long. And, of course, those slick outsiders approaching them with fat offers had done their research well, knew which buttons to push.

He heard people talking about money, large sums of it.

He saw strangers waving around thick contracts, along with far less precise verbal promises, filling the naive villagers' minds with grand dreams of dramatically altering their lifestyles.

That it could all come true for them was a special irony but didn't disguise the fact that any wealth soon to be theirs would be eclipsed by the sums accruing to those in charge of dispersing pieces of that particular pie.

*It used to be that they had food to eat and water to drink and warm clothes and this was enough, since elsewhere, starving thousands—*

That was changing.

It hadn't taken long.

The influx started with the first functioning well more than a year earlier, an event seized upon by the outside world's media.

And it had continued unabated.

But there were hints before any of this had happened.

People becoming dissatisfied as they thought about the wealth to the north of them, and the south, and the—.

"Why has God stuck us in this little spot and made life so dreary for everyone?" a middle-aged man asked one afternoon. "The only reason *anyone* comes here is to rob the graves of the ancient!"

Christians had been in control for many years by that point. Two church buildings, which were simply bigger huts, as it were, had sprung up, erected as a common community project. All copies of the *Qur'ān* were burned in a designated spot on the outskirts of the village, and rightly so.

*How much filth is permitted under the banner of freedom of the press and freedom of speech,* he thought. *But then that problem exists primarily in the United States and a few other Western countries. We here are not shackled by it if we don't want to be! We can avoid having a so-called freedom become an excuse for a kind of imprisonment for us—*

Conversations laced with "Praise God!" replaced references to Allah. The Christianization of that settlement had been gradual at first but had gained momentum as the years passed.

*. . . the only reason anyone comes here is to rob the graves of the ancient.*

Ironically the previous Muslim population not infrequently reacted in a somewhat similar manner, before Christians had assumed total control—this was during periods of devastating winter storms, or during varying degrees of food shortages that sometimes occurred in that region. But, as Bashir recalled, many of the villagers assumed that these circumstances were besieging the village mainly because of the growing colony of Christians who had begun to settle there.

"Allah surely will not bless us so long as those white devils reside in this our humble village," remarked that same middle-aged Muslim man, whose name he had long ago forgotten, and thankful that he had. "They are nothing more than messengers of evil, and they pollute the very air. Something must be done!"

"What would you propose to do?" Bashir asked sharply. "Cut off their hands, perhaps? Or—?"

He saw the other man's eyes widen at *that* prospect! The conversation ended shortly thereafter.

Eventually, the Muslim population dwindled, presumably because others left rather than stay and tolerate the Christians who had settled in the area, first as a colony of missionaries, then their numbers increasing as Muslims converted to Christianity, the ultimate sacrilege according to Islamic law. In time, the ratio reversed, and practicing Muslims were in the minority.

Bashir briefly wondered why anyone would want to come *to* such a place at all. It seemed so bleak, indeed, set as it was in a so-called no man's land between two neighboring and hostile Arab countries.

But, of course, he knew the answer well enough.

*Everything in the world that is old and fabled is supposed to be somewhere near here: Noah's ark . . . the Garden of Eden . . . lost cities buried by time.*

Scores of archaeologists came each year, or so it seemed, armed with sophisticated electronic devices and such basics as shovels and pick-axes. Each dreamed of finding the discovery of the century.

He chuckled as he recalled a group of Christian seminary students who spent their summer vacation in the area. They were certain they knew where the Garden of Eden was and were determined to return home with a most wondrous story of being *the* ones who had stumbled upon it.

"But we have the *latest* information," a blonde-haired student told him. "Computers have been a big help to us, sir."

Bashir had nodded, then, aware that none of the students was susceptible to being dissuaded at that point and having to admit that probably he would have acted the same way at their age.

*. . . at their age.*

How well he could attest to that, how well indeed.

*If they only knew,* he had thought, as he spent some time with them, half regretting his own secrecy about the day he himself came so close to finding what might have been that very spot.

It was years before, when he was only twenty. Bashir had set out alone, guided by not much more than tenuous local myth, telling no one what he was in the process of doing, because of a determination that the thrill would be very much his alone, not to mention credit for the discovery, and also wanting to avoid the ridicule that surely would have been heaped upon him otherwise.

He had been away only a few hours when something happened.

He thought he heard the sound of singing.

It was quite unlike any that Bashir had encountered before in the course of his young life.

Directly ahead of him was a towering mountain, part of the ancient range that dominated that region but not it alone. Behind him was the stretch of desert across which he had just traveled.

He saw a pass that cut through the mountain, hardly wider than his own slim body, the mountain rising quite jaggedly on either side, a little like the entrance that led to Petra, that ancient Christian hideaway several hundreds of miles to the west of his village.

As soon as he entered the pass, the singing rose in volume, as though a thousand speakers had been placed around him and their collective orchestral was coming at him from every direction.

*So beautiful,* he remembered. *So very beautiful . . .*

He could never ascertain just how long he remained there, listening, having fallen to his knees, tears streaming down his cheeks.

*The bells of heaven are chiming, and the angels are singing.*

That description floated in and out of his mind. Unlike other Muslims, he had had thoughts of heaven over the years that seemed closer to what little he knew of Christian beliefs.

*Fairest Lord Jesus, Ruler of all nature!*

Those words came to him in that moment.

*How could it be?* he asked himself. *Jesus was a great prophet, nothing more, certainly not the Son—*

He felt something touch his face then, and he looked up. Nothing.

The pass. The mountain. As before.

And the singing! The singing had ended.

He did not arise immediately but sat quite still.

*I feel so—*

Peaceful.

Yes, that was it.

*I've got to tell Yamma! I've got to tell her about this.*

He jumped to his feet and ran, ran from that pass, ran across the stretch of desert between the mountain and the village where his mother and he lived, possessed of an energy he could not explain, but there it was, propelling him.

"*Yamma! Yamma!*" he screamed as he approached their little home and saw her outside.

She reacted with panic when she saw him, when she saw his hair, which had once been black but now was totally white.

"*Yamma,* I have been with Jesus!" he told her once they were inside the humble dwelling.

She knew that *something* had happened, else his hair would not have changed. Once inside the family's house, she sat down in a chair, and he on the floor in front of her, and he recounted the experience that had had such impact.

After he had finished, his mother pushed him away rather frantically, screaming at him that he should never visit that house or speak her name again.

"But *Yamma,*" he tried to tell her, "it wasn't evil at all, it was good. I—I feel so clean."

"And why is that so?" she asked sternly.

"Because I accepted Him as my Savior and my Lord, dear *Yamma.* I asked Him into my life."

She let out a shriek then, clamping her hands against her ears and shaking her head wildly.

"*Go!*" his mother yelled, her voice rasping. "Go, before you have me dead at your feet!"

He turned and left that house.

# =3=

Fahid Bashir managed to leave the village not so very many years after the encounter on the mountain. It happened that a visiting archaeologist took a liking to him, and though Bashir was rather suspicious of his motives at first the man proved to be a committed Christian who was in that area to do research for a new book entitled *Origins of the Faith*.

His name was Sir Isaac Templeton; he was more than six feet tall, broad-shouldered, and completely bald.

"I had a Jewish mother," he said, "and an Anglican father. My father persuaded her not only to marry him but to convert to Christianity."

Templeton was genuinely appreciative of what Bashir had been going through in order to profess his own faith in Christ.

"Friends turned their backs on you, which is quite hard to endure after your family has kicked you out," he said one evening as they sat in front of the makeshift tent in which Bashir had been living since his mother ordered him away from her presence. "How are you managing to get along, Fahid?"

"Barely," Bashir admitted in flawless English, having been taught the language at an early age. "I am almost a beggar, you see."

"Almost?"

34

"Well, yes, I *am* a beggar here. A few brave ones give me food. But I have earned no money for months now."

"What about clothes?"

"Only what I had on my back until Dr. al-Fahazi slipped a few old shirts and pants to me."

Templeton started to puff on a pipe that he had lit moments before.

"Bad habit, this," he readily acknowledged. "I shouldn't be polluting even this aging body."

"Because the Holy Spirit indwells you?"

"Yes, *yes!* How could you have such a grasp of the truth?"

"Missionaries come through here every so often, sir."

"Call me Isaac, please."

Bashir smiled, grateful for the informality.

"They have been able to teach me much . . . Isaac."

Templeton looked at Bashir.

"You are examining me very closely, Isaac," Bashir told him. "That makes me a little nervous."

The other man chuckled.

"No need for you to be. I'm not *that* type of Westerner."

"No?"

"It's forbidden in Scripture. And I try to honor the Lord as much as I can while in this imperfect body of flesh."

Templeton cleared his throat as he added, "I do have money, Fahid. I am not, shall we say, fabulously wealthy, but I could buy up this village and support everyone in it for a long period of time if I had to do so. I suppose, by the standards of others in my world—well, there are many with considerably greater resources than I will ever have."

"What are you saying, Isaac?"

"Oh, in my own fumbling way, I am trying to get to the point. You see, I could have helped a few select organizations extensively over the years, but I haven't, settling for getting involved with quite a number."

"Why?" Bashir asked logically.

"Because when an organization or a community is infused with large sums all at once, and from a single source, two things happen: First, they become lazy, and, next, they tend not to spend the money as wisely as they should. Whereas an expensive computer would have been out of the question just weeks earlier, now, with this new money, it is feasible. Yes, I said feasible but I did not say necessary. But they get it anyway, and then there's something else, and another luxury item after that. The money eventually is wasted, at least to a certain extent.

"About the lazy part: They become self-satisfied, along with self-indulgent. They begin not to pray with the energy, the commitment that was once the case, simply because they think they have everything they need."

He saw that Bashir was comprehending everything that he had been saying but, also, by the young man's expression, that he was growing a bit impatient.

"My point?" Templeton asked before Bashir was able to do so. "There is an organization that could send you on a kind of knowledge-gathering trip, Fahid. It is dedicated to strengthening the foundations of the faith of young people like yourself in a dozen countries. I do help to support it. And I would like to sponsor you for such a trip."

Bashir looked at him blankly.

"Yes, son, I am serious," Templeton assured him.

In just two days, Fahid Bashir was literally on his way.


He traveled to cities such as Cairo, and spent time with the Coptic Christians there, and into Jerusalem to fellowship with some of the individuals who happened to be in charge of Gordon's Calvary, to which Isaac Templeton regularly contributed sizable support.

Bashir's first visit to the location of the tomb of Christ accepted as such by evangelical Christians proved more emotional than he might have expected.

"Go ahead and cry, Fahid," a thin, elderly man named Clyde Habersham told him as they both knelt inside. "I have been here often, perhaps as many as a thousand times, and I always weep.

"It cannot be otherwise for those who really care, you know. Think of what it must have been like two thousand years ago, for Peter, for Mary Magdalene, for others who visited this place expecting to see the shrouded body of Jesus, only to find this hole in the side of a mountain empty!

"And to learn, shortly thereafter, that no one had stolen His body but that He had arisen from the dead, as He had promised. Imagine their *joy!*"

Bashir knew similar joy himself, the joy of emancipation from the shackles of his former faith.

"I can see, now, how awful it was," he told Habersham.

"And I can understand why you feel as you do."

"You can? You've been a Christian, you said, for more than half a century. Even before your conversion, you would never have considered getting involved with Islam. How can you understand?"

"Because Islam is simply another religion that removes from Christ any possibility of deity. Think of it, Fahid! To say that our blessed Redeemer, the Son of God, was no greater than Jeremiah or Daniel or any of the other prophets!"

Habersham paused, then placed his hand on his young friend's shoulder.

"Are you aware that in the Bible there is discussion about just one sin that cannot be forgiven?"

"I am not. What is it?"

"There has been a great deal of speculation on that very point."

"What do *you* believe, sir?"

"I believe it is the sin not only of rejecting Christ as Savior and Lord but also of saying, in effect, that He was simply a fine man, a good man, a very perceptive man, but *only* a man, that Muhammad, who is even now in hell, was far greater."

Bashir was shivering.

"Forgive me for upsetting you," Habersham said.

"No, no, that is all right. A wound cannot be treated to any healing if it is not recognized for what it is."

Habersham died a few days later, in Bashir's arms. They were walking near the Mount of Olives.

"Fahid, how did you know that I was suddenly very weak?" he asked, his voice cracking.

Bashir was puzzled.

37

"I . . . I don't know what you mean," he said. "Do you want me to take you by the hand so that you can lean on me for strength?"

"Oh, Fahid, I thought that you already had done so . . ."

He turned, smiled, said only, "I love you in the Lord, my young friend," and died, Bashir catching him before he hit the ground.

*Clyde Habersham was buried in a cemetery not far from Gordon's Calvary. Several hundred people were in attendance-. . . Jews as well as Christians.*

*"If every Christian were like this man," a rabbi spoke to the multitude, "we all would have become completed Jews a very long time ago."*

*Some apparent Muslims were also there.*

*Bashir could hardly believe what he was seeing.*

*As the crowd was filing out of the cemetery, he hesitantly approached one of them.*

*"Yes, we are now Christians," the rough-looking man told him. "It was because dear Clyde Habersham was the Lord's instrument. Without him, who knows what would have been happening to any of us today. We certainly wouldn't be talking with you!"*

*"One man was responsible for—," Bashir started to say.*

*"Yes, for everyone here accepting Christ . . . Jews, Muslims, others. It is a wonderful thing, you know. How the heavenly host must have rejoiced as that man stepped into their presence!"*

*Bashir was looking at their garb.*

*"You thought we were still Muslims, did you not?" another interjected, a knowing expression on his face.*

*Bashir nodded.*

*"We still live in Muslim communities. We feel an obligation, therefore, to fit in as much as possible so as not to lose any opportunities that might be present to witness to them."*

*"Witness?" Bashir repeated, not having gone quite that far in his Christian walk as yet.*

*So the members of that group took him to the quiet residence owned by one of them and fed his hungry stomach as well as his thirsty soul.*

# =4=

Whentp
en Bashir returned to the village after that trip, a few
friends who were generally more forbearing than anyone in his
immediate family began to see in him the fresh hope that had
not come from Islam.

"Sir Isaac arranged for us to get pamphlets, Bibles, lessons," a friend named Omar Khladun remarked.

Bashir rejoiced with him.

"It was so wonderful," Khladun, who was just two years
older than he, said happily. "We read so much that concerns
us, this whole area."

"I heard that Iraq and that group of madmen were described in a prophecy in the book of Revelation," Bashir told
him. "Do you know whether or not that is true?"

"It may be, Fahid, it may be."

Khladun and Bashir were sitting in the little tent outside
the boundaries of the village. They were cold, but neither paid
much attention to this because the enthusiasm they both felt
for matters biblical had taken charge of them.

"Listen to this," Khladun said as he turned to Revelation
18:3: "'And the merchants of the earth have become rich
through the abundance of her luxury.' Fahid, that was speaking of the great whore of Babylon. But then Hussein claimed

all along that he was the successor to the king who built the great Babylon in the first place."

"Nebuchadnezzar!"

"Exactly. The merchants of the earth could easily be those greedy companies anxious to get in on the wealth Hussein was accumulating because of Iraq's oil revenues. But there's more."

Khladun went on to read the preceding verse: "'Babylon the great is fallen, is fallen, and has become a habitation of demons, a prison for every foul spirit.' What better description could there be for the evil that Hussein brought about, in Kuwait and upon the Kurds, against anyone who opposed him!"

And then he skipped to verses 9-11: "'And [those] who committed fornication and lived luxuriously [because of her] will weep and lament for [Babylon], when they see the smoke of her burning, standing at a distance for fear of her torment. . . . And the merchants of the earth will weep and mourn . . . , for [Babylon does not buy] their merchandise anymore.'"

He turned and looked intently at Bashir.

"Think of it, Fahid. Think of the scandals that arose when investigation revealed how certain companies—German and American and some from other countries—were selling Hussein not only his weapons of warfare but, in the case of the Germans, gas chambers modeled after those in the old concentration camps."

Both sat quietly for several minutes, feeling the stunning impact of such a prophesy written two thousand years earlier.

*Three days later, Omar Khladun was found nearly dead, having lost a great deal of blood because of both hands being cut off.*

*Six months after that, he was beheaded.*

# =5=

Bashir started conducting secret meetings during which he told those in attendance the truths he had learned from Scripture.

They all, Bashir and the others, knew how dangerous such activity was. Khladun had already experienced Muslim wrath. But this didn't stop them from going ahead, although the conditions were horrible, the threat of death or crippling seemingly awaiting them at every turn. It was only later, as their numbers increased, that they felt a bit more secure. Even then, there were threats.

Among the rest of the villagers, people he'd known as friends most of his life looked at him no longer *as* a friend or as a human being, either.

A Christian.

Many of them visited the spot where he had been converted and returned to the village, expressions of sarcasm on their faces.

"See!" they would say. "We are as we always have been. You were deluded. You are under the control of a seducing spirit."

"Salvation does not come because of a *place*," he tried to tell them. "It could have happened in an alley between two of

41

our homes. The Lord simply chose that time, that place, as He did with Paul on the road to Damascus."

But they turned from him, and walked away.

During the weeks and months to follow, Bashir came to realize that such treatment indeed was typical of his former Muslim brothers and sisters; if anything, it seemed almost mild, if that could ever be a word applied to their tactics. He learned of what other Muslims were capable of doing on a far greater scale.

The Sudan.

What was happening there eclipsed anything Bashir could have imagined. At first, he thought it was nothing more than anti-Muslim propaganda, but more details followed.

Genocide.

The Muslim military regime had instituted a policy of starvation directed at the Sudanese in the southern part of the country because they were not Muslims themselves.

"It is probable that 350,000 men, women, and children will die as a result of this government-mandated atrocity," one of Bashir's sources in the United States told him by letter after viewing a segment of the American TV series "60 Minutes." "Tiny babies will not live past the age of four months because of their Islamic doctrine.

"This calamity, which could have been avoided, will prove, in the end, to be ten times worse than the famine in Ethiopia."

Amidst the rough times of rejection and persecution, Bashir was assaulted by regrets. Not that he ever wanted to return to what was basically the old, dead heart of Islam. But there were certain moments, warm, tender, happy ones with his family that he could never regain. By giving up being a Muslim, he gave up any hope of getting back with them, and that made those times of reverie all the more bittersweet.

Ramadan.

The Muslim holy period.

A time of fasting and prayer in which they all rededicated themselves the principles of living and worship as set forth by Muhammad in the *Qur'ān*.

At its end, there was a celebration called *Eid-al-Fitr,* which meant "Breaking of the Fast," which involved cannons or drums announcing the end of Ramadan. Three days of rejoicing were to began.

Adults wore new clothes, and children received presents. In nearby Turkey, it was called *Seker Bayrami,* or "Candy Holiday," during which children received money as well as candy wrapped in handkerchiefs. In northern Sudan, children got as presents cute red candy dolls that held paper fans. And in Pakistan, the special treat was *sawaeen,* a kind of sweet spaghetti made of milk, flour, sugar, almonds, pistachios, and dates.

Happy moments in a bleak world.

But no longer.

# = 6 =

**H**ow long has it been, Yamma?

Bashir looked about his office, and felt very, very alone then, even after so long a period had passed. For his mother, there was no forgive-and-forget syndrome. She was forbidden from doing that by certain tenets of Islam. Years later, his mother had managed still to avoid any warm and loving contact with him, though he tried often to get through to her. Nor would he be able to spend any time with his father or his brothers, so effectively was he cut off from the other members of the family.

When his father died, he was barred from the funeral.

*Once they decide you're out, that is it forever, as far as they are concerned,* he thought, recalling the furor over *Satanic Verses* by Salman Rushdie—and how unwarranted it all was, his own opinions of that book much more mild than any voiced by his former Muslim family members and friends.

*What they see in others is only what exists in themselves,* he told himself. *They call their enemies by the name of Satan, when they are the ones with him as their father, their ruler, their guide, their king and master.*

Bashir shivered at a singular fact. It was one that no longer held sway in his life. And which he was glad to be rid of, though ashamed that he had been deceived for so long.

44

*I was once one of them. I once fell devoutly at the feet of Muhammad and worshiped from the* Qur'ān. *I thought that book of spiritual perversion to be divine, holy, and completely worthy for all of life's situations, a guidebook for peace and redemption when in fact its pages were rift with Satan's own—.* There was a large brass spittoon near his feet, and Bashir spat into it contemptuously.

*Praise God for showing me the truth . . . for opening my eyes about Khomeini, that monstrous enemy of everything good, and decent, and holy . . . and the rest of his kind, blind beasts leading others into the hell . . . damned by their mindless addiction to a so-called prophet who in reality deserved only the flames of perdition, the very ones that are now tormenting him for eternity.*

But Bashir recognized the differences between himself and Salman Rushdie.

*He speaks out, and must pay for the rest of his life. I do little except—*

Bashir smiled, realizing that he was, as he always tended to be, far too hard on himself, for indeed he had had to give up his entire family for the sake of his conversion to Christianity.

And along with them went those friends who also considered him a Judas, someone who was lower than a slug slithering its way through a pile of garbage.

*And yet here I am, years later, elected to my second term as constable by the populace of this village—*

That in itself was remarkable.

There was considerable opposition, of course; the Muslim remnant in the village tried to see to it that Bashir never lived to assume the post, or tried to intimidate him in a number of other ways.

*How many of my dearest, dearest friends no longer have hands because of me? How many have suffered because of the cause I took up, and yet here I am, a whole man?*

The memories flooded in, unstoppable just then, men and women maimed for life simply because they supported a *Christian* candidate.

Most, however, either remained in the village, or returned soon after the votes were counted, determined to be with him when he emerged victorious.

But the worst time of all, and Bashir would always think of it as such, for nothing could ever again prove to be quite as hellish, the worst time indeed came during one of the attempts on his life.

It wasn't that this was being done that in itself seemed so awful to anyone such as he, who was intimately familiar with the way Muslims lived their lives—he had expected it, in fact —but, rather, *who* the assailant proved to be.

His mother—his *yamma*.

She came on the pretense of a reconciliation, concealing the dagger under her garb. When he had turned away for an instant, she whipped it out, and the blade landed in his shoulder.

Seeing that she had failed to kill him, she turned the knife toward herself and tried to end her life. Though weak from his own wound, he managed to get the weapon away from her.

"Do you not see what your faith makes you capable of?" he screamed. "Do you not see how *evil* it is?"

He was nearly passing out.

"I am your *son!*" he said weakly.

She looked at him, then, without saying anything, and he saw in his mother's expression such hatred that he fell back from its dark countenance. It seemed almost that he was looking not at a human face but something quite alien, certainly not the face of the woman who had given birth to him and for twenty years of his life would have been willing to die for her son.

Finally his mother spoke, no emotion whatever in her voice, the words coming from her mouth—and *how* she said them—cold, flat.

"I have no son," she said. "My son is dead."

He ripped open his shirt, showing her the wound in his shoulder.

"I am not dead," he cried. "I am here. This is my blood. It flows from a *living* body, *Yamma.*"

His mother walked up to him, then, cocking her head for a moment. Bashir hesitated, not knowing what she would do.

She looked into his face, narrowing her eyes in concentration, as though studying every line in it, every wrinkle.

"You are not my son," she said finally, just before spitting at him. "You can never *be* my son. You are no better than a slimy serpent who has crawled out of some dung heap and whose stench makes me ill!"

*Yamma* turned on her heel and left, perhaps never hearing the cry of anguish that tore through his throat and kept on coming until he lost consciousness.

# =7=

His *yamma* moved away after that, and he had never been able to find out what had happened to her.

His brothers went with her, none of them ever turning back to say anything to Bashir but rejecting him as an outcast.

*And now here I am, divorced, and with no remaining family of my own. I protect a village that had been torn from one century into quite another.*

That it should be oil to start a massive turnaround in the local economy seemed ironic.

*After all these years, some archaeologists are digging around for dead bones and tap into liquid that is the stuff of new life itself!*

But now he saw the changes, the appearance of better clothes, automobiles, and newer ones to boot, the presence of many more foreigners, and so on.

*So loud,* he told himself. *So loud here these days—*

One of the beguiling factors of living in that village, if all the negatives could be ignored, was truly the quiet. It had been possible to stand out under the stars at night, and breathe in deeply, and feel a certain peace.

*Only desert animals could be heard . . .*

He turned from the window and looked back at his desk.

Sitting on top was a new computer.

The townspeople wanted him to have it. A new era was coming, they said, and computers were a part of the picture.

Bashir walked over to the desk and stared down at the computer as though it were a fierce beast ready to pounce on him.

*I have no idea what you can do for me. I don't know if I want you even to try!*

He sat down, staring at the blank monitor, the detached keyboard, the instruction manuals piled to one side.

*Connection with the outside world . . .*

He chuckled, remembering the old, black, nonelectric typewriter he had been using for nearly thirty years.

*And now—*

He turned the computer on and waited for the so-called C-prompt to show up on the monitor.

C:>.

There it was.

Which he followed with a code that accessed a word processing program.

Bashir started typing:

> Today, I am told, additional drilling formally starts.
> May we survive the miracle. . .

He leaned back in the chair, looking at those words, realizing that the message implied that he should have been rejoicing, but instead he felt as though he was constable of a dying town.

*A dying town. . .*

With the unprecedented potential of oil revenues pouring in, he should be rejoicing, sharing in the sense of anticipation that was rippling through his fellow villagers, and he tried at least to smile when one or another came up to him, gesturing, eager to tell him the latest "fact" that they had heard.

"They will need to build a motel to the north of our village," an elderly man had said. "Think of it, Fahid. Just think of that!"

49

"Not a motel," he had responded. "It will be a place for the oil workers to stay, with a very big wall around it, I'm sure."

"Yes, yes, a motel, as I told you," she said, her hearing defective.

Bashir gave up trying to convince her otherwise.

But that was only a small part of what could be expected, though it would prove to be one of the most visible.

I wonder what it will be like for all of us a year from now. Reply when you have time . . .

The message was then sent by modem to a friend of his in Switzerland, someone who worked at a special retreat near Geneva.

Bashir waited, but there was no immediate reply.

He was about to type something else into the computer when he heard the door to his office open and a familiar English voice call over to him cheerfully.

"Fahid, top of the morning to you," Derek Sparrowhawk was saying. "You intend to be present at the drilling site, do you not?"

Bashir turned around and looked at him scornfully.

"Why are *you* in such a happy mood?" he asked.

"I rejoice for this village," Sparrowhawk replied.

"You rejoice over a dying thing? What *are* you suggesting?"

"Just look about you, Fahid. It is apparent to the naked eye."

Bashir swiveled around in his chair and faced Sparrowhawk.

"You sound like an American," he said. "Please do not play games with me."

"Now who is talking like a Yank?" Sparrowhawk retorted.

Bashir broke out laughing.

"I do sound sour, don't I?" he said.

"It's a good thing that you're not made of milk."

50

The constable stood and walked over to his friend and shook hands with him.

"I *am* sorry, Derek," he apologized. "But I see what a few months have wrought."

"Actually, Fahid, I do tend to agree with you," Sparrowhawk had to admit. "After all, I did come here from London to escape the frenetic life, didn't I?"

"And soon it may reembrace you if you decide to remain."

"Are you planning on my possible departure, old bloke?"

"I wasn't speaking from my point of view, Derek."

The two men sat down and continued talking.

They had become close friends during the eight months or so that Sparrowhawk had lived in the village. Both had been through a wrenching divorce; both had seen their ex-wives take over custody of their children; both approached life with a touch of weariness brought on by pain that had been a persistent companion for a long time, the kind of pain that is born from the ashes of relationships that were lost forever, and which could never be duplicated.

"I get a woman I love, and the whole thing ends after a few years," Bashir commented. "I see her walk away, without even turning and waving back to me. She was like a robber baron with her booty, her spoils, the kids, and that was all she cared about."

Sparrowhawk threw his head back and looked up wistfully at the ceiling, with its cumbling plaster surface.

"I remember my first day here," he said. "The divorce papers had been signed by Angelica and me a week or so earlier. I *had* to leave my country, Fahid, no way in the world could I stay in an environment that was the least bit familiar. I had to get away from anything that I could recognize, any sense of familiarity invariably based so much upon memories that would involve the two of us."

"You never did mention why you chose *this* place, though, Derek," Bashir commented. "I agree with you that it was the sort of change a man sometimes needs in his life. But this area is hardly on the lips of every man whose marriage has just ended."

Sparrowhawk chuckled at that one.

"How right you are," he replied, rubbing his chin as he tried to answer honestly. "Let's see now: It was recommended to men by an oil worker employed by Americo. He came here periodically, liked the quiet, fancied himself an amateur archaeologist. I suppose the prospect of finding some hidden horde of artifacts proved quite a magnet for him."

"Then you and this man must have been quite a bit alike."

"Indeed."

Bashir had got a bull's-eye with that one.

Derek Sparrowhawk was a journalist, a very good one, and one of his principal assignments over the years had been covering important archaeological finds wherever these might occur.

*Finding a previously unknown Aztec settlement near the Amazon River was a highlight,* he recalled. *It was on a more vast scale than any unearthed in the past. But the battles! With environmentalists worried about the rain forest situation. With the natives, descendants of the original Aztecs, who considered the site to be sacred. With governmental agencies . . .*

Sparrowhawk told his friend what he had been thinking just then.

"We won't have them here," Bashir remarked. "There is no environment as such *to* save. We're on no one's list of ecological necessities, you can be sure of that."

"You don't think so?"

"I doubt it, Derek. We're old, we're isolated, and we have nothing to do with the greenhouse effect. The radical environmentalists go where the publicity is. I'm not saying they're opportunistic, mind you, but I do know they understand the value of media coverage. And I guess they're not above exploiting the Establishment they claim to detest!"

*. . . we're old, we're isolated.*

Precisely what had appealed to Derek Sparrowhawk.

He used to be one of that countless number of Brits and Yanks and Italians and Spanish and others who enjoyed London for its abundant antiquities, savoring the sheer joy of merely turning a musty corner in the White Hall district or Fleet Street or Chelsea or a dozen more and, in some respects, going back in time perhaps five hundred years, frequently much further than that because of some special building, yet standing on a spot where something infamous or otherwise had happened, the spot seldom changed from the moment of the original occurrence . . . and there was indeed the very smell of the city, unique in itself, like that of a tomb perhaps and yet different . . . the knowledge that Jack the Ripper and Winston Churchill had walked the same streets, once cobblestoned, the time that separated them actually very little indeed when compared to the totality of London's long centuries of being in existence . . . a city once littered with the hapless and pathetic victims of the Black Plague, or else tottering under the impact of the *blitzkrieg*, but now jammed to bursting with cars and buses and motorcycles and a variety of trucks, and the resultant noisy crescendo . . . hotel rooms that a decade earlier cost £27 per night having shot up to £120 or more, bachelor-type flats now going for thousands of pounds *per week*, lunches at Simpson's-in-the-Strand and Cafe Royle and Flanagan's and The Wig and the Pen joining the relentless inflationary parade and thereby eliminating London as once a city of special pleasures for anyone on a tight budget . . . and always, always, inexorably always the encroachments of certain styles of "newer" architecture eating away at the special atmosphere that was this city's and this city's alone, to the outrage of Prince Philip and other members of the Royal Family who cared about what their beloved London was becoming or, rather, what it was giving up at an accelerated pace to those insensitive individuals interested only in the bottom line of profit that was to be gained from so-called progress at their hands, and with no regard *for* or innate sense *of* history . . . yet that was not all. A once pleasant and untroubled walk along Oxford Street as late as midnight and beyond now turned quite perilous, Piccadilly Circus unsafe as soon as the sun went down, and, yes, Trafalgar Square—

"Jack the Ripper is a terrorist these days," he said.

"That's rather cryptic," Bashir told him.

"So is life."

*And now the cycle would soon begin in that little village . . .*

Derek Sparrowhawk felt inexpressively sad when he contemplated that eventuality.

He had drifted into silence for several moments. Fahid Bashir came up to him and tapped him on the shoulder.

"Are you all right?" he asked.

Sparrowhawk nodded.

"Oh, yes, if you don't qualify that question very much. I'm healthy, in a manner of speaking. I have enough income from various investments to be able to take on only those assignments that stir me to my soul, or to take none at all if that be the case. Yes, I would say I am quite all right."

"But are you happy, Derek?" Bashir persisted.

Sparrowhawk paused, wondering how he would answer that question, though not offended by the personal nature of it.

"Ah, you touch upon a very sore point, old chap."

"Then you aren't, I take it?"

Sparrowhawk looked directly at his friend.

"I will try to evade any direct answer by posing another question: Are you?"

"But I wanted to know about Derek Sparrowhawk."

"If your answer is no, Fahid, and, therefore, basically the same as mine at this very point in time, then I suspect it will be for much the same reason."

Bashir was prepared to object but knew he could not and remain honest in his relationship with this man.

"How did you know?" he asked simply.

"I watched you for a few moments as you stood at that window and looked out. If I could not see your eyes, then your body language nevertheless told me everything I needed to know."

Bashir's shoulders slumped.

"You are perceptive, my friend, embarrassingly so," he said rather forlornly. "Well, like me, you've seen what can happen. Can you blame me for my mood today?"

"No, I cannot," the Englishman replied. "I feel for you because I feel a similar pain."

Bashir liked this man, and was glad to have him as a friend; his perceptivity continued to be a source of astonishment.

"Ah, yes, there *is* pain, as you say, Derek. It's with me when I get up in the morning and, alas, when I go to bed at night. It doesn't seem to go away, lingering on like an uninvited mother-in-law."

Smiling a bit, Sparrowhawk stood slowly, stretching his arms and legs in the process, and turned toward the door.

"Let's go for a walk, Fahid, while we can still breathe air that is clean and pure."

As they emerged outside, Sparrowhawk said, "I'd also like to learn something about Wise One as we walk, Fahid."

"How did you hear about him?"

"Let's just say that it was what I *overheard*, my friend. Two chaps were playing a game of chess in the town square, and a small crowd had gathered. Near where I was standing, a man and his wife were wondering what had happened to Wise One."

Bashir was silent for the first part of their walk.

Sparrowhawk didn't press him; after years of being a journalist and interviewing thousands of people, he had developed enough of a sense of human nature to know when to let matters coast a bit, and this was one of those occasions.

The village was literally in the middle of an inhospitable Middle Eastern desert, where the temperature alternated, depending upon the season, between oppressive heat and extreme cold. It had been assumed, for decades, to be just barren territory, like so much else in that general region, suitable for only the most hardy and misguided individuals, except for one peculiar attraction.

Archaeological finds.

Those brought a trickle of visitors over the years, enough to keep the village from extinction altogether and to justify some semblance of hospitality, however hypocritical, toward strangers who otherwise would have been approached with substantial caution and not a little hostility.

55

But at its best, or its worst, and the two were indeed one and the same, it was not much of an oasis, just a haphazard grouping of old houses of stone or, in a few instances, dried mud blocks covered over by thatched roofs, layers of dust and sand filtering inside and resting on whatever furniture was present, on the floors, on curtains and cooking utensils, and whatever else.

Centuries earlier, the village had been the hub of a trading center for a number of countries dealing in exquisite silks and other goods, but time and circumstance had erased its value as such, dooming the ancient routes as most others had been since the days of the Phoenicians and even earlier, and causing the whole region to become a mockery of what it was once, betraying the threadbare spectacle of nameless, weary human beings wandering like finite phantoms through a forlorn graveyard of passed-down memories and a few crumbling parchments filled with epic tales of splendor from generations long gone, all that was left of what once thrived, and no way to discern the true from the mythological.

Months before, when he had been in the village only a short while, Sparrowhawk felt motivated to provide Bashir insight into why anyone would want to spend so much as a few minutes in an area such as that, which would have seemed alien to any but lifelong inhabitants who had had no choice but to stay.

"When people become disenchanted with the modern world, they try as much as possible to return to some ancestral roots, perhaps," Sparrowhawk said over dinner at Bashir's house one evening, a meal which Bashir himself had cooked, one of the few postmatrimonial tasks at which he was able to excel.

"I will agree that this entire region seems to belong to another century entirely," Bashir replied, "but I always thought that that was a shortcoming. I would not have believed it would become an attraction, especially to someone like you, who has traveled so much."

"Oh, you are wrong, Fahid," Sparrowhawk insisted. "Smell the air—it reeks of the ancient. I had a similar sensation when I crawled inside the Great Pyramid outside Cairo.

But there it was oppressive, maddeningly so. I experienced claustrophobia for the first time in my life. All I could think of was what you might call the weight of the centuries. And, of course, I was surrounded by someone's *tomb.*"

He chuckled briefly.

"Here I have the pleasure without the pain. After all, Fahid, look what you live in the midst of!"

"Can we be so sure?" Bashir replied, as he took a toothpick and worked at a piece of lamb that had become stuck near his wisdom tooth. "I have heard most of my life about Noah's ark . . . and the Garden of Eden, as well as a fabled and wicked city that was destroyed by God, in addition to the well-chronicled instances of Sodom and Gomorrah, and which had become buried over the centuries.

"Yet, apart from a few artifacts, nothing much has been retrieved from a hundred miles in any direction. But that is not a daunting issue, it seems. People continue to come here, in dribs and drabs, again and again, drawn by the hope of monumental discoveries!"

He turned and looked at the other man.

"Including you," he said, "all the way from England, and yet that's not the entire reason, I know. For you, Derek, the artifacts and antiquity and all that are not nearly as critical to you as wanting to be separated from the rest of civilization for a while, or it might be just the present civilized world, which is why *other* civilizations draw you. Has it helped, my friend, has it helped at all? Answer me honestly now."

Sparrowhawk assured him that coming to and staying in the village indeed had done exactly that.

"I've been able, to a certain extent, to empty myself of some not inconsiderable junk," he remarked. "I had begun to feel, you know, like a garbage can after a while back in mother England."

"And what was being thrown into the can?" Bashir said, trying to go along with the other man's terminology.

"A great deal, Fahid, a great deal indeed! I saw first hand the pitiable degradation of our ancestral heritage, that once sublime respect for tradition for which we had a special zeal now a vanishing part of life. I am English, after all, and such matters are terribly important to me, for they constitute pride, the best kind of pride, pride in my country.

"But that even changed for me. I would have to say, now, that I *was* proud of England, of what she *once* had been. Arrogant, perhaps, autocratic to the extreme, yes, but basically endowed with a belief in honor, in integrity, in acts that were right and just, some semblance of the Judeo-Christian standards of conduct yet remaining.

"Take the book publishing business, for example. Fifty years ago, doing books was still a gentleman's game, as it were. Quality remained important, a quality of content as well as the binding that held each book together.

"Now books have gone the way of the tabloid press, Fahid—sensational stuff, lurid and revealing, usually with as much sexual revelation as can be dredged up somehow.

"Nor is the degradation in other areas hidden either, detectable only with great effort. It is all around us—the terrorist attacks, riots in the streets, protests over one thing or another."

Once Sparrowhawk witnessed directly one such melee from a window in his flat near Buckingham House.

An antinuclear group had clashed with a pro-Thatcher crowd, which was the larger of the two. Hundreds of men and women were involved on both sides as they later would, on another occasion, with supporters of John Major, her successor.

"It was quite awful," Sparrowhawk said, his voice trembling a bit. "People were trampled upon, kicked, beaten. Some were blinded for life. Others had broken ribs, arms, cuts and bruises. But I remember even more vividly the two who died."

"You *saw* them killed?" Bashir asked.

"No, but I saw what was left of their bodies after the bobbies arrived and cleared the area. Fahid, they were such a young couple. They had been holding hands apparently. They fell that way in one deadly instant, their fingers still intertwined. Their eyes were open, as though looking up at a night sky filled with stars, and yet it was high noon at that time. There was no pain that I could see, and that was the most

58

extraordinary thing, you know, such peace as to be beyond comprehension, with not one whit of any fear, though they died so violently. I could almost believe that death came so quickly that it bypassed pain—but the calm they manifested, you have no idea how that looked!"

"How do you suppose it was that they could have died like that," Bashir asked, nudging his friend ever so gently, "in the midst of such utter chaos as they had been?"

"I never found out, unfortunately. I can't really imagine. But it was nonetheless a strange sight, and an abysmal waste of such young lives. But then that sort of thing has become typical. There is an accelerating loss of decency everywhere, Fahid, in even the simplest of business dealings, integrity sacrificed at the altar of commerce."

Sparrowhawk paused, a sad expression on his face but no tears just then.

"I keep speaking of everything in the past tense, don't I? And yet no funeral has been formally announced!"

Bashir nodded.

"The toughest part will be after I leave here, after I land at Gatwick, continue on into the city, and spend the next few days getting back into the swing of things again. I know, of course, that nothing will have changed. Everything will only be worse, it seems to me, and that thought fills me with the greatest possible dread."

"But perhaps *you* will be changed, Derek. Then you can react to the circumstances far differently, because you will be feeling better, much better since having been here."

Sparrowhawk rolled that thought around in his mind.

"Perhaps you are right," he acknowledged. "I desperately do want to feel better, as you can well imagine, since I have not felt very good for a long time now."

Sparrowhawk's mind started to wander a bit as he had to admit, though not to Bashir, that feeling better was not quite the same as feeling well. Once, weeks before, while on an amateur "dig" of his own, he had actually managed to unearth a human skull, and sat there, with it on the sand in front of him.

"We all end up like this," he had said somberly, with no one around to hear him. "Perhaps a few thousand years from now, some amateur archaeologist will be poking around, and come upon *my* skull, and say, 'We all end up like this.'"

He had felt unbearably lonely then, and cold, as though an ice storm had suddenly whipped into his very soul and every inch of him was reeling from the force of it.

"And a few thousand years after that, it will be *his* skull that is discovered, and—and—"

On and on the cycle went, ancient and hopeless and never ending, people living for a brief while and then becoming whitish piles of bone that the centuries covered, all beauty as dust, love and hatred both destroyed by the same awful and inexorable progression of events that keeps on, and on, changeless.

"There is no more to any of this," he had said as he stood, looking around at the base of the mountain that stretched to his left and to his right. "The mountains outlast us. The streams continue on their predestined course. Trees are living long after we are dust."

He could feel something wet on his cheeks.

"I, Derek Sparrowhawk, of long and noble lineage, could die right now, and fall at this very spot, and few of the seven billion on this planet . . . would ever know that I existed," he said, his voice breaking. "Most of those who did either wouldn't care or would be inclined to say, 'Good riddance to that boring old bloke!'"

He had let out a holler that echoed across the mountain.

*Good riddance . . . good riddance . . . good riddance.*

"That's all there is," he whispered as he left that lone skull on the desert sand and started walking back toward the village. "Dust and death and fragile old bones. What's the point of anything? What's the point of living another day?"

In the distance he could hear the mournful call of a creature unknown.

# =8=

Sparrowhawk's and Bashir's walk had taken them to the village's center, a nearly round area where there were no buildings of any kind, nothing except tents from which merchants located in the village itself or from the surrounding area sold their wares in a ragtag enterprise known as a bazaar, the Americanized versions of it in the States bearing little resemblance to those that proliferated throughout the Middle East, a fixture of Arab communities that seemed identical regardless of the community, only the size denoting the importance of the particular location.

Small.

In the village of Fahid Bashir, the bazaar there had only a few hawkers of silks and linens and some exotic birds plus one man with an old camel that he should have been giving away instead of trying to sell to an unwary customer.

Musty odors dominated, as throughout the rest of that village, even the young children smelling of these somehow, a circumstance of living in an ancient place.

"So little gives me pleasure anymore, Bashir," Sparrowhawk commented. "I am reduced to digging in the sand for the bones of long-dead strangers."

"But you have seemed quite happy doing this, at least much of the time," Bashir observed.

"I may be a better actor than I am a journalist."

"We all experience bouts of melancholy. About which I personally have known a great deal, I assure you."

Not only over his own divorce and the strain of those early battles with Muslims who were once brothers; not only over the wall between himself and every Muslim who remained in the village; but also about the future of that place, the loss of—.

"And what have we seen in this brief walk may give you some clue as to the depths to which my own emotions have been sinking, Derek."

. . . *what we have seen.*

Men walked around dressed in thousand dollar silk suits, with five hundred dollar hand-tooled leather shoes and an air of utter arrogance as they projected the notion that the potential of billions of dollars in oil revenues should take precedence over environmental and other considerations.

"Money can buy as much culture as you want," one of them was overheard telling a group of villagers. "Money can buy all the things you've always wanted."

The English journalist and the former Muslim looked at one another knowingly as they moved on.

"I want to show you something," Bashir remarked, "the site of a major turning point in my life."

"Lead the way, constable," Sparrowhawk said agreeably.

They stood, briefly, in front of a typically modest residence on the outskirts of the village.

"This is where my family and I used to live until I was turned out," he said simply.

He had told his friend the story of the time when he was twenty years old and the experience he had had in that mountain pass, together with the awful rejection that had followed by every member of his family and nearly all the rest of the village's populace.

"You've not shown this to me before now," Sparrowhawk observed.

"I could not."

"Why?"

"It was too painful."

"After so long?"

Bashir nodded.

"Why is it less so now, Fahid?"

"I have the feeling of late that there is something *more* painful waiting to take its place."

"More painful than losing your family in the way you did?" Sparrowhawk asked. "Are you feeling saying *that?*"

Bashir carefully considered what the Englishman had just mentioned.

"I think so," he said finally. "What we are seeing at this moment is more recent, the corruption of my people."

"You may be overreacting, Fahid. If you're wrong, won't you feel more than a little foolish? Right now, I can't equate your own mother's attempt to murder you with some villagers buying automobiles and a few good pieces of clothing."

"The hangnail that pains today supersedes the viper's bite yesterday."

"That sounds like ripe old Middle Eastern whimsy," Sparrowhawk replied, laughing sympathetically as he did so.

"It is," Bashir told him but in a far more serious tone.

His manner suggested that more than one memory was surfacing as he looked over every inch of the front of the house.

"I can almost hear her voice," he said. "My mother had a wonderful laugh, you see. In the midst of this place, so cold and hot, depending upon the season, she was always the same, ready to laugh given the slightest excuse."

"She may still be alive, Fahid. You shouldn't talk of her as though she's dead. There might be some—"

"—miracle waiting to happen?" Bashir interrupted. "How I would like to think that, yes, I would. But it's been more than ten years now, and there has not been so much as one letter."

In front of them was the desert, now tinged in spots with a light coating of frost.

"I dislike this particular season of the year," Bashir remarked, changing the subject but not very artfully. "It seems so much like the time just before death, cold and harsh and—."

He turned and looked back at the village.

"How much longer?" he asked. "How much longer before the oil interests totally and, I fear, indiscriminately have their way with this village and we are gone as a community?"

"Who can say?" Sparrowhawk replied. "Take Hawaii, my friend. I've been there innumerable times over the years. On each occasion it seems a bit more ravaged, a little less Hawaiian in the purest sense of the word, and more like the pretended Hawaii you find in patches of the United States and even in England when they try to create something that could be labeled Hawaii-like. I am sometimes reminded of a studio sound stage at Shepperton, for example."

"Your point, Derek?"

"My point hasn't been reached yet, thank you," he said with mock-offense. "Yet even in the midst of all this degradation of a very special natural resource, you know what?"

Bashir shook his head.

"There is still *something* left, the residue of old memories," Sparrowhawk continued, "perhaps only that, I grant, but I am much inclined to doubt that it stops there, Fahid. It may be that Hawaii will never be totally debased. It may be that patches of what once was will be allowed to remain, the developers' concession to things truly Hawaiian."

The Englishman wiped his eyes with a handkerchief that he had retrieved from a trouser pocket, then added:

"And we can go to those patches and stand wistfully in the midst of them and somehow relive the past we cherished in the nostalgic corners of our minds because we have been able to cling however tenuously to a physical remnant of it, indeed small, nothing more than a patch really, and quite surrounded by symbols of the very forces that have whittled it down to that tiny, tiny—some would say, pitiable—portion, a crumb from the tables of those who have done the plundering."

"Are you saying that something may endure of what we've had here for many centuries?"

Bashir would have liked very much to believe that. Even such a place was not without its virtues, and he had never known anything else except for those brief periods of travel. Certainly Romania offered no viable options as far as he was concerned.

"Perhaps, Fahid, perhaps," Sparrowhawk commented. "Who am I to offer up convenient little prophecies? I can scarcely tell what next month will bring."

"There was someone, you know."

Bashir turned back toward the desert, and pointed in the direction of the peaks in the near-distance.

"Out there," he said.

"Wise One, I gather?" Sparrowhawk repeated, pleased that the direction of their conversation was finally pointed in the direction he had hoped for the past hour or so.

"Yes, Wise One," he said. "Wise One came down from the mountains and told us, or tried to do so anyway."

"You didn't heed the warning, I gather. But then how would that have been possible. None of you dug the tell-tale hole. It was some strangers. You had no control over any of that."

"Or forgot that there was one in the first place."

"You lost me, I'm afraid."

"I mean, conveniently forgot that there had been a warning to begin with."

*"You want everything on the spot," Wise One said, a sneer in his voice, "and yet you claim to be unlike so many other villages and towns and cities in this world at present, untainted by many of the excesses of modern civilization."*

Bashir repeated those words for his friend.

"That's not a prophecy, as far as I can tell," Sparrowhawk remarked. "It may be a judgment perhaps, but nothing other than that."

"There is more," Bashir said. "In the context of what happened, it was indeed foretelling."

When he had finished recalling for the Englishman the details of that afternoon two decades earlier, Sparrowhawk was stunned by what he had heard.

"Pretty miserable treatment for the old guy, wouldn't you say?" he commented.

"Oh, yes, I agree, Derek."

"Where were you when all this was in progress?"

"In the crowd, I'm afraid, watching. I suppose you might say I was a silent member of the vocal majority."

Sparrowhawk sighed.

"And what you just told me happened *after* this place had become predominantly Christian?" he asked. "What about all those tenets of the faith? Helping people rather than casting them out? And a score of others even I seem to have memorized over the years?"

"It's a shameful fact to have to admit, but the answer is yes, some devout Christians treated Wise One just as I have mentioned," Bashir told him. "About the only thing I can say, and only in the feeblest defense, I have to admit, is that the Muslims surely would have treated him far worse than we did."

Bashir paused, remembering the details of that day with particular clarity.

"The saddest thing, I suppose, is that Wise One must be dead by now, and I will never have a chance to make it up to him, if that had ever been possible."

"It's amazing that you remember everything," Sparrowhawk remarked, "every nuance."

Bashir tried to smile at the compliment but didn't succeed.

"The old man had been called Wise One years before by village children who used to flock to him whenever he came down from the mountains," he continued. "In those days he seemed to be dispensing only mythological-type stories to charm their innocent attention spans. None of us knew anything about him, actually, but then no one felt threatened, either. Wise One seemed harmless, an eccentric old codger, a little like the village mascot."

"Or idiot, perhaps?" Sparrowhawk interpolated.

"I'm afraid so," Bashir had to agree. "As long as he could be held somewhat at a distance, as long as he made no exceptional demands on our tolerance, he was acceptable. It cost us virtually nothing to be kind to him, after a fashion, anyway.

"Then he dared to judge us, dared to see through the facade that we had constructed around our hypocrisies. We couldn't let him go unpunished for that, and, thus, we shouted the worst kinds of accusations against him, naturally so that we wouldn't have to deal with the truth about ourselves that he had laid out before us."

"I can imagine how you feel," Sparrowhawk agreed. "I can—"

His face went pasty-white all of a sudden, and he became dizzy, and had to lean slightly on Bashir to steady himself. The spell passed in less than a minute.

"What happened?" Bashir asked, deeply concerned.

"It's nothing physical," the Englishman replied.

"What makes you say *that?* How can you be so sure, Derek? Please, you should seek—."

The other man's expression made him cut off his own words.

"It has to do with my own nightmare as a youth," Sparrowhawk recalled. "You had yours, and it was awful, I admit. Here's mine . . .

He had been on assignment in Pakistan and had noticed a woman in her mid-twenties.

"I found her to be more than a little attractive," he said, smiling as her face came back to him in memory. "Through various machinations, I arranged to meet her. Within a matter of a few days, we fell in love, Fahid, deeply in love."

He noticed the other's questioning expression.

"Ah, yes, your Christian sensibilities, sorry! I hadn't met my wife, so our relationship wasn't adulterous, my friend. Nor did we share the same bed, ever. She was too much a product of her strict Islamic upbringing for *that* to be a part of the story."

*She was taken from me before we could make love. We held one another. We kissed. We caressed.*

67

*But word that was distorted and evil spread too quickly in that part of Pakistan and—*

"They stoned her to death, Fahid. That may not surprise you, of course, since you were once a Muslim. The trouble is that they *assumed* we had been to bed together. And they refused to believe otherwise. She had committed a mortal sin, in their minds, and—"

He started sobbing, and Bashir came over to him and put his arm around the Englishman.

"I didn't do anything to prevent what was happening," Sparrowhawk continued. "Of course, I would have been greatly outnumbered, me against the population of an entire village."

"What did keep you from—from—well—," Bashir tried to speak, failing in the process.

"From at least trying to help her?"

Bashir nodded.

"It was quite simple, actually," Sparrowhawk continued. "They made me unable to be a father, and left me for dead."

"You were castrated?" Bashir asked, horrified.

"I didn't want to be too specific."

"Not all Christians have their heads stuck deep in the sand, Derek. My own view is that being doctrinally conservative, which includes believing in the fundamental inerrancy of Scripture and all that that entails in one's life, *and* having my eyes open to the world around me are, well, not mutually exclusive, by any means.

"Christians who ignore the latter because they think it is somehow contradictory to the former are, shall we say, Satan's easiest targets. As far as he is concerned, anyone who knows little about his tactics is ill-prepared when he does attack, as invariably he will."

"You believe in the devil, then?" the Englishman asked. "You're that far into this sort of thing?"

"This sort of thing?" Bashir replied, offended.

Sparrowhawk blushed, and apologized immediately.

"Sorry, governor, really sorry. But I haven't thought about Satan a great deal over the years, you know. I equate

68

him more than anything with those Hollywood and British horror movies that have been ground out over the years, I suppose."

"But knowing what happened to your friend, isn't it impossible to see that in any context other than direct satanic deception?"

"Deception on whose part?"

"On the part of a belief system that came into existence, we might say, at the very whim of Satan, a brain-child that has entrapped countless millions through yet another of his false prophets!"

"Extremely strong language for someone who embraced Islam for the first twenty years of his life!"

"That is *why* I feel as I do. I have seen the bone-and-marrow-and-sinews of this so-called faith, seen how utterly bankrupt and evil it is, seen how this prophet Muhammad, whom they revere so greatly, is someone deserving contempt rather than adulation, speaking peace and joy and much else while fomenting heinous acts."

Sparrowhawk was startled.

"You aren't going to write a book, are you?" he said, obviously taken by surprise at Bashir's passionate display.

"I shouldn't allow myself to be tempted, Derek, by you or anyone else, since I just might decide to do such a book." Bashir's face was reddening as the emotions built.

"Here's a clear-cut example of strong, redemptive, life-changing light as opposed to the darkness every Muslim stumbles through day-after-day," he said, "like someone who is not blind as such but merely too stupid to open his eyes. Remember when Christ stopped at least one stoning, according to Scripture? He spoke of those without sin being the only ones who could inflict such treatment, which is nothing more than an execution, if you get right down to it.

"And yet my former brothers in the faith engage in that abominable practice more often than either of us could possibly count, that and other atrocities you know about as well as I do."

The Englishman did, for sure he did, and from vivid personal experience, experience that had opened his eyes about the true nature of Islam, a religion to which he had once been drawn.

Sparrowhawk was shivering.

"It is very difficult, Fahid, to look at things in strictly theological terms when . . . when—"

He was shivering as he spoke.

"One of the bonds my wife and I had, ironically, was what had happened to me. My emotions were still quite raw when we met. I was beginning to wonder, Bashir, if they'd ever heal, although my body itself had become well enough by then."

He wiped his eyes with the back of his hand.

"Angelica was so wonderful. She pulled me through, made me realize that virility could be measured in more ways than one. That woman enabled me to regain some self-respect, of which I had little or none left before we met. And, of course, I had the greatest of admiration for her, for her own womanhood.

"We were determined that what happened wouldn't be *allowed* to go on affecting either one of us. You see, for Angelica and me, surviving and constructing a worthwhile future that would not give those Muslim monsters new victory became a mission of sorts between the two of us. We weren't going to allow them to . . . to . . . totally ruin life for the two of us."

*He recalled some of those wonderful moments shared with Angelica. She was so sensitized to his feelings, so aware of how compromised he felt as a man.*

*"Children will be a part of our relationship," she told him.*

*"But not my own children. They'll be taken from some other man. I don't know if I can cope with that, Angelica, I just don't know."*

*"You won't . . . alone," she assured him. "We will, Derek, the two of us."*

*He thought, with such a woman by his side, that he could conquer anything in life that crossed his path, no matter how devastating it might be.*

"But you ended up being divorced," Bashir mentioned as gently as possible. "What caused so strong a bond to be broken?"

The Englishman answered to softly then that Bashir couldn't hear what he had said, and asked his friend to repeat it.

"My work . . . ," Sparrowhawk commented. "My dear beloved Angelica could cope with anything but having her mate on the road so much. She assumed, with little justification—and please believe this, Bashir—that being a journalist-world-traveler meant more to me than whatever it took to be the sort of husband she *needed* as well as a devoted father to the adopted children we had been responsible for bringing into our home.

"Angelica couldn't abide anything to the contrary, you see, unable as she was to roll with the punches, as the expression goes."

"So she gave up trying?"

"I'm afraid so," Sparrowhawk admitted. "She gave up trying to alter her life . . . that is, her life with my playing any part in it."

There was real weariness in the man's tone then. Bashir picked up on this instantly, and let the matter drop.

# =9=

Derek Sparrowhawk was tired that night after he returned to his little cottage, although to call the place in which he had been staying for months by any such designation seemed far too generous under the circumstances, a glorification of what, in reality, it actually was—a three-room structure barely a cut or two above a simple mud hut.

Few "houses" were any different in that village or others like it; this one had been unoccupied since the owner, one of the handful of remaining Muslims, had moved on a year or so earlier, leaving it unceremoniously behind, as though glad to be rid of the hovel and, more particularly, to get away from the "infidels" who now controlled the village's governmental structure.

The odor of dried earth had greeted him when he first moved in, and it remained eight months later. He had to pump his own water and use a ramshackle outhouse. There was no heat except whatever he was able to coax from a fire in a well-nigh crumbling fireplace.

He should have been thoroughly depressed. He certainly should have returned to London seven months ago, for he could name a hundred people in his acquaintance who would scarcely have stayed the first night or two without making other arrangements.

72

*But here I am, and even now I've not decided when to leave,* Sparrowhawk remarked to himself.

He sat in one of only two ancient chairs in the entire place, looking around at the very basic interior. Back in London he had a radar oven, a sound-surround stereo system, a large screen projection TV, and much else.

But here—

*What am I learning?* he had asked himself at one stage in his stay. *What have I gained? How foolish am I being by not just admitting that coming to this village was a bad idea from the word go?*

And then Sparrowhawk decided to stop the circuitous route of procrastination that he had been taking, and started using the little manual portable typewriter he had brought with him, knowing from long experience that he should never trust the tenuous legibility of his handwriting. What he had begun that morning proved to be the first chapter of a long novel, which was a deliberately sharp departure from his proven track record of nonfiction works.

That was six months earlier . . .

He reached out and picked up the pile of paper from the folding table in front of him.

"Here it is," he said, "the very best work that I have ever been able to do."

Leaving through the pages, Sparrowhawk smiled as he reread one paragraph or another.

*. . . the very best.*

He was still a chapter or two away from completing it, but he had little doubt that doing so would not take a great deal longer.

*Why here?* he asked himself. *In the middle of nowhere, as the expression goes, I may be creating a masterpiece. But in the midst of the city of Shakespeare, Dickens, and a host of others, I tried to do so and came up with the worst sort of dribble. There I was, with ten thousand pounds worth of computer equipment, and yet all I had to show for it was mindless nonsense, fluff no more substantial than bubbles blown by a child through a—*

But in that village, after a month that had been spent unproductively trying to persuade himself that he shouldn't have come in the first place, he sat down that one morning, not expecting to accomplish more than he had the day before and, abruptly, the prose that poured forth was soaring, lyrical, an *opus profundis* beginning to take shape on a bargain-basement typewriter that was stiff to use in comparison to what had been at his disposal back "in civilization," so stiff and slow that his fingers began to feel slightly numb after a few hours daily.

*But there is soul within these pages,* he acknowledged to himself. *There is life, there is passion and—*

Fahid Bashir had been part of the reason.

Sparrowhawk disliked having to admit this to himself because he then would have to proceed to the next link in the chain of reasoning, and that would bring him face-to-face with Bashir's Christianity.

The two could not be separated.

"I've tried," he said, again out loud. "I've tried to look at the man without the necessity of involving that bloody slaughterhouse of a religion to which he insists upon clinging and yet—"

*How can he take any of that claptrap seriously? As far as I've ever been able to tell, religion succeeds only in one area, that of pitting deluded people against one another. And yet Fahid can still go on babbling about the beauty of salvation through Jesus Christ as Savior and Lord.*

*An intelligent man like him given to the most absurd near-ravings! How can that be?*

Sparrowhawk put the pile of papers back on the folding chair and stood, stretching his legs.

He was tired. He needed to sleep. But instead he walked outside, at an hour past midnight, and looked up at the sky, which was what it tended to be all the time in that part of the world, a clear and beguiling tapestry littered with stars.

*Three wise men . . .*

He found himself whispering those words, surprised that they had been remembered at all, since the last time he consciously repeated them was surely back in his childhood.

"So long ago . . . ," he started to say, but stopped, not wanting to wade through the memories.

Many of those were pleasant. He had spent much of his early life with his parents in Scotland. The three of them had worshiped in a Scottish Presbyterian church at the base of Edinburgh Castle. To get to it meant walking through a marvelously atmospheric cemetery.

At first he was scared. Then he came to regard it as a special place. He enjoyed looking at the headstones and trying to find the oldest one.

And he loved Edinburgh itself, a city filled with wonderful little restaurants and quaint, unspoiled alleys that did seem to have sprung out of a Charles Dickens novel. By entering them, it was nearly as though he was actually going back in time a couple of hundred years!

*So happy . . .*

The memories were still as fine as ever. But the good times they embodied ended tragically when his mother died of cancer and was buried in that ancient cemetery. It no longer seemed special to him. It had swallowed up his beloved mother's body and wouldn't ever give her back to him.

*I believed in You then,* he thought. *I thought of You as our Protector, our Comforter. I came to You so often on my knees, with the faith of a child, asking for Your healing—Please, please heal my mother, Lord—. She believed in You. She kept telling me not to worry, that she was going to heaven and would be waiting for father, for me, and when we were reunited, it would last for eternity.*

He knelt suddenly on the soft surface of sand, but not in supplication or worship, not that at all.

"But that wasn't all, wasn't it, *Lord?*" he whispered as sarcastically as he could. "You really didn't care about me later any more than You did when I was a boy. I was one of those poor souls that somehow always slipped through the cracks of that so-called divine plan of Yours.

"First, my mother—you treated my prayers as though they were the ravings of a nitwit. Perhaps that was what they amounted to if they were spoken with any hope of a miracle from You!

"But then neither were You anywhere around when that sweet little butterfly was killed by a group of evil men whose religion surely must be among the greatest of blasphemies in Your eyes," Sparrowhawk said plaintively. "Two thousand years earlier, You condescended to save a common harlot from the same bloody fate—but, more recently, such a beautiful, fragile, innocent creature . . . You . . . You allowed her to be sacrificed on the altar of intolerance."

Anger was rising, anger that caused his body to be covered with perspiration, even as the evening chill wrapped tightly around him.

"She did nothing evil," he went on. "She did in fact try to break away from the corrupt delusions of a belief system that had been enslaving her. Yet that wasn't enough for You, was it?"

He let out a low cry.

"Tell me now: What is it that the two of us didn't do that we *should* have done in order for You to condescend to show a few drops of that mercy for which You are so famous?"

Sparrowhawk stood, his hips arched in a stance of raw defiance, as though demanding to hear forthwith some *verbal* reply but not really expecting one either, recalling an instance he'd heard about an irate former patient who had challenged her ex-doctor to prove that he was not a quack, while believing fully that he indeed was just that.

When there was no response, the Englishman spat on the dry ground, and turned back toward the—

He halted in mid-stride, and as an afterthought, looked out over the desert, and, beyond, to the mountains.

"Do *you* have any answers . . . Wise One?"

He paused, sighing, then added: "Are you even alive?"

For a moment, he could almost see an ancient form in the darkness, with a long, thin beard and a head of hair pure white, a weathered old face with eyes that seemed deep pits of wisdom.

"Is that you?" the Englishman said, the image so vivid in his mind that he stopped just short of the doorway, turning his head and peering with mock-intentness into the clear Middle Eastern night. "Have you perchance been overhearing my idle ruminations?"

Derek Sparrowhawk shook his head as though to clear it of some inner fog and chuckled as he glanced one more time at the sky.

"Or perhaps You, God," he said cynically, "yes, perhaps You."

# = 10 =

The ground-breaking ceremony for yet another of numerous projected wells was supposed to take place at noon the next day. It seemed an unnecessary contrivance but undoubtedly was done to make sure the people felt involved. And it seemed to work, as it had done for the other half-dozen wells, since everyone in the village was present, residents as well as those who were visitors, such as Derek Sparrowhawk.

The oil field had been discovered barely a mile away, in close proximity to what was essentially an extended series of rock piles nearly two miles long. There seemed to be no direct connection with the nearby mountain range, eliminating the possibility of volcanic eruption spewing forth lava as far away as that, without some perceptible link. And since the rock piles weren't man-made, there was no possibility that they had been tombs erected by unknown rulers of that region many centuries before.

This spot was where most of the archaeologists, professional and amateur alike, started in their separate quests.

That was so especially after a series of tunnels were discovered underneath one portion of the site; in the tunnels were found striking evidence of what looked like a secretive community in exile, one not mentioned in a single historical chronicle.

Bashir and Sparrowhawk both had been to the catacombs on the outskirts of Rome, where even the Englishman was profoundly affected by the "mood" that seemed to predominate there.

"Similar, wouldn't you say, Fahid?" he remarked as he stood for the first time before a rock wall lined with little sections that had been chipped out of it.

"More than that," Bashir assured him. "I would think, Derek, that they were virtually identical if I remember correctly."

But there had been no large-scale group of Christians escaping persecution throughout that entire part of the world, at least according to any records with which the two of them were familiar.

"There have never been any clues," Sparrowhawk asked skeptically, "not in the slightest?"

"Whoever lived here did so in total anonymity," Bashir replied, with a touch of awe, "though there were stories passed down centuries later, chilling little anecdotes, to be sure."

Sparrowhawk wondered if his friend had arrived at the same speculation as he.

"Could we be talking about one-and-the-same impression, Fahid?" he suggested to his friend.

"I wouldn't doubt it," Bashir replied. "But you first!"

"They were evil undoubtedly," Sparrowhawk continued, understanding the irony that he, an agnostic, would ever use such a term as other than purely a psychiatric generality.

"Do you realize that *everyone* who ventures down here comes to the precise same conclusion?" Bashir pointed out. "It's always the same, my friend. And no matter how many times I myself stand here, I feel the same way, the intensity not lessened in the slightest."

"You say everyone. Even those doubting Thomases who scoff at the very existence of evil in any form?"

"Especially those."

"How so?"

"You see, they just aren't prepared for any of this, Derek. They find their rationalizations about myth and legend

79

slipping like greased pigs between their unaccustomed fingers."

Evil . . .

Not just in the odor of things ancient and unknown. Nor in the near-total darkness that played with vagrant childhood fears about what might lurk a bit beyond human sight. Nor the strange sounds that could be heard periodically, all of which could be explained by underground air currents and scampering rodents and other creatures.

But what had been carved on the rock walls.

Drawings of the most bizarre sort. Strange shapes. Scattered messages in a language no one had been able to translate.

"Why hasn't more been covered in the media about all this?" Sparrowhawk mused out.

"Because practically no one talks about the experience. They leave, and crawl into their beds at night, and shiver for a while, then somehow manage to go to sleep—though not without some predictable tossing and turning."

"But whoever lived here, whatever they did, all that is thousands of years gone. It is silliness to—"

Bashir looked at him with an amused expression.

"Then why are your teeth chattering, Derek?"

"So you say! That's ridiculous, they're not—"

He suddenly realized that Bashir was correct.

"It's the cold down here," he said lamely.

"It's hardly cold enough for that!"

Sparrowhawk didn't speak for a moment as he walked up to one of the carved sections.

*Strange shapes . . . distorted . . . human only in the sense of a modernistic abstract painting, yet done apparently countless thousands of years before Picasso and others like him were born.*

"Amazing," he said after a few seconds. "I feel uneasy merely *looking* at what whoever it was had been trying to communicate."

*The faces are the worst, bizarre and grotesque, like age-old representations of demonic malevolence . . .*

Rubbing his left arm, which felt as though it had suddenly gone quite numb, Sparrowhawk turned to the other man.

"Did that Wise One chap *ever* mention anything at all about this place?" he asked.

"Never," Bashir told him. "Not during that final day, certainly. Nor any previous to it, as far as I can tell."

"I wonder what he *would* have said."

"What are you getting at?"

"I mean, everyone went from utter surprise at his apparent wisdom to accusing him of being in league with evil forces."

"A connection between Wise One and—?" Bashir said, then added, "If so, we could ponder for a long time which side—what is it the Americans say?—ah, yes, which side he would have come down on."

Sparrowhawk interrupted by shaking his head and muttering, "Who knows, Fahid? Do not consider what I have said as anything but pointless, and irrelevant, and probably somewhat foolish to boot."

"Too bad we have to assume that Wise One is no longer with us," Bashir remarked with a curious melancholy, a detailed picture of the old man so sharp in his mind that it was hard indeed to believe so many years had passed since that last encounter.

"Too bad indeed," Sparrowhawk agreed. "Now let's get out of here before we start imagining all manner of nonsense!"

# =11=

For a very long time, the mystery of that settlement had been pondered by anyone brought face-to-face with it, none ever being able to forget what he had seen, or what he *perceived*, however vague. To date, nobody had any theories that were other than patently irrational, many falling into the "chariots of fire" category that often refuted basic Bible tenets.

*Nothing that happens in this world can ever be contrary to what God has declared would occur,* Bashir told himself each time some bizarre new theory was "bounced off him" by visitor and resident alike. *Anything that may seem contrary, for the moment, has either been misunderstood or is an outright deception originated by Satan himself.*

He had learned to think that way in a land and with a people who were rift with superstition, which once had held sway over his own life.

*Oh, how sanctified the* Qur'ān *purports to be,* he thought as he recalled the long hours of so-called study, of meditation over pages that were supposed to be directly from Allah through His most holy Prophet. *I wallowed in its deceptions like millions of other blinded souls. I took the words of Muhammad, and they became as life itself to me. But I never suspected their true nature,*

*my senses dulled as I bowed in worship and honored a man, noth-*
*ing more than a man, never more than a man, a deceiver who—*

If true religion were based upon God, and God was truth, then the extent of falsehood and error in Islam was enough, in itself, to condemn Muhammad as the father of infamies spread over the centuries.

*To speak about Christ as a great prophet on the one hand, and then condemn those who followed Him, calling upon Muslims to bring death to any Christians who got in their way, that alone should open the eyes of the most casual observer.*

*How easy it is to cry, "Holy war! Holy war! Holy war!"*

*For the Shiites, centuries of hatred toward any and all people who are not Muslims has molded them into one of the most evil sects on earth, possessed of a fanatical desire to establish a pure Islamic kingdom.*

*Thirteen centuries after Muhammad's death—or his ascension into heaven, as the Muslims believe—the Shiites still have not cut off enough hands or performed enough decapitations to satisfy their blood lust.*

Bashir realized he might still have wallowed in this outlook if not for that one encounter, so strong that it—.

More than once, he went to the portion of the New Testament that told of Saul's Damascus Road experience, and how, afterward, he became Paul.

*From persecutor to defender to champion . . .*

Bashir smiled, thinking how much he paled in comparison to Paul, though he had such a similar experience in a spot that was quite close, as distances in the Middle East went, to where the apostle underwent his own transformation.

He wondered, often, why he had never returned to that place and why he had never heard of others who had had the same experience, though there were any number of times that he started across the stretch of desert between the village and the mountain range.

Always he stopped. Always he turned around and went back.

Once, during the heat of the day, he collapsed, and in the wave of unconsciousness that engulfed him, he thought he heard the sound of many wings but assumed, later, that this had been imagined.

*Many wings . . .*

"What was that?" he said, jolted out of his reverie by someone tapping his shoulder.

The ceremonies were over.

The switch had been thrown, and yet another well was in operation. A number of others would soon be activated and in full operation within the next month or so, pumping oil by the thousands of gallons each day.

Everyone, it seemed, had gone on to the village square where a tent had been set up and a buffet-style meal was being served.

Sitting next to him at one of the picnic-type tables was a tall, wiry American named Stuart Brickley, an executive vice-president with Americo, the huge international oil company involved with the new oil find.

"I was saying, Fahid, that I can't imagine how excited you are about all of this," Brickley, who must have weighed not more than 150 pounds, commented with obvious enthusiasm.

Bashir turned, and studied the man's face for a moment.

"Is that what you think we should be—excited?"

"Why, yes, your land can be turned into a real wonderland."

"And what do you consider to be a wonderland, Mr. Brickley?"

"Call me Stuart. I used *your* first name, didn't I? No formality is necessary, as far as I am concerned."

"All right, Stuart, explain to me the sort of wonderland for which we should be grateful."

"Poverty will be eliminated."

"Would you suggest that our existence before you arrived was what you would call poverty-stricken?"

"Well, I daresay it wasn't like Kuwait, certainly!"

"Before or after Saddam Hussein?"

"Before, of course."

Brickley's large protruding eyes narrowed a bit.

"I must say I detect a degree of hostility for which I wasn't prepared," he remarked.

"Because you thought all we needed was money, is that it, Stuart?" Bashir retorted.

"Money can buy you anything you want, my friend."

"Including an army to protect us if some unfriendly government wants to overrun us?"

"No, that was proved in Kuwait," the other man said, his face reddening. "What it *can* do is get you property elsewhere."

"Oh, you mean, so that running away won't leave us homeless?"

Brickley was becoming exasperated.

"You will change your tune, Mr. Bashir, that is, when you see what happens here."

"No more Fahid, Stuart? What happened to the first name routine? I thought formality wasn't your bag, as the expression goes!"

"I can only assume you fell for that nonsense."

"What nonsense?"

"That the old doctor mentioned."

"About Wise One, you mean?"

"Yes."

"But that was twenty years ago."

A bemused expression crossed Brickley's face then.

"I mean, the more recent, shall we say, 'visitation.' Surely you've heard about what happened last night."

Bashir's mouth dropped open.

"Ah, the man loses his cool finally," Brickley said. "You must learn that even someone such as yourself doesn't know everything."

Bashir knew that he had been properly chastised.

"I *am* sorry," he said sincerely. "I suppose the original incident has been on my mind ever since."

"I see! Then the news that Wise One allegedly visited that doctor in the middle of the night as recently as a few hours ago must be quite startling."

"Especially since I thought he was dead a long time ago."

"Wise One may be just that, in fact. The whole thing could have been a delusion on the good doctor's part, I mean, that *is* a possibility at his advanced age."

Bashir had to admit that the other man was right.

"You have a point, Stuart," he agreed.

"I am a rationalist," Brickley told him. "Old men die when they're supposed to do so. They do not live on mysteriously past an age when everyone else has fallen victim to the Grim Reaper. It just doesn't happen that way, and I am much inclined to doubt that your so-called Wise One is any different, Fahid."

# $=\!\!12\!\!=$

As the festivities continued, Bashir noticed that Derek Sparrowhawk was not present, nor had he been at the dedication itself, though such an absence was odd for the consummate journalist. However abhorrent the various implications were to some individuals, including the Englishman and Bashir, the event was a notable one, and Sparrowhawk by all rights should have been there.

*I wonder . . .*

The last time Bashir recalled having seen the other man was back at the tunnel site.

*I cannot believe that he returned there. I'll have to stop at his residence and see if he's—*

But first he knew he had to see the doctor, to find out about this supposed visit by Wise One, who should have died many years before.

For the moment, however, he returned his attention to the square, and the surge of activity within it.

What had once been a quiet place in the center of the village was presently filled with activity, people dancing about, the odor of liquor in the air, prerecorded music coming from large loudspeakers.

A celebration.

*How easily the old restrictions fall,* he thought. *How these collapse before the onslaught of mammon.*

He stood quietly for a moment, watching the gluttony as men and women experienced what it was like to have plenty to eat, and, yes, that was understandable in view of the very basic foodstuffs to which they were accustomed. Now it was caviar, now it was prime rib, now it was Dobos torte for dessert. All of this could be looked at within the framework of human nature and provide no surprises.

But deprivation had brought with it a precious kind of spiritual discipline, for Christian and Muslim alike, which made the present revelry seem a bit like what Moses must have encountered after he came down from Mount Sinai with the Ten Commandments on tablets of stone.

Bashir was reminded of something else as well, the story of what happened to a small colony of monks living in a monastery near Geneva, Switzerland.

They had been utterly dedicated to serving others, which provided their only reason for ever leaving their fortress-like home. Otherwise they all would have been quite content to have no contact of any kind with the outside world.

"We could be so happy here, away from the shameful ways of the rest of society," they would say among themselves, "and yet Jesus Christ has give us a sacred mission that is utterly contrary to our own desires. Therefore, we are compelled to add this further denial to a long list in the hope that He somehow will be pleased with our conduct."

There was still among these men a shackling works-orientation, but it seemed, for them, to have been turned into a genuine desire to seek His will, and to do it, to offer their bodies a living sacrifice in every sense.

So they expanded their ministry beyond the confines of the monastery and worked with the poor, not simply in Switzerland but elsewhere, in the surrounding countries, providing clothes they had made, food they had cooked, and spiritual counsel.

Though not large in numbers, they achieved notable results that seemed beyond the capabilities of much larger organizations with ample high-powered personnel, advanced equipment, and respectable budgets for the various needs.

But then, as they entered a period of cutting back that was initiated abruptly from the Vatican, they had had to come up with a larger percentage of the money needed to survive. So they started to sell small jars of preserves: boysenberry, apricot, and others.

Word spread about the sublime taste, unmitigated by additives of any kind. People started writing to them, asking for large numbers of jars. The letters were from a dozen different countries.

Finally the monks received an offer from an American manufacturer. Initially they turned it down as smacking of commercial exploitation, especially since it was obvious that the company's *only* motivation was profit—always accelerating profit—aided by marketing techniques that would be state-of-the-art.

"We will not bury our mission under a pile of cash register receipts," Father Francesco declared to the others. "Can we hope to honor our sweet Savior if that happens? Once there is no honor, once it lies in a heap at our feet as we stand mockingly over it, laughing, once it has been drowned out by the purveyors of exploitation, the door will be wide open for dishonor to come rushing in on cloven feet to destroy all of us.

"My dear friends, one of Satan's mightiest weapons is greed, and we dare not allow that to envelop us. What we have is too precious!"

. . . *what we have is too precious.*

And that was something special indeed.

They had in fact few real links remaining with the Vatican, but they had not made a big thing of the changes in their outlook so that the monolith in Rome left them pretty much alone, though there were some of the brothers who thought that the financial cuts were more in outright punishment than the others realized, and, if the truth be known, very little having to do with the Vatican's troubled economic straits.

They were more than content to be off by themselves, loners each and every one, but perceptive enough to comprehend that *total* separation could have been in violation of the Great Commission, so as they fed and clothed the poor, as they consoled the bereaved, as they treated the ailments of the sick, they also preached a strong salvational gospel, a gospel of light and truth and redemption.

And, in doing so, they eschewed some of the most pivotal doctrines of Roman Catholicism.

"We cannot follow the example of our dear Christ," Father Francesco had said some years earlier, "if we have to carry with us all the baggage of our man-made theology."

"But, pray tell, what then can we consider to be biblical, and what is no more than finite dictums conducted by the legalistic maneuvers of sinful men?" asked one of the monks.

"We have only one way of knowing," Father Francesco replied.

"And that is from a thorough reading of the Bible as the inspired and inerrant word of God," offered another of the eager brothers, pleased that he knew the only correct answer.

Father Francesco looked at him, touched by his unerring grasp of the truth, and then broke out weeping.

"What is it, Father?" they all shouted in concern.

After a few moments he had calmed down, the tears still glistening on his ample cheeks.

"The beauty of God Himself shining through in this humble gathering is just too much for me to bear without tears, my good and dear coworkers in the vineyard of souls."

They were never closer than in that special moment.

But it was not to last.

Ultimately there was more expansion, leading to more products, more income, more hoopla.

They found it necessary to incorporate, to have a governing board of directors, to become—

"A business!" Father Francesco said at a point before the activity intensified. "The only business we should have is that of bringing souls to Christ for His reception. This other—"

But the monks had tasted of what was a kind of forbidden fruit for them. They liked that taste, which soon became addictive, manifested by the good reviews, the enhanced income, the fact that they were being asked to do media interviews. Most now spent more time *outside* the monastery.

"We are being asked to attend a convention, Father," one of them told him. "They think we should have a booth and that the response to our products would be quite wonderful."

Father Francesco looked at the man with great sorrow.

"I have been to one of those . . . conventions." he recalled. "I have walked the aisles. I have seen the shame."

"The shame?" the other monk repeated, puzzled. "I do not understand, Father. Please enlighten me."

"The shame of making His name the stuff of cheap trinkets, the shame of people scrambling almost on their knees for the favors of publishers, distributors, bookstore managers."

"But the Vatican sanctions bingo games in dioceses all over the world, and holy water from vendors at its very gates!"

"The fact that those who govern Mother Church aid and abet the very forces attempting to dull its spiritual sensitivities into mere useless and endless proclamations that are as plentiful as the holidays that give rise to them—"

"Father Francesco," the other monk said, "you are rambling. Are you feeling ill?"

"Ill? Ah, yes, my friend, my brother in Christ, ill indeed, ill of the spirit, and bereft of hope that the process of deterioration can be stopped."

Father Francesco was dead a week later, apparently as the result of a massive heart attack.

Within a year, the monks had entered the restaurant business, with a series of franchises. Followed by a company selling gardening supplies. With other corporate entities on the drawing boards.

They exhibited at their first Christian convention six months later.

And no one seemed to remember what Father Dominick Angelo Francesco had tried to tell them.

No, that wasn't the case actually.

They remembered when they simply couldn't forget. But by then it no longer mattered.

91

# =13=

That night, Dr. Abul al-Fahazi had been sitting in the front seat of the new car his wife and he had ordered from a dealer in London.

A brand-new cherry-red Jaguar Sovereign.

He looked at the wood trim on the dashboard and along each door, smelled the odor of handsewed leather, leaned his head back on the seat, and closed his eyes and wondered if it could be true.

*Twenty years . . .*

That was how long it had been since he had seen his first Jaguar while attending a medical convention in Milan, Italy.

*I don't have to stay in this humble village,* he thought, *because my services would have be in demand anywhere else, but I've done that all these years, sacrificing for my people. Now I'm being rewarded. Praise God, the shower of blessings has begun.*

He remembered hearing a certain radio preacher over his shortwave, the broadcast beamed into the Middle East by satellite. He had started to listen long before the discovery of oil, his mind filled with words about material blessing coming in on the wings of angels.

"You see that new car! Tell the Lord you want it. That's all it takes, brethren. Once you become a Christian, all you have to do is ask *whatsoever you will in His name, and it shall be granted to you!"*

Dr. al-Fahazi had no idea what the man looked like. He just knew that kind of message turned him off.

At first.

But each time he left his office or the living quarters adjacent to it and walked the old streets of his village and saw the cracked and sometimes gradually crumbling old houses, saw camels dripping green or white slime from their mouths, stepped on camel dung, or smelled the odor of raw sewage, he thought back to that radio preacher and another, this one with the most seductive doctrine of all.

Possibility thinking.

"Explore the possibilities!" the baritone voice declared over the radio's tiny speaker. "You know what the key is? Faith in the God of possibilities, and faith in the possibilities of God.

"Unlock the potential *you!* Pull yourself up from the melancholy that has plagued you. Get rid of any mind-set that says you are incapable, because you *are* capable of *everything.* You can master your own existence. Being a Christian makes you master of your world. Think of the possibilities. Think of the money you could earn. Think of the fine clothes you could wear. Think of the places you could visit.

"Forget any talk of punishment or judgment. Turn away from those who try to get you to wallow in the blood of Jesus. Wash your hands of that stuff. It's not relevant in this world of ours. Christians should *demand* that God—"

That was when al-Fahazi turned off the radio the first time or two. But he became captivated. The preacher began to talk about Jesus now and then. Perhaps he wasn't so bad after all.

It was also when al-Fahazi started to dream, started to think of leaving the village, started to feel that his sacrificing days were over, that he had gone far enough down the road of denial and it was time he grabbed hold of some possibilities!

One medical convention a few months later was being held not far from the second preacher's church. So al-Fahazi decided to attend.

*I was so impressed. The hymns were right. The opening prayer. The sermon itself. So fine . . .*

And that building!

An extraordinary architectural achievement.

Most of it was glass, held together by aluminum beams, the glass treated with a photo-grey chemical that helped to block out the sun, like a giant pair of sun glasses.

It was shaped like a pyramid. Some of the American fundamentalists pointed out that this shape was a key symbol of the satanic New Age heresy and that the new church seemed to fit right in.

But the preacher lambasted that sort of narrow thinking. He deftly contrasted the gloom-and-doom of their outlook with the joy, the vibrancy—yes, the *possibilities*—that his own approach to worship brought forth.

The doctor came away convinced that *this* preacher had the right idea.

*And that he did, he surely did,* al-Fahazi told himself as he opened his eyes, taking in the wood, the leather, the smell of the Jaguar's interior.

After getting out of the car, he did a little dance step before returning to his office. That night, he dreamed of a gold-plated hood ornament.

*He wasn't prepared for the visitor he had a few hours later.*

*Not prepared at all.*

# $=\mathbf{14}=$

The door to Dr. Abul al-Fahazi's office was ajar. Bashir hesitated before opening it farther.

The doctor was sitting in a chair. On the dirt floor in front of him was Derek Sparrowhawk. The Englishman raised his index finger to his lips, and Bashir did not speak.

He sat down next to Sparrowhawk.

The doctor was speaking in a low voice, not much above a whisper.

"He was here quite a while, this time, you know. That was so different. He always seems to appear and then is gone in an instant."

There were tears on his cheeks.

"I told him how much I regretted the treatment he had been accorded previously," Dr. al-Fahazi continued. "He said he was only trying to warn us, and we were too blind."

Sparrowhawk reached up and placed his left hand on the old man's knee.

"Did he say anything else?" he asked, his tone tender.

"He repeated what he had mentioned earlier and then added, 'There is so much pain ahead. You have no idea how much will be required of you.'"

"Was that all?" Sparrowhawk prodded. "You just said that the two of you spent much time together for a change.

However what you have just told us could have been spoken in minutes. What about the rest of Wise One's visit?"

"We didn't talk, Mr. Sparrowhawk. We just sat together. Words seemed superfluous somehow. I could *feel* things from him."

Bashir shook his head, and finally spoke.

"I do not know what that means, Abul. It sounds metaphysical, and I cannot accept that. Do you really mean to say that Wise One read your mind?"

"No, no, it was nothing like that. I could feel only a spirit of love coming from him, at the beginning, and then that turned to deep and terrible sorrow."

"But how could you *know?*"

Dr. Al-Fahazi looked down at him, smiling.

"What is the Body of Christ?" he asked.

"Believers gathered together unto Him."

"And is there not supposed to be unity?"

"Of course, but—"

"With Wise One, I experienced the most sublime unity I have ever known with another human being."

"Listen to him," Sparrowhawk pleaded. "Don't discard what he says without *really* considering it."

The irony of that moment did not escape Bashir: Sparrowhawk the agnostic urging him to pay heed to words that professed spiritual significance unlike any he, the Christian, had heard in a very long time.

*If they were to be believed . . .*

"And then we both stood. Wise One turned toward the east, toward those tunnels, and he said, 'Did you know, Dr. al-Fahazi, that, as early in time as the original Eden, before the Fall, they happened to be the location of great evil. You see, it was in that very spot that—'

"Wise One did not finish that sentence. He simply shivered, his face more deeply lined than ever, and then he opened the door, and started to walk off, back to the mountains, but stopped, ever so briefly, and looked at me, as he said, 'The original name—remember that, and it will tell you much.'"

Sparrowhawk's eyes opened wide, protruding more than usual.

"Do you know, sir?" he asked. "Do you know that name?"

Dr. al-Fahazi nodded.

"I do. Roughly translated, it meant, 'where evil began its march.'"

*After they had gone, Dr. Abul al-Fahazi took out a strongbox and opened it, then surveyed the contents. When he had finished, he held the heavy box tightly to himself, not wanting to let go.*

# $=15=$

Fascinating!" Derek Sparrowhawk said as they sat in Fahid Bashir's office the next morning. "I don't believe I got a wink all night thinking about what we've learned."

"Nor I," Bashir assured him.

"But I'm puzzled, Fahid. Why didn't you know that such a name was associated with that place?"

"Remember, Dr. al-Fahazi is much older, and he has a hobby of sorts."

"Hobby? What kind of hobby?"

"Building up a collection of folklore."

"Folklore? That's an interesting term."

"How do you mean?"

"I thought Christians weren't especially keen on that sort of thing."

"They shouldn't be. Folklore tends to be anti-biblical."

"I don't get it."

"For example: the Apocrypha."

"Ah, the Middle Testament."

"Some have called it that over the years. But it has been rejected as nothing more than folklore, fanciful tales that—"

"That Satan tried to sneak into the inspired canon in order to discredit the whole Bible in later years."

Bashir looked at his English friend with pure amazement.

"You really don't cease to surprise me," he said.

"I'd wager, right now, that you think I'm perhaps only a step or two away from what you call salvation."

"Something like that, yes."

"Don't count on that. I've seen too much pain, suffering, and outright moral garbage in this mucked-up world of ours ever to be able to believe in a God who would *allow* all of that.

"After all, Fahid, if God can bring a whole universe into being with just the wave of His hand, so to speak, then surely He can stop Satan with the fleck of His little finger!"

"Then you believe, instead, in the indomitable spirit of man himself?" Bashir offered.

"Not even that," Sparrowhawk replied, "in fact, least of all any such spirit. When left to his own devices, the average human being is a pretty sorry creature in matters of ethics and the like. I mean, look at the Ivan Boeskys, the Michael Millikins, and many others who proliferated in America this past decade, dispensing their 'Greed is good' philosophy.

"Deregulation of various industries or else lax enforcement of existing statutes generated a hoard of scum interested only in grabbing a piece of the economic pie, as large a piece and as quickly as they could."

"If not God, if not man, then what else, Derek? There is hardly a surfeit of choices."

"True. And that's what makes life so depressing. People like me, people who *care* about a matter such as personal integrity are beginning to feel that there is no hope."

"But humanism said that human nature was the one, the true, the ultimate hope for mankind."

"I was never a red-blooded humanist, Fahid. I am one of a group of realists, and since we are what we are, we could never be humanists or religionists. The former mandates faith in humanity, the latter faith in God. We eschew both. If anything, we are perhaps nihilists."

"You could band together with others who feel as you do. You could achieve some degree of security through harmony with one another. Surely, my friend, you *could* do that."

"Certainly. But, *as* realists, we do recognize fully that we all are human—just as is every corrupt politician, every Middle Eastern tyrant, every kiddie porn addict, every—"

He sputtered off into silence for a moment, and Bashir could see deep emotion playing across his face.

"Let's change the subject," Bashir suggested then.

"Let's *not* do that," Sparrowhawk said abruptly. "We happen to be touching upon a personal area that I have not been able to discuss with another person before now."

He clasped his hands together, trying to steady his nerves.

"When I see myself in the line with men, if you could call them that, the likes of Stalin, Saddam Hussein, Noriega, and others I could mention, and I realize that, in a species sense, we are indeed related, well, it terrifies me. If they are capable of what they have done, then I must be capable of heinous acts, too, for we are links in a human chain."

"But that chain includes Schweitzer, Salk, and Mother Teresa."

"Yes, of course, but when you think of it, what we are talking about amounts to a kind of Russian roulette. Spin the chamber and pull the trigger, and out comes Florence Nightingale . . . *this time!* But do it again, and out pops Adolf Hitler. It's a dangerous game, Fahid, dangerous and tragic."

He was holding his hands so tightly together that Bashir could see the knuckles turning white.

"What is worse to contemplate, almost impossible to do so, I would say, Fahid, is that the behavioral seeds of a Hitler are buried as well within a Simon Wiesenthal, however bizarre that may sound. If all human beings are capable of infamy, therefore, nothing *truly* separates the death camp commandant from the poor Jews he had been murdering by the hundreds of thousands!"

"Behavioral time bombs, Derek?"

"Oh, yes, yes, yes! Precisely that! The settler in the Old West who got his jollies from collecting Indian scalps admittedly could be the same family man who went to church and absorbed teachings that included the Golden Rule and the Great Commission."

Sparrowhawk paused, obviously giving his friend a reasonable opportunity to respond.

"You have just given a strikingly accurate recitation of what the Bible has been telling us over the centuries about human nature," Bashir commented after a moment or two.

"And next, you're going to tell me that Jesus Christ offers the only hope any of us have."

"That's what I believe, Derek."

"But I'm not willing to risk dying for a Man I've never met, or having my hands cut off, or anything of that sort. With this Jesus in my life, as you would say, I don't obviate my personal anguish, my apprehension over the future, but add yet another source of both! I want to bury them, Fahid, not compound them!"

He chuckled a bit, actually snickered was more like it.

"I can't picture myself hanging on a cross," Sparrowhawk said. "That takes a special sort of man, Fahid, and I just don't qualify."

# $=16=$

*Their culture as they know it may be destroyed . . .*

Stuart Brickley read those words in a fax received a minute or two earlier, then crumpled the sheet of coated paper and threw it into a nearby wastebasket.

"Always the same wherever we go," he said out loud, though there was no one else in the tiny temporary office to hear him.

Whether in Alaska or the Caribbean or the Indian Ocean, whatever the location, the destruction of a culture occurred as perhaps an inevitable consequence—if not a calamitous oil spill, then it was the rape of virginal forest land, so to speak, with trees cut down and wildlife wrenched out of their natural habitats, or it took the form of a variety of other instances in numerous locales across many thousands of miles—and, ultimately, the substitution of a strictly monetary value system in place of whatever it was that once existed, often a way of life quite simple and basic but sacrificed at the altar of the Profit Motive.

Brickley remembered the discovery in the 1980s of a supposedly massive oil field on a Sioux reservation in the American West. It could have been argued that the influx of revenue pulled that particular tribe out of abysmal poverty, and at last they finally could buy enough food, buy automobiles that worked instead of breaking down repeatedly, afford proper health care, and so much else that had been denied them for a very long time.

*Ten years later . . .*

His mind went back to what the passage of a decade had brought the Sioux: a high crime rate and dramatically increased rates of alcoholism, born not of the crushing humiliation of being poor but, rather, of their inability to absorb in constructive ways all the money that had been thrown at them over the years.

*Nightclubs, ah, the nightclubs!*

Inevitably, despite alleged controls, a certain powerful Mafioso family became involved, and gambling crept in, along with drugs and alcohol, a "natural" consequence that had been repeated on a larger scale elsewhere in the nation, especially in Las Vegas and, more recently, Atlantic City.

And there was that other ingredient, the violence that proliferated as another mob family tried to tear a piece of the action away from the first one. Indian men, women, and children died in the crossfire, their blood staining the spanking new concrete sidewalks, that is, where those hadn't been demolished by car bombs.

So it was that white men, wearing expensive suits and hunched together in different smoke-filled rooms at different times, decided the future of that tribe of Sioux, each group with its own agenda aimed at grabbing a tempting chunk of the Indians' newfound wealth, yet another piece of the lucrative pie.

There were the fast food franchises offering hamburgers and pizzas and tacos . . . the liquor store outlets . . . the supermarkets . . . the automobile showrooms . . . yes, the nightclubs . . . business after business . . . dollar after dollar spent on the products being offered, and all of it coming from Indian pockets, whether needed or not, the Sioux methodically bled of money they had had little experience in handling, and everything conducted according to what was dictated by the computerized, demographized marketing plans of the companies involved.

But then the wells went dry.

The result was that after just ten years personal bank-ruptcies of Indian families soared, while businesses run by the white bread management of Fortune 500 companies closed up shop and moved away, deserting those who had been meal tickets for that period of time.

*And some professing Christians were included!* Brickley ex-claimed to himself, the words laced with not inconsiderable contempt. *They were wearing crosses from their necks, getting in there along with the greedy corporations and the Mafioso, some of the meetings even opening and closing with prayer for God's guid-ance.*

He suspected that Christians of that stripe could justify virtually anything because—

*The Indians were heathens, after all, worshiping a substitute Creator through a pantheistic religion.*

He shook briefly with anger as he recalled overhearing precisely that statement from a TV evangelist.

"We have an obligation to win them for Christ," re-marked the overstuffed white-haired chap who had a Sunday morning program on a cable network. "But if they resist, then in fact they deserve whatever judgment God brings upon them."

Brickley had been tempted to search out that so-called reverend and shake him by the lapels of his hand-tailored jacket, and then punch him senseless, but decided he didn't want to open up the likelihood that the guy would become a martyr of some sort, the latest victim of the secular media.

But it wasn't the only hypocrisy that he witnessed from various Christian groups.

Numbers.

Denominations and evangelistic associations and others *competed* for the largest number of converts, their methods of-ten resembling the TV media's competition for ratings.

*Especially that one deceitful monster, far more obnoxious than the other TV evangelist . . .*

Brickley's body tensed at the image of this second man surfacing in his mind, that robed, self-parodying form strut-ting from one end of the Italian-marbled podium to another, hands waving in the air, his voice bellowing out over the loud-speaker system as the cameras cut from him to the congregation in the vast cathedral that he had had erected three years earlier, a structure of spectacular appearance, shaped like two Egyptian pyramids joined together in the middle.

*They were so impressed, a poor Sioux tribe thrust from poverty to a stunning display of grandiosity that sent an indelible message to them—become a professing Christian, and God will continue to bless you because He wants you to partake of all of the possibilities that life has to offer, especially the ones concerning your bank account, for our Creator is the best treasurer of all . . .*

Brickley smiled cynically as he came to the punch line, the hook that this pompous and conniving fool added to make sure that as much of the disposable wealth of the Indians ended up in his own already overflowing coffers.

*You cannot outgive the Lord, brothers and sisters in Christ. Turn over to Him your tithe, and He will send it back to you twice over. Talk about compounded interest! Give to Him sacrificially, and look at the possibilities, the sanctified possibilities of what will be in store for you from the very banks of heaven itself.*

Brickley wondered how Fahid Bashir could ever explain away such intolerable deceit, such—

*Those Indians deserved nothing better so long as they persisted in their satanic deception.*

He stopped himself, sensing that he was doing the other man an injustice.

*No, Fahid seems more rational in his faith. He surely must be as repulsed by such opportunism as I was. And I cannot believe he would tolerate the kind of behavior manifested by those who were Christians in the group of businesspeople, preparing as they were to fully exploit that tribe of naive Indians, as white men had done for a hundred years, in one way or another.*

And so the tribe was soon enough seduced by the various "modern" influences and fell headlong into a materialistic mind-set, many of them converting either to a seed faith or to a possibility thinking approach to worship only to find the promises that once had been part-and-parcel of those heresies quite transitory.

He saw what remained of the tribe after the wells ceased giving up barrel after barrel of "black gold." The nightclubs had been boarded up; supermarkets as well; no more gas stations remained in the area; homes were repossessed and remained unsold to new owners afterward, primarily because no "respectable" white family would consider living amid such deprived conditions. Men, young as well as old, stumbled about with liquor bottles grasped in their hands, shouting deliriously at the empty air.

Brickley was about to get into his car when a man in his late thirties approached him, asking for money.

"I need it to buy food for my family," the Indian told him.

"I think not," Brickley replied. "You're just going to fill your gut with more poison."

The man stood there, thinking about that in a dazed sort of manner, and then said, "Yeah, you're right mister. But what else I got? Ain't got no family any more."

"What happened to them?"

"I shot 'em both this morning, blew their brains out."

Brickley's eyes widened in horror.

The man started laughing.

"You fell for that, ha, ha, ha!"

"They're not dead?"

The man looked at him, his face no longer twisted with laughter, now with no emotion at all, a cold, hard, human mask.

"Not yet."

The man turned and shuffled off, mumbling to himself . . .

But the people of that tribe weren't the only examples of the aftermath of oil interests invading a region, far from it. There was quite another instance, equally unsettling in its implications.

He was thinking, specifically, of what had happened in the Amazonian rain forest a few years earlier. There had been warnings about the environmental impact after an oil find in a nearby patch of land. But economic concerns dominated, and the tireless scenario of billions of dollars of income flooding

106

into a region not accustomed to such riches was replayed once again.

Brickley shivered as vignettes came to mind.

*Entire villages decimated by an insect population that was displaced from one habitat and had to go out in search of another.*

"Oh, that may have been the worst," he said. "That indeed was . . .

Massive outbreaks of disease.

A plague in South America to equal the bubonic plague in Europe in the Middle Ages but on a smaller scale.

Thousands of people died, and never less than horribly, not a quiet and dignified death at all, a death of convulsions, of sores like leprosy, of brains addled, of teeth swollen and gums festering and—

*Some people refused to go to the hospitals but stayed home, thinking they could escape*—he said, this time to himself, with no words uttered audibly.

Brickley personally saw one such family, saw its members in a state that surely would remain in his mind for the rest of his life, saw them dead and rotting away in a house that was crammed full with expensive furniture, original oil paintings, plush carpeting, modern appliances of every sort, as well as piles upon piles of money stuffed into shoe boxes, under mattresses, in wall safes—there were twenty in that house—and, even, in a huge freezer in the basement, between chunks of meat. The bodies themselves were almost completely covered with money, their hands frozen around clumps of bills in various denominations.

*The love of money . . .*

He felt disgusted, and literally ran from that house, ran from his job with Americo, ran away to some isolated spot in the western United States after returning from Brazil—until he came in contact with a group of militant environmentalists, at least a group that *seemed* to be hailing such a cause.

*They seemed so dedicated,* he thought with more than a touch of wistfulness. *They seemed willing to endure any sacrifice if it meant achieving what they believed in, a goal so noble that it would have been foolish for me to ignore what they were about.*

Brickley was with them barely a week when he overheard a conversation that left no doubt as to the true nature of the group.

*They weren't environmentalists at all but simply a guerrilla group of sorts funded by an oil company rival, one that sought to embarrass Americo and other competitors, and whose efforts got out of hand. The diseases that spread over such a large area were—.*

Always the blood drained from his face when he recalled that ghastly truth.

*—released on purpose!*

Brickley pushed himself away from the roll-top desk and stood, stretching his legs.

"Those bloody fools!" he said, angry even after all that time had passed. "Those insane idiots!"

He managed to contact a regional office of Americo that was relatively nearby and was advised to remain with the group until more evidence could be gathered.

Finally, after secret tape recordings and pilfered documents of one sort or another, everything necessary was in hand and he got away from the group without injury.

When the story was released, he became an instant hero and was welcomed back into the Americo hierarchy.

*Fahid Bashir thinks I am someone to loathe, thinks Americo is essentially a principal villain in the scheme of things. If he only knew the full extent of what had happened . . .*

Brickley spun around and strode back to the desk, reaching for the phone on top, intending to call Bashir.

*He must know that he has no enemy in me,* he thought. *He must know that right away.*

The phone rang several times before Bashir answered.

"Constable Bashir?" he asked.

"Yes, this is he."

"This is Stuart Brickley."

"Yes, Mr. Brickley?"

"Is there a possibility that we can meet, perhaps for breakfast, in the morning? I do apologize for this short notice but I'm hoping, in any event, that you can oblige me."

"What is there that you want to discuss?" Bashir asked, his tone guarded. "I'm not sure that there is anything we could cover that would be, as the diplomats say, very constructive, given where you and I are coming from."

"Could we cover that tomorrow? Let's just say it's a somewhat personal matter. Are you able to join me?"

A pause, then Bashir agreed to do so.

"How about the Americo temporary building?" Brickley asked. "The food is really quite good, I must say."

"That would be acceptable."

"Is seven thirty convenient?"

"I'll be there."

"Very good indeed."

The connection was broken then.

Brickley stood, his fingers still holding the receiver of the ancient phone.

*Why am I doing this?* he asked himself, not at all sure of what the answer might be. *I thought I had become desensitized, with little or no potential of being motivated by my conscience.*

He replaced the receiver on its cradle, having momentarily forgotten that he was holding it. He looked about the interior of that very old structure, anxious to leave its mustiness and move on to quarters that were far more Westernized, as part of the Americo building being constructed nearby.

*And now I'm here,* he sighed, *probably for years to come. Oh, well, weekends in Rome or Paris or Zurich will help . . .*

Brickley decided to take a walk and stretch his legs.

Hoping to avoid contact for the moment with any villager who might be inclined to stick yet another petition in his hand, he headed toward the back door rather than the one in front, which opened on what laughingly could be called the village's main street.

*Nothing more than a back alley in a hundred other communities I could mention,* he sneered.

As his hand closed around the knob, which was so loose it nearly came off while he turned it and opened the door, he abruptly jumped back in surprise.

"Where in the world did you—?" Stuart Brickley started to ask, totally unprepared.

His words were cut off as he reacted to encountering a tall, broad-shouldered old man standing directly outside, as though just about to knock, an expression of unfathomable sadness on a deeply lined, weathered-looking face.

## ═ **17** ═

Bashir awoke an hour before the scheduled breakfast meeting. He had not slept well, both curious and wary about what Stuart Brickley could possibly be interested in discussing.

*He wants to bribe me as he likely does everyone else,* he thought wearily, *to offer me some modern equipment—or enough money for me to get anything I want—to be willing to look the other way when something occurs that I might otherwise have opposed.*

Bashir sat up in bed, took his Bible from the little nightstand to his left, and started reading in the midst of Job 28:

> *But where can wisdom be found?*
> *And where is the place of understanding?*
> *Man does not know its value,*
> *Nor is it found in the land of the living. . . .*
> *It cannot be purchased for gold,*
> *Nor can silver be weighed for its price.*
> *It cannot be valued in the gold of Ophir,*
> *In precious onyx or sapphire.*

He paused, closing his eyes for a moment, grateful for that particular passage at that particular time. And then he went on to read another few words:

111

*. . . Behold, the fear of the Lord, that is wisdom;*
*And to depart from evil is understanding.*

Bashir closed the Bible, and put it back on the night-stand.

*The fear of the Lord . . .* he repeated prayerfully. *Some-one like Stuart Brickley probably doesn't believe anything the Bible offers, let alone ever fearing You. As far as he is concerned, evil is nothing more than a collection of simple human shortcomings—if he goes even that far.*

Bashir finally climbed out of bed and started toward the back door, then the well outside, but stopped, the muscles at the back of his neck abruptly tightening.

*. . . And to depart from evil is understanding.*

He dropped the white porcelain-coated water pitcher that he had been holding in his right hand.

In a few seconds his entire body was covered with perspiration, his heart beating far faster than normal.

He tried to stand completely still, fighting an attendant dizziness, but ended up collapsing to the warm sand, disorientation shaking him perhaps for a couple of minutes or so.

*The fear of the Lord . . .*

As he looked about, his vision steadying, he half-expected, in a moment of fading anticipation, to hear a multitude of angels nearby, their wings beating in unison as they came to gather him and other believers for the rapture.

*Why do I feel as I do now, Lord?*

In his mind, the images still wondrously fresh after those twenty years that had passed, was the experience he had had among the towering Middle Eastern mountains. He turned toward their misty forms in the dawn-shrouded distance, tempted to forget altogether about Stuart Brickley, and breakfast, and everything else in his life at that moment, and return as though for the first time to the place where that very life, at least whatever of it was of value, had begun.

The water felt reassuring against Bashir's face. He had been retrieving the cool liquid from wells like that one all his life. Switching to a full-fledged system of pipes and faucets would be convenient, but, somehow, he found that walking outside first thing in the morning, inhaling deeply, and looking around at that expanse of desert gave him a true sense of the remarkable nature of Almighty God, for that was just one desert out of many on the planet, each one stretching on for a vast number of miles, whether in the United States or in Africa or Australia or elsewhere, and that little village completed the picture—hundreds like it in the Middle East alone—and he was one man out of hundreds of millions living under those or similar conditions, unimportant indeed to people in London or Paris or Rome or Madrid, people with civilization towering around them, its massive structures—

*Most have never known such a simple joy as getting morning water at a well and suddenly thinking back to the time of Christ and the woman at the well who came to know Him as her Savior, and realizing that nothing, nothing whatever, has changed. Oh, it's a pump now instead of a simple bucket lowered down into a hole in the ground, and I carry a porcelain pitcher instead of an earthen vessel of some sort—but curiously it's the same.*

*When Christ walked the earth in His human form, the mountains then were as they are now. The desert was as barren then as now. The goats baaed, and the camels spit grime slime, and dirt-smudged little children walked the streets barefoot. Even as He ministered in villages and along narrow country paths, He could pause for a moment and smell the ancient odors . . .*

Bashir decided to walk the mile or so to Americo's so-called temporary headquarters, which was a collection of trailers of varying sizes, all one-story but some quite long and wide, located on the outskirts of the village.

Village life was just awakening from the night.

Women carried water bags on long wood poles across their shoulders; children emerged from their homes to play games. And the men went out and polished their brand-new automobiles.

Bashir stood for a moment and watched this phenomenon, three sedans in a row, one white, one red, one yellow, their owners standing proudly before them, hands on hips, heads thrown back, proclaiming their satisfaction.

In a short while the three gathered together and compared notes. Bashir saw how quickly simple pride could turn to arrogance as each boasted of the equipment that came with his particular model, how much it had cost, how long the warranty was, the gas mileage, and other factors.

*Six months ago, there wouldn't have been that kind of rivalry between them,* Bashir observed. *They would have tended to their goats and sheep and been content.*

Unlike the other villagers, he had been able to get away periodically, and had seen the pursuit of greater and greater acquisitions, with bigger homes and more cars and hand-tailored clothes and multicarat diamonds taking center stage in the lives of so many.

He also remembered the economic collapse years before that had followed the then-latest Middle Eastern crisis, and what had happened to oil prices, with spot market figures climbing to $60 a barrel or greater.

Many lost their *things.* Many couldn't cope. They committed suicide, presumably because they couldn't face life without the walls of a thirty-five-room mansion around them. Or a $150,000 car parked in the driveway. Or closets packed full of furs and silks and whatever other apparel had caught their fancy as they went shopping on Rodeo Drive or the Champs-Élysées or Oxford Street.

He saw the three men arguing, boasting, gloating.

*Oh, Lord, it has begun, yes, it has.*

114

# =18=

Erected around the compound was a steel-girded fence, with guards patrolling it at regular intervals.

*Still dangerous,* he thought. *Nothing has changed after so many years.*

Indeed the Middle East was every bit as dangerous as during the war with Iraq or any of the other conflicts that had despoiled the region for a very long time, not just the Muslim-Christian controversies but those involving Jews and Muslims and, not inconsequentially, various Muslim factions. Anyone who expected a prolonged period of peace was following a deluded line of thinking!

*Someday, we'll be caught up in the midst of it. Oil wells and refineries are always targets of any conflict in this region. We used to be ignored because we were not of what could be called strategic importance. But that is no longer the case. My people may someday die in the rubble of their wealth.*

Bashir imagined that Christ might have felt the same way as He stood on the Mount of Olives, and looked at His beloved Jerusalem below and in front of Him, and saw the centuries of destruction and pain that were ahead, and yearned to gather her under His wings and protect her but knew that that was not what the Father intended.

*Turn your eyes upon Jesus. Look full in His wonderful face.*

115

He was at the front gate of the compound now, and looked back, briefly, at the village behind him.

*How much of that will they do, Lord? Or will it all be forgotten as the money spigot is opened wide?*

Word had been left for him, and he walked through the main gate and headed toward the building indicated by the guard.

Inside, he could see an entire room given over to computer equipment, powered, as everything else in the compound, by huge self-contained generators that had been flown in on cavernous cargo planes from Germany.

Dozens of men and women scurried about in other rooms. Phones were ringing, fax machines in full operation as well.

After turning down one corridor, followed by another, he entered the rather smallish room that served as an executive dining quarters of sorts.

Suitable for holding not more than thirty people, it was filled to capacity, except for one empty table at the opposite end.

Bashir was amused by the variety of "types" present. There were the silk-business-suited Americans like Stuart Brickley himself; a few Japanese men; a couple of Arabs in their normal garb; the rest not easily discernible in terms of country of origin.

The headwaiter approached Bashir, and he identified himself.

"Mr. Brickley has not arrived as yet," the man said. "Would you mind waiting at the table, or would you prefer to be outside?"

"The table would be fine," Bashir told him

"Follow me, please."

Bashir, whose hearing was unusually acute, picked up bits and pieces of conversation as he walked behind the head waiter.

*"These villagers will be easy . . ."*

*"You think so?"*

*"Oh, yes. They have nothing. We're going to be giving them everything . . ."*

116

*"You're right. They shouldn't present a problem at all."*

He was tempted to stop right there, and confront the two Americans who were speaking in that manner. But he decided it was more important, for the moment, to find out what was in Brickley's mind.

*"OPEC seems to be a bit more reasonable these days . . ."*

*"Can you blame those guys? Saddam taught them quite a lesson . . ."*

Bashir smiled, and continued past.

*"Remember what Sadat tried to do?"*

*"The three places of worship?"*

*"Yeh, the mosque, the synagogue, and the church . . ."*

*"Correct. What a great idea for here! Terrific marketing ploy, don't you think?"*

Bashir felt his tact and reserve almost shattering with that one.

*Matters of faith now treated as a marketing ploy!* he thought. *Father, forgive them . . .*

He was at the sole vacant table now, and sat down, thanking the headwaiter.

Awaiting Brickley's arrival, Bashir decided to sit back and survey the rest of the group in that room.

None of them would be there if it hadn't been for the discovery of oil. That didn't require enormous perception to understand. They went where wealth lured them. It was unlikely that any had even slight interest in the *people*.

For Bashir, that was the most hypocritical and unsettling aspect of the situation now involving his birthplace. There would be pleasant smiles, hearty pats on the back, dinners and special gifts and, yes, hefty royalty checks along with so-called civic improvements and a great deal else, and his people would be lured, as already was happening, into thinking they had made deals with a generous company.

*Carpetbaggers,* he said to himself, remembering something he had read about the aftermath of the American Civil War. *They come to us with their Trojan horse routines, and we fall for it like the—*

He sighed, weary, and closed his eyes for a moment.

"A decade from now, nobody will recognize this place," someone at the next table was saying. "There won't be those awful huts they call home. Here's a bet: The first time everybody gets running water, they'll declare a local holiday. Everybody will be celebrating!"

The tone of the speaker seemed condescending at best.

"I hear this particular village converted to Christianity from Islam," he continued. "Is that so?"

One of the two men with him murmured agreement.

"Good," he said. "That'll be helpful. I have some friends who can keep them supplied with—"

Bashir turned around in his seat. Three men sat at that table, all of them apparently Americans. The one who had just spoken was extremely large, to put it mildly, dwarfing his two companions, his weight probably exceeding three hundred pounds.

"I heard what you said," he remarked.

The man looked at him through eyes that seemed surrounded by a heavy layer of fat that pressed his lids nearly shut, leaving only the tiniest of slits for him to see through.

"I see that eavesdropping is another talent we must expect of the local populace," he sneered.

"You talk of these people as though they are mere statistics in some demographic analysis," Bashir replied.

"Does it matter, as long as we pay you guys a few billion over the next twenty years?" he rumbled.

"Is that what it takes, in your opinion?"

"What are you talking about?"

"Money."

"To do what? You asked me if that is what it takes? I'm afraid I don't understand."

"I'm talking about destroying a heritage of many centuries for a whole group of people and leaving nothing more than piles of money behind."

"Nothing *more* than that?" the man repeated, incredulous. "Money buys clothes, food, better homes to live in. Money buys the best medical care. What is so wrong with that?"

"It's what they have to give up that is wrong, a culture smashed into little pieces in the wake of this so-called prosperity."

The man noticed the cross hanging from Bashir's neck.

"You're wearing a cross. Your original faith had to have been destroyed in order for you to start wearing that, unless it's just some kind of ornament, which any good Muslim wouldn't be found dead with. You don't seem depressed over that part of your heritage collapsing. And you can't tell me that you think it has been replaced with anything of lesser value. Surely you wouldn't even *try* to say such a thing!"

"My faith has nothing to do with my heritage. You are confusing the issue."

"It has *everything* to do with it. All you have done is be selective. You've decided which part of that heritage is valid, which is quite disposable."

"But it wasn't *forced* upon me. I could choose to accept Christianity or reject it."

"Your people are free to take our money or leave it," the other man retorted. "In either case, their lives are never the same again. Traditions are sacrificed inevitably at one kind of altar or the other."

He seemed to be gathering energy for the discussion, his face flushing with enthusiasm.

"Besides, of what value, really, is tradition and culture and all that? Weren't they the very elements in life that Jesus rebelled against when He was repeatedly so critical of the religious leaders of His day, who had allowed tradition and legalism to dominate everything they did—and, consequently, everything they *expected* of others?"

Everyone in the room had stopped eating and was listening to the two of them. Bashir could sense their scorn, could sense exactly where their value systems were anchored.

"Are you honestly comparing monetary wealth with spiritual things?" he asked. "Is there no difference in your mind, sir? Are you trying to say that—?"

"I'm trying to say that there is nothing in the money itself to corrupt anyone," the other man interrupted. "Doesn't your own Bible make matters a bit more specific by referring to the *love* of money as the corrupting element? Are the only uncorrupted people in the world those who are poor and have been that way all their lives?

"If *that* is what you would have me believe, then give me some of your time, and I'll personally introduce you to some hookers, some druggies, and others who are *very* poor but also *very* corrupted."

The man was intent, the words coming out in rapid blasts.

"I see no inherent nobility in poverty," he went on, "but I *can* find some real goodness, some authentic dedication, to helping the poor simply by introducing you to a few millionaires *who give away a huge percentage of their income!*"

His manner was that of someone who realized he was onto something and would not let it drop.

"How many of the poor you and I have met over the years would do anything at all with, say, a million dollars, if that individual suddenly were given that sum, except merely buy the goodies *they* have been missing over the years? Answer that, Mr. Morality, or whoever you are! If you can't, then shut your mouth and let me get on with my breakfast!"

Bashir had to admit to himself that he had not expected *that* sort of response, and he didn't answer immediately.

A few seconds passed.

The heavyset man at the next table started grinning broadly.

"Thought so!" he said, looking at those sitting with him. "This guy is great, yeh, but only if he's arguing against some fool who doesn't know the facts."

Then he faced Bashir again.

"Tell me this: What are you *doing* about your convictions?"

He paused for effect, then: "Is it possible that you are taking some piece of the pie for yourself, however grudgingly, while bellowing on about what that same pie is doing to your friends and neighbors in this area? If you are, then who happens to be wearing the shoes of a hypocrite? Not *me*, I hasten to add. You know *exactly* where I stand. *And I act accordingly!*"

Bashir was trying to think of something to say in rebuttal when the headwaiter walked up to his table.

"Mr. Brickley has not arrived as yet," he said rather obviously.

"Yes, I know," Bashir replied. "Any message from him?"

"None but . . . but—," he said nervously. "But someone's over at his residence now, trying to find out what happened to him."

"What *happened* to him? You mean, he's disappeared?"

"That seems to be so, sir."

Another voice spoke up.

"May I be of assistance?" the heavyset man said as he stood, with some effort. "My name is Otto Kuhlmey. I'm the chairman of the board of Americo."

The waiter explained the situation.

"Of course, Constable Bashir will go. And I will join him."

"You knew who I was?"

"From the first moment of our debate, I detected that you were articulate."

"But I'm afraid you outclassed me by a significant margin."

"That's only because I had the element of surprise in my favor. You never expected a fat man like me to talk like that."

Bashir was blushing at this candor as he said, "That didn't enter my mind, Mr. Kuhlmey. It's just that—"

"You have something in which you believe very strongly, and sometimes words prove to be quite an unsatisfactory conduit."

Kuhlmey said good-bye to the others at his table. Bashir and he left the room and, in a few seconds, the building itself.

"We could hop in a car," Kuhlmey pointed out, "but, trust me, Fahid, I need the exercise."

He reached out one large hand.

"By the way, you can call me Otto."

# =19=

Gone.

Stuart Brickley had left apparently with whatever clothes he had been wearing at the time, everything else remaining behind.

"I don't understand," Otto Kuhlmey admitted, scratching his forehead in puzzlement. "Stuart's wallet, his toiletries, his laptop computer, it's all here."

He turned as he heard Fahid Bashir calling to him from the rear of the little structure.

A line of footprints. In two separate rows but very much together as they extended side-by-side out into the desert . . .

"Look at that! He didn't even put on his shoes," Kuhlmey observed. "He just walked off in his bare feet. Believe me, when I say this man's not the type to act like that, he just isn't. I can't imagine what caused him to do this."

He turned to Bashir.

"You know this area," Kuhlmey said. "Could he have been attacked, anything like that?"

"I doubt it. There was no apparent struggle, at least any that I can see just now. Just that second set of prints. Otto, seems that it's not as deep into the sand as the other one."

"What does that tell you?"

"That the other individual was either very young or very old, and didn't walk as heavily. If he were old, he may have been suffering from some arthritis."

"Now what makes you say that?" Kuhlmey asked, appreciating Bashir's powers of detection.

"Some of the prints are irregular, possibly as though he had to walk with effort, sometimes with more strength in his legs, sometimes with less strength."

"You're sure that Stuart was met by someone then?"

"Unless the man grew an extra set of feet, I doubt that there is any other conclusion, frankly."

"Touché. I deserved that."

"You surely did."

Ordinarily Kuhlmey would have bristled with anger at that kind of remark, but this time he was inclined to let it go, having developed a degree of instant respect for Fahid Bashir.

"I'll get some men together and go after Stuart."

Bashir hesitated as he glanced out in the direction in which the footprints seemed to be heading.

*The mountains.*

*He felt something touch his face then, and he looked up.*

*Nothing.*

*The pass. The mountain. As before.*

*And the singing! The singing had ended.*

*He did not arise immediately but sat quite still.*

*I feel so—*

*Peaceful.*

*Yes, that was it.*

*There was no sorrow when he thought of his father, only the greatest joy imaginable.*

Bashir shook his head, clearing it.

"Are you ill?" Kuhlmey asked.

"No," he said, nearly whispering. "Not at all, Otto. I was just thinking about the mountains."

"Do you suspect something?"

"Nothing that I can say right now."

Bashir hoped that didn't amount to lying.

"Well, back to headquarters then," Kuhlmey remarked. "I'll set some things in motion and—"

"I'd like to go alone," Bashir interrupted. "I feel that way without quite knowing why, I must admit, Otto."

"That doesn't make any sense. You have no idea, Fahid, what you might run up against."

"It doesn't matter. I have a feeling about this."

"A *feeling?* Come on now, you don't expect to appeal to my sense of so-called spirituality or whatever with a statement like that, do you?"

"I'm as surprised as you are that I want to do it this way but I . . . I just don't feel that we should be so alarmed."

Kuhlmey looked at him with amazement.

"There go the *feelings* thing again! Stuart Brickley may have been abducted, and you think you can handle the situation entirely on your own but, of course, I shouldn't be getting all upset like this?"

"I can't say, Otto. My own reactions puzzle me."

"Fahid, try and be lucid, and tell me exactly what *are* you talking about?"

"I'm not sure, but I really do doubt that you'll need anything resembling a miniature army."

Bashir started to walk away.

"Hey, there," Kuhlmey said, "I don't know that I can agree with what you suggest."

Bashir kept on walking, back toward his own office.

Kuhlmey stood there, looking at his back, not quite sure whether to become angry or to trust someone like Bashir, who seemed then more akin to one of those head-in-the-clouds Middle Eastern mystics than anything else, a breed with which he had never learned to have much patience, despite years of bumping into them in one Arabian locale or another.

Kuhlmey went back inside, hoping to find some sort of clue.

He stopped short as soon as he had reached the doorway.

The short, thin Americo employee who had sent back an alert on Brickley's cellular phone was standing in the middle of the dirt floor, weeping.

"What the devil is wrong?" Kuhlmey asked.

The young man didn't answer at first, his face contorted as though in some intense pain.

"I asked you a question, son," Kuhlmey said, his voice a decibel or two louder. "And I *do* expect an answer."

"I think I . . . I saw . . . I saw—," the other stuttered.

"Come out with it!"

"Sir, you'll think I'm crazy!"

"I'd rather think that than suspect you of insolence."

The young man took out a handkerchief and wiped his eyes.

"I . . . I saw . . . I mean, I thought I saw—"

He looked frantically at Kuhlmey.

"I saw an angel, sir. I saw it so clearly, standing right in front of me, its wings shimmering with color."

"You saw—!" Kuhlmey started to repeat, at first thinking that, surely, the man was engaging in some kind of practical joke, not knowing that his boss had no sense of humor.

"At first I wasn't sure. At first the shape seemed to be that of an old, old man but then I don't know for sure and—"

Kuhlmey became angry, and interrupted.

"You'd better answer me correctly *now*, and in a coherent manner, or you'll no longer be—"

The young man's sobbing stopped in an instant.

At first he said nothing further but merely stood there, awkwardly, surveying Kuhlmey's corpulent frame.

"Are you going through some sort of breakdown?" Kuhlmey asked somewhat stupidly. "I don't like the way you're—"

He cut himself off.

"Your face—!" he said.

"I think I know what you're about to say," the young man gently interrupted. "My face . . . it must be glowing, sir."

Kuhlmey could say nothing, astonished by the expression he saw now, blue eyes wide and—

"I feel so peaceful, sir, and . . . and so ready," the other continued, his voice a trifle hoarse. "It came over me just now, oh, sir, it truly did!"

"But why, son?" Kuhlmey asked. "Can you tell me why?"

"Something awful is going to happen."

"And you feel peaceful about that?"

"But soon afterward, oh, sir, Christ will—"

"Christ will what? You're not talking about after the Tribulation, are you? I happen to believe that—"

"*No!*" the other yelled with exasperation. "That's not what I mean when I say that something awful is—"

The young man was visibly trying to control himself but not doing very well at it.

"Son, the Bible says that no man will know the day or the hour," Kuhlmey said as soothingly as he knew how.

"That's right, sir, but the Bible also talks about the seasons. When autumn comes, when the leaves die and drop off the trees, can winter be far off?"

As he had been speaking those last few words, he started to walk somewhat uncertainly toward the very broad man in front of him, reaching out both arms toward him, so single-mindedly that Kuhlmey backed away a few inches.

"This joy I feel within me, sir," the young man proclaimed, his tone exultant, "I would that you could experience it as well."

With that, he collapsed, falling forward, into an astonished and unprepared Otto Kuhlmey's arms.

*"Mr. Kuhlmey, Mr. Kuhlmey!"*

Abruptly, coming from just behind the two of them, there was a shrill, frantic voice urgently shouting, "Thank God you're here, sir. There's been a second disappearance apparently. That Brit, the journalist . . . *sir, he's gone, too!"*

# $=20=$

Derek Sparrowhawk had no idea that anyone had come into his modest little room and was standing by his bed. There were no creaking door hinges, nor any footsteps, no sound of breathing . . . nothing of the sort awakened him, at least as far as he could tell.

Yet he awoke anyway, earlier in the morning than ordinarily so, which was especially irritating since one of his joys was sleeping measurably later in that isolated village, with its enveloping habitual quietude, than he ever would have been able to do in the middle of London, where trash cans were collected, loudly, at 6:00 A.M., and intrusive traffic noises were unavoidable, along with the loud and inconsiderate chatter of rude early morning passersby who walked blithely past the front window in his Cadogen Square flat.

Even after his eyes were somewhat tentatively open, he didn't see the white-haired old man or suspect his presence.

Since Sparrowhawk had been asleep on his right side, he was turned in the opposite direction from where the intruder stood, and remained in that position for some little while, reluctant to concede that nighttime was over and something was prodding him to forget about his usual pattern of staying in bed until the last possible moment.

*Not this time*, he thought.

He groaned a bit as he looked at the clock on a rickety old table next to the bed.

7:12.

"What in the world?" Sparrowhawk said. "Why am I awakened at this ungodly hour?"

He yawned twice, grumbled irritably to himself, and turned over on his left side, intending to give the act of going back to sleep his very best effort.

Just as his eyes were shutting again, he dimly saw the old man, thought this was his imagination, then realized that it wasn't, and shot up to a sitting position.

"Who are you—?" he started to say, startled.

No answer.

Yet, somehow, Sparrowhawk knew an instant later. Somehow he found himself relaxing as soon as the realization of the old man's identity hit him.

*It's him! After hiding out, apparently, for two decades, he's now back in the village.*

"You're whom they've called Wise One, aren't you?" he asked, scarcely believing that the encounter was taking place, indeed half-suspecting that he had not awakened after all but that it was still night, instead of morning, and he was actually in the midst of a compelling dream that must have been based on an intense desire one day to meet this elusive Wise One.

The old man nodded.

"It has been assumed, well, very unlikely by everyone with whom I have spoken that you would still be alive," Sparrowhawk observed candidly. "I thought perhaps that we might stumble upon your grave one day. Or, more likely, that we could well pass by it without ever knowing. That seemed so sad, frankly."

Wise One continued to be silent.

Sparrowhawk studied him for a moment, trying not to be obnoxious or obvious about this.

Quite tall, certainly over six feet. Thin-faced, with gaunt cheeks, long, narrow nose. Eyes that were rather too small for the size of his head. Thin lips. Skin that gave testimony to his age: wrinkled to an extraordinary degree, scarcely an inch free of lines, whether deep or not, blotched with liver spots, veins showing near the surface of his cheeks, yet curiously robust as well.

The hair!

Long indeed, and thick, trailing down past his shoulders.

And of such a pure white color that he found himself impolitely staring at it and having to restrain himself from giving in to an urge to reach out and run his fingers through it.

"You are more than a hundred years old, are you not?" Sparrowhawk asked with uncustomary gentleness.

Wise One's eyes narrowed briefly, as though examining the Englishman, and deciding whether or not the question deserved to be answered.

"I am," he replied simply.

"Permit me to ask, sir, why you have come here just now," Sparrowhawk asked, "that is, so many years after that last time? To me, and the good doctor earlier, and it may be that there are others of whom I am not unaware?"

Wise One turned and started to walk toward the back door.

"Wait! Let me go with you," Sparrowhawk said hastily, nervous that he would lose contact just as quickly as it had begun.

Wise One spoke nothing, nor did he break stride. Within a second or two, he had reached the door, and opened it, and was heading outside, his stride not that of someone as old as he.

"Please!" Sparrowhawk pleaded. "Please, Wise One, let me go with you. Let me do that, will you?"

The Englishman scrambled out of bed and put on some heavier clothing than the relatively light pajamas he had been wearing all night. Then he slipped into a white designer sheep-skin jacket that he had bought one rainy afternoon during a special sale at Harrod's days before leaving for his stay in the Middle East.

"Wise One," he shouted a bit frantically. "I'm coming. Wait a moment! Please wait, won't you?"

The old man didn't stop but continued on toward the distant mountains.

# =21=

Fahid Bashir looked at the old snub-nosed British Bulldog in his desk's middle drawer, not quite sure whether the pistol worked anymore, yet, for a moment, thinking that he should take it with him because Kuhlmey may have had it right when he warned that none of them knew what to expect in terms of the two disappearances, especially if one or both of the men had been abducted.

There had been no warnings from any of the remaining Middle East-based terrorist groups but, still, this sort of thing amounted to a signature of theirs, behavior of which these thugs had been guilty numerous times in the past, what with their disastrous bombings of businesses owned or operated by any country or firm they happened to be angry with at a given moment, or it was the use of hostages taken in return for political concessions of one sort or another, or whatever method of terror seemed appropriate in their warped minds, often with the justification of a *Jihad* giving them continued impetus.

*But I don't believe that he was, Lord—abducted, that is. I believe that You somehow—*

Bashir slammed the drawer shut without retrieving the Bulldog, or the large, brutal-looking hunting knife beside it.

He grabbed only a piccolo inlaid with ivory along its ebony-colored surface.

130

It was, he remembered, a very special piccolo, apart from the apparent craftsmanship of whoever created it.

*The old man from the mountains took out a hand-tooled piccolo from one pocket in his rough-hewn animal-skin garb and started playing a tune, and a lively ditty it was.*

*In a matter of minutes, many citizens from that town heard the sounds coming from the doctor's place of business and decided to investigate. They found the doctor and the old man dancing as though they were very young and lithe.*

Wise One had put it in his pocket, but as he turned and walked away from the village, back toward the mountains, the little instrument had slipped and fallen to the ground.

Bashir, though past his teen years by then, was still decidedly brash, had rushed back to that spot, and picked it up, and taken it back home with him, never letting anyone else in the village know that he had found it. He would sneak off just beyond the outskirts of the village and play certain melodies on it, including a few rather raucous ones that he had concocted on his own.

*If anybody had found out, I might have been forced to dispose of it since everyone supposed, by then, that Wise One was not a good man after all, and anything that had belonged to him must have been somehow suspect.*

Bashir slipped the piccolo into the pocket of the warm, plaid, flannel jacket he had been wearing, walked to the front door of his office, and started to open it.

*Dr. al-Fahazi!*

*Perhaps he would like to know where I am going, so that he could decide whether to come along.*

He shook his head.

*The man's too ill and too old and—*

Bashir decided at least to go by his friend's office, since it was only down the street.

More and more activity was showing up outside, villagers with a growing number of new cars, several Harley Davidson motorcycles, the odor of gasoline befouling the air.

And he heard something else.

Language. Mostly bad.

131

Their isolation once had been so complete in that remote place that the way they spoke was totally unaffected by any negative influences from the outside world.

And yet, now, it was a radically different story. Over the course of a few months, they had been able to afford so-called literature from a number of publishers in America and England, often thrillers that were littered with the worst language imaginable, four-letter words and other examples of profane and dirty talk.

*So easily,* Bashir thought. *They pick it all up so easily, discarding the ways of the past like so much litter on the highways of their lives.*

He felt sad enough in that instant to be tempted to return to his office, and get that old pistol, and press the open end of the barrel to his temple, and end—

*N-o! That thought in itself is a sin, and I ask for Your forgiveness, Father!*

He was only a few hundred feet from the doctor's office when he saw a battered old bus stop a block away. A group of casually dressed men and women got out.

One of them spotted Bashir, and waved at him.

"You're Fahid Bashir, aren't you?" the youngish dark-haired man said as he trotted up to him.

"Yes, I am," Bashir acknowledged. "How did you know?"

"My name is Jerome Godesmith. I edit CMPE's trade magazine."

"What is CMPE?"

"Christian Media Publicity Experts."

"Oh," Bashir replied, notably unimpressed.

"Scores of book and magazine publishers, radio and TV producers, evangelistic associations, record companies and others, as well as individual churches from a couple dozen countries all over the world have hired my company to make the Christian public aware of what they have to offer, products or whatever. Anything that is *communicated* in the name of Jesus Christ, well, we like to say that we have some part in it, however obliquely sometimes."

*In the case of an evangelistic organization,* Bashir thought, *do you happen to count salvation itself as simply a product?*

"What can I do for you?" Bashir asked out loud, with no particular enthusiasm.

*"Everything!"* Godesmith told him.

"I don't understand, sir."

"Call me Jerry. Do you have a few moments?"

"Actually I don't. I . . . I have to do something now, of a rather critical nature."

"Just five minutes, I promise. Won't you carve that much time from your busy schedule?"

The other's condescending manner quickly irritated Bashir, but he nevertheless decided to delay seeing Dr. al-Fahazi for not more than the five minutes requested, and find out what this self-important young newcomer had in mind.

# $=22=$

Ve want to open up a small Middle Eastern office here," Godesmith told him as soon as they had sat down.

"In the land of Islam?" Bashir asked, incredulous. "We are not what you would call a population center, in any event."

"Ah, but that is the very place where our missionaries need to go. After all, from what I understand, you once were a prime force behind the conversion of this village, were you not?"

Bashir felt uncomfortable accepting the lion's share of the credit for what had happened.

"I really do not deserve—," he started to say.

"I see! *And the meek shall inherit the earth.* Very good, Mr. Bashir, very good indeed."

"I have to be going now."

"Just one other little detail."

"What is it?" Bashir asked, his impatience growing along with his blood pressure.

"We want to find out all about the entire history of this area. It seems to be veritably overflowing with biblical significance. For one thing, as I understand it, wasn't the Garden of Eden supposed to have been near here?"

Bashir was beginning to perspire.

"Some say that that was the case."

"And there's that . . . that place of evil, that puzzling network of underground tunnels which must have been dug many centuries ago, probably an understatement in itself.

"Believe me, there's been a lot of speculation in the United States about that one, Fahid! Why, *Christianity Always* magazine sent a team of three noted archaeologists all the way here, you know the type, pretty stuffy but very smart, and they stumbled upon something quite interesting."

"And what was that?"

"The tunnels lead only in one direction."

"All right, I'll bite. Where?"

"Toward that group of mountains we passed on the way into the village."

Bashir's expression betrayed his surprise.

"I see that something *does* stir you, my brother. But, now, you amaze me in return. How come you of all people didn't know what a few strangers were able to find out?"

"It was never something we had much interest in, to be honest, beyond some initial curiosity. When you live next door to something for generations, it loses its appeal. That is a pity but it's true.

"All of us assumed the tunnels went on for many miles, or else didn't go very far at all. Some over the years did try to explore them to a certain extent but gave up before getting very far at all. They claimed that the tunnel walls, except near the entrance, seemed ready for collapse at any moment. Further on, there *had* been such a cave-in, and the remainder of the tunnels could not be penetrated, I assure you. The risks clearly overrode all other considerations, even among young people who were normally rather impetuous."

"That may have been so, yes, I can see that," Godesmith went on, "but I assure you, Fahid, ah, the best is yet to come."

He opened a burgundy leather attaché case that he had been resting on his lap and took out a single eight-by-five-inch glossy photograph, handing it to Bashir.

"Yes, the writings on the walls just beyond the entrance," Bashir observed as dispassionately as possible.

"Obviously, then, you don't know what the content of any of them happens to be."

Bashir shook his head.

"But, surely, you do know what that very place has been called over these many years."

"Of course. *Where Evil Began Its March* . . ."

"Absolutely correct, Fahid, absolutely! Now, think for a moment: What is it that was supposed to have been located somewhere in this region lo those countless years back into antiquity?"

"I suppose you mean the Garden of Eden."

"Correct, between the Tigris and Euphrates rivers."

Bashir was frowning, not pleased in any way with how he was being toyed with by this stranger.

"I'm not one for idle games of this sort, Mr. Godesmith. Get to the point, will you?"

"All right, here are the pieces, Fahid, as I see them, anyway: Take the Garden of Eden, admittedly as yet undiscovered and, therefore, unauthenticated, but if it still exists at all, then it is probably somewhere among the rugged peaks and valleys of those mountains yonder . . . and then add—and, remember, here is the most crucial part of the puzzle—*Where Evil Began Its March.*"

Bashir was drenched in perspiration by then.

"That place of the tunnels, as we might call it just for the sake of discussion, was where—," Godesmith said slowly, in a rather obvious attempt at achieving maximum effect, "during one awful year way back in infamy, if time had any meaning then, Lucifer and his countless thousands of demons plotted—"

"—the total corruption of the human race . . ." Bashir said with equal slowness but for an altogether different reason.

"—from which he marched on to Eden," Godesmith carried on the sentence, "and appeared as a talking serpent to deceive the first humans, Adam and Eve! There you have it, what I might call, if permitted, *maximized revelation!* What do you think of that, my brother?"

136

# =23=

J erome Godesmith finally left, and Bashir sat at his desk, thinking over what had been said. In his right hand was a manila folder that the other man had given him.

He idly leafed through the contents. Inside were press releases, advertisements, newspaper clippings.

After just a few examples, Bashir knew he had correctly caught the gist of what Godesmith was about during their conversation, which ended up lasting more than half an hour, the clippings and such only reinforcing his impression.

*Experience.*

That was what had been happening in the Christian world beyond the little village where he had remained for so long. Experience was beginning to be more important than Scripture. Instead of judging experience *by* Scripture, the reverse was becoming more and more the norm.

And experience was such that it had to have its material as well as emotional props in order to be sustained. But experience was eventually doomed as an approach to Christianity unless each successive group of props topped the one that preceded it.

"Only Scripture can form the backbone of a healthy Christianity," Bashir said out loud. "Anything else is cultism or the occultism. Anything else prostitutes the name of Christ."

*In the United States, experience-hunting was rampant,* he told himself, remembering alarming reports that he had heard over the last few years, and realizing that Jerome Godesmith was the embodiment of what was going on.

*And now he's come here, to continue the spiritual pollution of this little village, which will stop being so little sooner than I dare to admit to myself.*

Bashir picked up an advertisement that he imagined had been written by Godesmith personally:

AN AUTHENTIC PIECE
OF GORDON'S CALVARY
—THE VERY PLACE
WHERE OUR LORD
WAS CRUCIFIED

No surprise there! The offer was being made by Godesmith Enterprises.

Bashir studied a number of other ads, some of them four-color and every bit as splashy as any he'd seen from the Madison Avenue hypesters, offering an array of items ranging from pint, quart-, or gallon-sized bottles of Jordan River water to tiny pieces of wood from the same kind of tree that had *probably* been used to build the cross upon which Christ had hung.

He had begun to feel sick early on, as Godesmith was spouting off, but not nearly as much so as after reading those ads from supposedly genuine ministries forced, it seemed, to engage in questionable pitches in order to raise funds, including one ad that seemed especially obnoxious because there was no mention whatever of Christ:

POSSIBILITY THINKING SPECIAL!
YOU, TOO, CAN UNLOCK
THE ENORMOUS
HUMAN POTENTIAL FOUND
IN THIS BRILLIANT
NEW APPROACH TO
YOUR DAILY LIFE!

All of what Bashir saw was discouraging, some kind of pitch or another, a few disguised in specious sanctimonious language, but others out in the open, crass and manipulative.

Some offenders were more flagrant than others. One especially flamboyant preacher went so far as to promise a limited quantity of vials that contained his own tears, tears shed while praying for the needs of Christians who belonged to his worldwide organization!

Repeating itself in his mind was something Godesmith had said, the real intent behind his trip to that region, and why he intended to open up an office in the village.

"For a thousand miles in all directions, there is a gold mine of locales rich in meaning for Christians," he had spouted off. "But let's take just what you have *here!*"

It was obvious that Jerome Godesmith was "into" what he was proposing.

"Think of it, my brother," he went on. "*Where Evil Began Its March!* What a classic tourist attraction! Imagine how many thousands of visitors it will draw into this area."

"When there isn't a war, of course," Bashir had interpolated, mindful of Kuwait, the Suez, and the Golan Heights.

"There hasn't *been* a war for years," the other man retorted. "In the meantime, all that potential revenue is unrealized."

"Does everything have to have a price tag?"

"Are you suggesting that the experience of seeing that monumental discovery be *for free?*"

But, unfortunately, that wasn't the only scheme Godesmith seemed to have in mind.

"Hey, there are two other really good ideas that we are going to be implementing."

Bashir waited without saying anything.

"Tours!" Godesmith said triumphantly.

"To see that spot *Where Evil Began Its March,* I suppose."

"Yes, that's part of it, Fahid, but not nearly enough of an enticement by itself. The people my associates and I intend to package tours for will come by the thousands if we just make it one that is billed with some *pizzazz* as—"

He reached into his attaché case and brought out several sheets of computer printout paper, which had been left attached to one another.

Bashir reluctantly took one end, and Godesmith the other, and extended them to their full length.

JOIN THE TOUR
OF A LIFETIME!

HUNT FOR THE LONG LOST
GARDEN OF EDEN

That was when Bashir, disgusted, had asked Godesmith to leave the office without delay.

"I have more," the younger man said as he folded up the sheets and put them back into his attaché case. "Let's see now—"

"Not as far as I am concerned," Bashir interrupted him, with no pretense about being impolite.

"Here, my brother," Godesmith went on, as though not hearing what he had just said.

"You are *far* from being my brother, Mr. Godesmith."

"Judgmental, are we?"

"Testing the spirits, I would say . . . or perhaps discerning the fruits of those spirits is more like it."

"I'll leave this behind. I want you to look at it. Let me know what you think. Later, perhaps, you'll tell me what you know about the subject himself."

Godesmith started to hand to him an unmarked little cardboard box roughly six inches long. Bashir took it and, without hesitating, threw it to one side.

"Not interested!" he declared.

"Doesn't matter," Godesmith told him. "We've already started to manufacture this baby in Taiwan. It's going to have *major* curiosity value. Already I am getting a load of inquiries from perspective buyers who are wondering what it's all about. They're fascinated when I tell them a few of the details. An intensive media campaign should commence in a few weeks."

140

Godesmith turned then, and walked with wide steps to the front door.

"I'll be real easy to find, Fahid, yes, sir, I will," he said confidently over his shoulder, as he was opening the door. "We're setting up a fancy tent to the east, less than a mile from the village. We researched the design rather carefully. It looks quite Arab, I must say, and glows some very attractive colors at night. Come on by, my brother, and visit with me anytime! We'll have some fine fellowship."

Shaking by the time the other man had closed the door behind him, Bashir almost lost control of his temper, which had come close to exploding with not a little volume behind it. He managed to rein it in but only barely so.

Bashir's gaze drifted momentarily from the crumbling plaster ceiling on which he had attempted to train his attention, rather than Jerome Godesmith's back, to the little box that had split open as soon as it hit the hard dirt-and-rock floor.

A small figure was now exposed, carved out of what might have been light oak.

Bashir reached down, and picked it up.

*Thin-faced, with gaunt cheeks, long, narrow nose. Eyes that—*

On the beige marble-like base, directly below one of the ancient symbols of Christianity, were just two words:

**WISE ONE**

Next to them was a square ivory-colored sticker that read: $12.95.

# =24=

At dusk, Bashir decided to take a rather extended walk, with the hope of being able to converse with as many villagers as happened to be on the streets at that hour. He had been doing this periodically ever since the days when the conversion to Christianity had begun to take place among them.

With a population that had stayed so small over the years, it was not difficult for him to get to know many of the residents, but, even so, some he hardly ever had contact with, in large part due to the fact that even there, with just a few hundred citizens, falling in with only a limited group seemed natural enough. For Bashir, the members were people who managed to get beyond the confines of the village itself, who considered it very much home but who nevertheless realized that the outside world could be interesting as well. Some had gone with him to Romania. Others had joined him in a trip to London, tagging along, admittedly, but happy to do so, to see a broader view of what civilization was.

*How fortunate I have been,* he thought. *In contrast, a majority of the people here live and die without ever knowing what even a small portion of the rest of the world looks like.*

He knew that that would change, as more oil was pumped out, and more revenue pumped in, undoubtedly some of the people buying their own private jets, for one thing.

Those he met during that walk at dusk seemed happy enough, a few inviting him into their homes where, without exception, they would stand in the middle of the primitive structure and breathe a sigh of anticipation for the day when a better home would stand in its place, a home with five bedrooms and three bathrooms, running water, and certain appliances that were either missing now or sitting in corners because there was no electricity to run them!

All seemed thankful to the Lord for His blessings, giving Him considerable praise, honor, and glory, but then he noticed a subtle change as he joined several in prayer, prayer that went beyond any acceptable "if it be Thy will" hopes, and which seemed more like spending time shopping through a mail order catalog, with the expectation that the Lord would allow them to make a selection, and all they had to do was sit back and wait.

Some talked about their investments more than the spiritual direction of the community, stocks and bonds and real estate taking the place of any discussion about soul-winning, for example.

*Not once has anyone talked about starting to support missionaries,* he realized. *A tithe would mean tens of millions of dollars being released to fund those dedicated to advancing the Great Commission.*

He returned to his own home after a couple of hours, not comforted by what the villagers he met seemed to be telling him or, rather, not telling him.

*After so little time . . .*

He winced at the thought.

*What will it be like five years from now? No more huts . . . no more dirt streets . . . televisions in every home . . . cars everywhere . . . a model for others to follow, as my people enter the twentieth century . . .*

He got into bed early that evening, but he didn't sleep well.

He dreamed.

About Wise One.

About that mass-produced little statue, with the $12.95 price tag.

He dreamed of Wise One coming back to the village, to try one more time to warn the people, but then Jerome Godesmith got hold of him, convinced him to go to the United States and use all the media available to spread the message he wanted to expound, with particular emphasis upon Christian radio and TV stations as well as the print media.

A media star.

That was what, in Bashir's dream, the Wise One soon became. Godesmith set up a central office of operations in Wheaton, Illinois.

*No! No!* Bashir screamed, this time trying to warn Wise One against taking the bait.

But in this dream, in this nightmare, Wise One fell into an entangling web of delusion, just as virtually everyone else had who ever stooped to cooperate with Jerome Godesmith, the latter's lack of genuine Scripture concerns a kind of infecting plague that spread insidiously.

At a hundred-plus years of age, Wise One became an instant celebrity in the American world of razzle-dazzle Christianity, where the demands of show business supplanted the soul business of true Christianity. He attended broadcasters' and various other conventions, regionally and nationally; and did numerous TV and radio interviews. His prophecies were daily features in many newspapers.

And he *loved* it, the attention beguiling.

Hundreds of thousands of dollars passed through his hands.

He was accompanied everywhere by an entourage, including two bodyguards, a manicurist, a hair stylist, and a secretary.

Eager to satisfy the readily apparent demand, Wise One began to make up new prophecies, which were devoid of any authenticity, but no one seemed to notice, or guess, what was going on, most of these cleverly aimed at some point in the future when he would be dead and couldn't be held accountable for the fraud.

But then one day Wise One ran dry, of the "real" ones as well as the phony prophecies, and had nothing new at all to dispense to anyone.

The public turned away from him, for he could give to these people only one thing that was of any value to them, and when that pipeline, so to speak, became empty, they deserted Wise One instantly, and this included the likes of Jerome Godesmith, who went looking for some new individual whom he could groom to take over, leaving him a sad and broken old man, aged and dying in the midst of Manhattan as he walked, dumbfounded, across Broadway, looking up at the man-made peaks all around him, smelling the dirty air, with a faint whiff of marijuana past his nostrils, his ears clogged with the noise of civilization, and hardly feeling the impact of metal as the taxi ran him down.

Bashir awoke in the middle of the night, shivering.

*Oh, Lord, please, not him, not Wise One!*

# =25=

It was late, and Jerome Godesmith was tired, but he wanted to finish unpacking so that he would be ready for business in the morning.

Many boxes had arrived ahead of him. Bibles were in some, jewelry in another, with an emphasis upon ornate crosses that people could wear from chains around their necks.

Other boxes contained various Christian books.

*I hope I had enough evangelical stuff shipped,* he thought. *After all, I've got to satisfy the hard-liners.*

He chuckled to himself.

*The people I have to rub shoulders with in order to get anything accomplished these days!*

He stood for a moment and looked at the piles of items.

Godesmith had not had much time for ethics or good taste or anything like that in recent years. Perhaps it had been different for him at the earliest stages of his career, at a time when his youth made him significantly more naive, certainly not as jaded as he was to become.

But then he saw what many so-called Christian business-es were like behind the scenes, supposedly witnessing about Christ one minute, and "maximizing" their profits the next, whatever it took to do that.

And they seldom found it necessary to attempt any justification of the way they conducted their affairs, but when they made a half-hearted attempt at that, they often did so under some specious scriptural umbrella that usually involved taking one or more verses out of context, particularly the ones dealing with God's blessing on and, therefore, sanctioning of their prosperity.

After witnessing repeated instances of such conniving, Godesmith made a conscious decision to abandon any attempt at real virtue in his own dealings and go with the flow, making as much money as he could manage. Or, as he told an associate a few months ago, *"When in Rome . . . that's my motto, that covers it all."*

*The ringing of cash registers more and more seems as important as church bells,* he acknowledged, while ignoring the part he himself may have been guilty of playing in this trend. *How "Christian" we all must continue to seem to the unsuspecting, the poor suckers in the vast American marketplace, not yet aware of this business of new product development that we are foisting upon them. But that's OK. I can act the part as well as anyone. If I do say so myself, I have become quite adept at saying, "Thank you, my brother, God has blessed me with your business, and may He be with you every step of the way," and having everyone believing I meant it from the depths of my very soul!*

Godesmith was so good at the hypocrisy that he had been able to double his company's business each year for nearly a decade.

*The Bible colleges, oh, yes, how many has it been whose presidents have been so eager to invite me to speak, to inspire their students to follow the example I set before them.*

And the evangelistic associations who took him under their wing and helped his career mightily!

"Now I'm here," he said as he wondered if there was any likelihood that that village somehow could be turned into a Middle Eastern version of Heritage, U.S.A., with an amusement park, a luxury hotel, a shopping mall, and a long line of awaiting limousines.

*I can dream, can't I?* he thought without compunction.

147

After finally completing the process of unpacking and, feeling a bit restless, Godesmith walked outside.

Just beyond the little building he had taken over, he could see the outlines of the oil well towers.

*These people finally have such a chance here, at last, to get rid of their stupid camels and bring in some Jaguars instead. They'll be so much healthier because there will no longer be raw sewage in the streets, and there'll be a clinic with the latest equipment and medicines, and a staff that knows what it's doing, not some glorified witch doctor!*

*But Fahid Bashir is resisting. And I suspect he's not alone. When they were poor, he claims, they were happier than when billions of dollars started to pour into the local economy.*

*How could it ever be more desirable for people to have little in the way of material things? What is so wrong with—?*

"They are being corrupted."

The sudden sound of another voice startled Jerome Godesmith.

"But then you are no stranger to this sort of thing, are you?"

He swung around, and saw a shape in the shadows between the building where he was setting up shop and the one next to it.

"I didn't know you were there," he said.

"You do not know many things," the voice added.

The figure moved a bit, more into the moonlight, and Godesmith could see the old man clearly enough to recognize who he was.

"Wise One!" he exclaimed.

"As you say."

"I . . . I . . . ," Godesmith started to babble, losing the self-control he had developed over a long period of time.

"Does it make you so nervous to be as close as this to the pot of gold at the end of the rainbow?" Wise One asked him pointedly.

"I don't know what you're getting at," Godesmith replied, angry at the apparent insult but not eager to respond in kind, knowing that he could do nothing that would make the old man disappear again.

"Oh, but you do, Jerome Godesmith."

"My name? How did you—?"

"That is unimportant. I know far more about you than you could ever have imagined."

Wise One studied the other man's face.

"You do look quite harmless," he acknowledged. "Your seeming innocence is your biggest weapon, I suspect. But I am very much afraid that, sadly, it masks nothing more than a vain and opportunistic heart."

Godesmith was beginning to lose some of his discipline.

"Is it proper that you should be talking to me in this manner?" he asked with forced politeness.

"As opposed to reaching out my hand and letting you pour fistfuls of money into it?"

"I unlock possibilities."

"You unlock *avarice*, Mr. Godesmith. *That* happens to be one of your vaunted possibilities."

"I didn't give these people their new wealth."

"But you intend to take advantage of every dollar of it that you can get your hands on, is that not so?"

"Listen, Wise One, at least ten percent of what my firm earns goes right back into the Body of Christ, and always to help support missionaries worldwide, as well as to feed starving children."

"While you cavort with what the other ninety percent is able to buy, is that not correct?"

"We are taught by Scripture to tithe. That is what I do."

"That is what you are obligated to do in obedience to Him. But what about sacrifice, Mr. Godesmith? What about giving up a few luxuries in order to show the Lord that you are willing to go beyond mere obligation and manifest, in addition, the love that should be in your heart?

"You have so much, sir. You have health. You have money. You are extremely well known. And you have a measure of power. But the Bible says that without love, you might as well—"

"Don't start throwing Scripture at me like some street corner prophet," Godesmith interrupted.

The look Wise One gave him was one of such over-whelming pity that he was forced into silence for a moment by the sheer emotional impact of it.

It was then that Wise One started to weep.

"You are a vulture, sir," he said, his voice trembling, "and quite the worst variety. You are a vulture, yes, but first an especially loathsome sort of parasite as well. You drain away what is clean and good and healthy, replace it with moral and spiritual poison, and then when your victims are spent and lying dead in the dust, you circle overhead to see if there is anything left on the bones that you can swoop down, and pick off, and then fly away with!"

Godesmith strode forward and raised his fist directly in front of Wise One's thin old face.

"I do *not* have to submit to—," he started to say.

"Another individual has tried the same thing this night, and I respond to you in the very same way."

The old man grabbed the other's wrist and held it tightly.

"But there *is* a difference between the two of you: *He* will be redeemed through the atoning blood of Jesus Christ and, at some hour soon, joyously welcomed past the gates of heaven by a chorus of angels," Wise One said, "but not you, Jerome Godesmith, despite what I can imagine have been your assort-ed proclamations of faith.

"You see, all your trinkets and bottom lines and media blitzes will do nothing for you. There is one place into which you cannot bribe yourself, and quite another from which your cleverness will never be able to gain release for you!"

He let go of the wrist but as he did so, in the same mo-tion, he flung the younger man backward.

Godesmith nearly lost consciousness as he was slammed against the side of the little building. Dizzy, he tried to stand, but couldn't, and fell back.

He heard a sound, quite delicate, soft.

*Like the rustling of a pair of wings!*

He shook his head, trying to clear it, then blinked his eyes several times.

Wise One was gone!

"What the—?" he started to say.

150

Still wobbly, Godesmith managed to get to his feet.

*My wrist . . . it's so sore. The strength he had. The—!*

He hurried back inside.

*I have got to get to the manufacturer of that little statue in time,* he thought, then uttered, almost by reflex, a prayer for God's help.

He used a shortwave radio and managed to make contact with his company's branch in London.

"Nigel, Nigel, this is Jerry . . . Get to the guys who are doing the Wise One statute. It's not accurate enough. Believe me, I've just met him in the flesh. I want real authenticity here. We've got to—"

And he gave the man named Nigel some details.

"Got it now?" Godesmith asked. "Do your best. I want to avoid the recasting fees if I possibly can."

He was assured that he had acted in time.

"Praise God," he said, then broke the connection.

*Thank You, Jesus, thank You, Jesus,* he told himself as he breathed an audible sigh of relief, grateful for answered prayer having come so quickly. *Praise You, blessed, blessed Lord.*

He scribbled a note as a reminder to his secretary, and which he would call her about in the morning:

> *Ask Sherry to up our contribution to 11 percent for next month. Check with me about what should happen after that.*

Jerome Godesmith sighed, quite pleased with himself, then snapped his fingers in irritation as he realized that he forgot something in the note, which he quickly added:

> *Make sure Sherry leaks this out to our usual media contacts. Remember, the girl's real new at this sort of thing and might not be aware of how some things are done. But I think she's smart. She'll learn quickly enough. Or she won't have her job for long.*

He went to bed a few minutes later. As he was sitting up, thinking, for a short while, he recalled part of what Wise One had told him.

151

*. . . all your trinkets and bottom lines and media blitzes will do nothing for you. There is one place into which you cannot bribe yourself, and quite another from which your cleverness will never be able to gain release for you!*

Having no idea what the old fool could have meant, Jerome Godesmith decided to go to sleep, for there was much to do over the days to follow, and he needed as much rest as he could get, especially with jet lag now hitting him full force.

But not before engaging in the little ritual of saying his prayers.

As always.

# =26=

Derek Sparrowhawk stood in the middle of the narrow mountain pass. Wise One had stayed a bit in front of him throughout the three-hour journey from the village to the edge of the mountains, the Englishman amazed that someone as obviously aged as that could have such a sure, rapid stride.

Then, directly ahead, Wise One had turned around a corner of rock and was gone from sight. By the time Sparrowhawk reached the spot, the old man could not be found.

*Yes, but where?* he thought.

He looked back, deciding that he could find his way back alone if he had to do so.

*What have I done? Talk about wild goose chases!*

That was when he caught the sound of someone sobbing. He stopped breathing for a few seconds, concentrating on where it might be coming from.

He had never heard such pervasive sorrow before.

*What could have happened to make whoever it is feel so—?*

The path widened somewhat a hundred yards or so ahead.

Sparrowhawk continued on up to that point.

The sobbing was louder.

The Englishman himself was beginning to feel the emotional impact of the other person's anguish.

"Is that you, Wise One?" he yelled, thinking that it could scarcely be anyone else.

And then he stepped out into a scene quite unlike any he had encountered in a lifetime.

*"Where in the world did you—?" Stuart Brickley started to ask, totally unprepared.*

*His words were cut off as he reacted to encountering a tall, broad-shouldered old man standing directly outside, as though just about to knock, an expression of unfathomable sadness on a deeply-lined, weathered-looking face.*

Brickley was astonished that he had been confronted by Wise One after being so eager to meet this stranger. He could not let on to anyone that he felt this way—not to his superiors at Americo or to Fahid Bashir—because they would wonder, for the most opposite of reasons, about his motivation.

*Ever since I heard about you, old man,* he thought, *I prayed that I could—*

Wise One reached out, and touched his cheek in the gentlest, nonsexual manner that Brickley had ever experienced from another human being.

"So much pain," Wise One said, his voice showing his age but not hampering the compassion it conveyed.

"How could you possibly know that?" Brickley asked, taken aback by the other's insight.

"When you live more than a century, especially this century, you realize a great deal about people," Wise One replied, a bit wearily. "You look at the lines to the side of each eye, you look at the forehead, you look at how they hold their body . . . you look, and you see, and you know."

"In just a minute or two?"

"In only seconds . . ."

"It's as though, Wise One, that you're able to look through into a person's mind!"

"Oh, no, Mr. Brickley, I cannot. I surely cannot do that. Only our Lord has that ability."

Brickley looked at him with astonishment.

"How is it that you know my name?" he asked.

Wise One smiled then, enjoying some kind of joke of which only he was aware.

Then Brickley noticed the little label on his pajama tops.

"Oh, I see," he said.

"You seem to expect everything from me to be shrouded in mystery, Mr. Brickley."

"You are a mystery, whose presence even in absentia has been lingering over this village for more than a decade. Yes, I would say you are correct. Word about you has gone beyond just this one little spot on the globe."

Wise One seemed genuinely surprised by that.

"I see," he said, rubbing his beard a bit.

"What brings you back, after so long?" Brickley asked.

"May I come in?"

Brickley stood quickly aside.

As Wise One entered the little building, he sighed as he sniffed in the air inside.

"I am glad it's gone," he said. "It seemed oppressive after a while . . . very hard to get used to, I found."

"What's gone?"

"The odor."

"What odor?"

"Manure."

"Manure? I don't know what you mean, Wise One."

"Cow dung was used as paste to hold the packed pieces of earth together."

Brickley looked at the walls, sniffed.

"Are you certain?"

"Oh, yes, I have built many of these over the years."

"Where, Wise One? I got the impression that you never spent much time with the villagers, let alone help any of the earlier ones do any construction."

"You are correct. But I have not always lived here. I have been elsewhere in this part of the world."

"Where were you born?"

Wise One did not answer.

"I'm being too pushy, aren't I?"

Wise One nodded.

155

"But won't you at least tell me what it is that you want? After all, you were the one standing in front of the door when I opened it a few minutes ago."

"If I did not tell you, I would be playing the part of a fool, Stuart Brickley."

"I would tend to agree with that."

"But I will not tell you here."

"Why is that so?"

"Because what I have to tell you is not so important as what I have to show you."

"Did you bring whatever it is with you?"

"No."

"Then—."

Wise One reached out and touched Brickley's lips in a silencing gesture.

"I must bring you *to* it, not the other way around."

"Where must we go?"

Wise One had been sitting in the only other chair inside. He stood, then, and walked over to the back door, and opened it, pointing toward the mountains in the distance.

"There, Stuart Brickley, is where we go."

"But that's hours away. I have responsibilities here. I just can't go on a jaunt because it might strike my fancy. Surely you must realize that, Wise One."

The old man turned and faced Brickley.

Tears.

He could see tears trickling down Wise One's cheeks.

"Are you ill?" Brickley asked, alarmed.

Wise One shook his head.

"No, it is not that, not that."

"Any pain? Should we—?"

Wise One waved a vein-lined hand through the air.

"Hardly the kind of pain to which you refer. But, yes, I *do* have pain, a great deal of pain."

"Please help me to understand what you mean. I must confess that I don't."

"It is pain about which you know a great deal."

*Brickley personally saw one such family, saw its members in a state that surely would remain in his mind for the rest of his life,*

*saw them dead and rotting away in a house that was crammed-full
with expensive furniture, original oil paintings, plush carpeting,
modern appliances of every sort, as well as piles upon piles of money stuffed into shoe-boxes, under mattresses, in wall safes—there
were twenty in that house—and, even, in a huge freezer in the
basement, between chunks of meat. The bodies themselves were
almost completely covered with money, their hands frozen around
clumps of bills in various denominations.*

"You *are* reading my mind!" Brickley exclaimed. "I
thought you said that—"

"No, it is not your mind," Wise One interrupted. "It is
your soul that comes through your eyes into the very air
itself."

"I don't believe in such things."

"You believe in evil, do you not? You have seen it often
enough as you journey about this planet, searching for the life-
blood of industry everywhere."

"I wouldn't have used that word."

"Evil, you mean?"

"That's right, I would never have used evil to describe
what I've seen."

"Greed, corruption, opportunism, selfishness, insensi-
tivity—those are some of the words then?"

"Those are precisely the words."

"But what they describe all are a part of the evil of this
world. One cannot be separated from the other."

Brickley's expression betrayed his skepticism.

"But then words are seldom adequate in such matters,"
Wise One said, sighing. "It is that which you must *experience*
for yourself."

"How do you know I even care?" Brickley asked. "Aren't
you guilty of some wishful thinking?"

"You care, Stuart Brickley, hence, your anguish."

The old man turned, his very manner suggesting that
Brickley should follow him.

"You have more important things on your mind, don't
you?" Brickley said, with a sudden tenderness that he thought
he was incapable of any longer expressing to another individual.

157

"As you shall see, my brother."

"But I am not your brother, Wise One. I cannot possibly *be* your brother."

"And why is that so?"

"Because . . . because I have seen so much pain, so much betrayal, Wise One. There is little goodness in this world, there may be none, I suspect. There is only greed. There is only—."

"But you are a part of that greed, are you not?"

"Yes, I—"

"And your pain comes from the pain of others, the pain of people whose values are corrupted. In your mind, you represent the serpent in Eden, isn't that so, Stuart Brickley?"

"That never occurred to me."

"What *did* occur to you?"

"That we would go in and give people a chance to be lifted out of their poverty."

"And money would do it?"

"Yes, it would. Money would make—"

"—everything possible."

Wise One's eyes narrowed.

"As it did with the Sioux on that reservation?"

*He saw what remained of that tribe after the wells ceased giving up their barrel after barrel of "black gold." The nightclubs had been boarded up; supermarkets as well; no more gas stations remained in that area; homes were repossessed and remaining unsold to new owners afterward, primarily because no "respectable" white family would consider living among such deprived conditions. Men, young as well as old, stumbled about with liquor bottles grasped in their hands, shouting deliriously at the empty air.*

"How did you know about that?" Brickley asked, stunned, as though he had been violated in the most intimate manner imaginable.

Wise One smiled with great irony.

"I was there," he said. "I held many a dying man or woman in my arms as they cried themselves to death."

"But I never saw you."

"But you were never there, were you? Except at the very end. It was the same with Heinrich Himmler, you know. He ordered the construction of the Nazi death camps, and near the end of the war he visited one for the first time . . . Auschwitz. It has been said that even such an arch-Nazi was so overcome, from that moment on, that he seldom slept a full night."

"You compare *us*, Americo and me, to the Nazis?" Brickley asked, his adrenaline starting to surge.

"You all have blood on your hands," Wise One told him. "It is Indian blood in your case. And the blood of others as well. But not the Jews. *That is the only difference!*"

Brickley was enraged, folding his fingers into a fist and reaching out to strike the other man.

"You *are* what they accused you of years ago," he yelled, his face red. "A raving—."

Wise One closed his own fingers around Brickley's wrist, stopping him in mid-air.

"Your strength!" Brickley exclaimed, as he tried to break the other's hold. "How can you be so *strong!*"

Wise One let go after a few seconds.

"What I said is true," he commented.

"But how can we be brothers then?" Brickley asked him. "You said earlier that that was what we were."

"I spoke of tomorrow."

"We will *become* brothers?" Brickley added.

"Yes. We will. Brothers in Christ."

Brickley started laughing.

"You may be strong, Wise One, but your age has caused senility. You are no different from anyone else in that regard."

His face was twisted up in an expression of contempt.

"I saw Christians shedding blood but not in the way that you would mean it," Brickley went on. "I saw them bleed those Indians. They did it in the name of the Christ you mention."

He leaned forward slightly, a sneer remaining.

"And they justified everything, every bit of their behavior because, after all, Indians, whatever the tribe, you know, were only paganistic savages really. Didn't everyone who was a white man, a *real* American, a real Christian realize that? Indians were like dogs, to be given crumbs from their masters' tables, but there any charity was to end."

159

"Stuart **Brickley**?" Wise One interpolated.

"All right, we've already established that as my name," Brickley replied, annoyed. "Why do you repeat it?"

"Before you left for this village," Wise One said, his tone gentle, his eyes narrowed, "while you were still in Dallas, what did you say about the Arabs here?"

"That they were—," Brickley blurted out, then realized what the old man was telling him.

"How could you . . . know?" he asked.

"Is that so important?" Wise One replied. "Isn't *what* I know that which truly matters?"

The old man placed his hands, bony with a century of living, gently on the young one's shoulders.

"Say it, Stuart," he asked. *"Please,* say it."

"I told Otto Kuhlmey, the CEO of Americo, that . . . that—"

He did not want to repeat those words, often tried to avoid admitting them to himself, let alone utter them now before a stranger, such a stranger as this.

His eyes cast a look of pleading at the old man.

Wise One smiled, in an expression so kindly that Brickley knew he could not hold back tears any longer.

"I said to that man, my boss, that the Arabs would be easy to manage, that those pigs would—"

Brickley hesitated, wanting very much to end this wrenching revelation, to break away, emotionally as well as physically, but he could not, no matter how hard he tried in that brief time, he could not, and he knew, then, that the words were unstoppable, for, in a sense, they had their own momentum.

"—that they were only heathens, just . . . just like the spicks on that island, and the stupid niggers in Uganda, and . . . and the lousy chinks and all the other—"

"What were we saying about blood, Stuart? There is no blood on your hands? Is that what you were saying?"

Tears came to Wise One's eyes as well.

*The natives were scattered by the hundreds across the field. Another tribe had coveted their wealth, and war had broken out*

160

*between them . . . the huts in the middle of the oil field on a Caribbean isle were torn down, and those who once lived inside waited for the government to pay them, but no money came, and they left, and joined the rebels . . .*

"Why are *you* crying?" Brickley managed to ask.

"Because I have felt your sorrow, and it is now mine."

Brickley leaned forward, his head bowed slightly, his face pressed against Wise One's bony old chest.

"My blindness, my hypocrisy . . . how can I be forgiven?" he sobbed. "I *need* to know how I can be forgiven! Or . . . or I shall not be able to get through this day."

"I can tell you now," Wise One said. "But you must listen, and to every word."

He did.

# $=27=$

Just before walking up the street toward Dr. al-Fahazi's office, Fahid Bashir stopped for a moment and looked east, at the mountains.

*Like a storm on the horizon,* he thought.

"Or an oasis," he said aloud.

"Pardon me?" said a middle-aged woman passing by.

"Nothing," he said, smiling. "Just thinking out loud."

She was wearing a new diamond-plus-ruby encrusted ring, and saw him looking at it.

"Beautiful, is it not?" she asked.

"Oh, yes, indeed," he told her.

"My, how the Lord has blessed," she muttered with ill-disguised pride. "Praise His holy Name."

"How is your health, Mrs. Halrouk?" he asked.

The woman had started on her way again but stopped, momentarily, a puzzled look on her face, and answered with obvious haste that it was just fine, then continued walking.

"Praise God!" he said.

She didn't break stride this time; it was as though she had never heard him.

*Diamonds and rubies more than—*

The thought died of shame as he brushed it from his mind.

Ahead, a small crowd had gathered in front of Dr. al-Fahazi's tiny office.

One of the villagers saw Bashir and ran up to him.

"Sir, sir, *the doctor is dead!* I found him just three minutes ago. We were about to summon you."

Dr. al-Fahazi was lying face down on the dirt floor. A dagger had been plunged into his back and was still protruding from it. He had apparently been in the act of running away, a leather pouch clutched possessively in his right hand.

Empty.

The pouch was empty except for one small coin and a single gold pendant.

"He was in the act, the very act itself," said the same man who had rushed up to him.

"Did you recognize the intruder?" Bashir inquired.

"No! An outsider, for sure."

*A modern bandit!*

"But why here?" the other man asked. "We are so—"

"Not anymore," Bashir snapped. "There will be more of this, I'm afraid."

"More robberies, sir?"

"Oh, yes. And worse. We are becoming well known, you know. The media are going to be on the prowl."

The man bowed his head.

"Because of the oil?" he asked.

"That, yes, and how we have chosen to display the wealth it has brought us."

"It was supposed to thrust us into the twentieth century."

"And it will do every bit of that, my friend. A twentieth century that has seen the AIDS and the drug epidemics, alcoholism, graphic murders, hostage-taking, and so much else. We will eventually *embrace* the twentieth century, yes, you can be sure of the fulfillment of *that* part of what they have told all of us here."

"But what about the good things?"

"There will come a day when we will be holding our wallets in one hand and the obituaries of our loved ones in the other."

"I don't understand, Bashir."

"Nothing, nothing. Just the rantings of an embittered spirit. Pay no heed."

"But you sound so convicted. What are you going to do about your feelings?"

Bashir considered what the other man had just mentioned. It was a valid question, albeit a cruel one.

"I once would have given up my life," he said finally. "I was so brave that—"

"You lost everything, Bashir. You were thrown out by your family. You were instrumental in bringing many of us to Christ. What has happened to the fervor?"

*Can reformers become pallid mirror images of that against which they once fought so hard?* Bashir asked himself. *Can they set themselves up for someone to fight against them?*

"Are we fine and good and devout when evil is at its most obvious, yet less so when Satan's tactics become seemingly more oblique?" he mused out loud. "Are we soldiers of the King only so long as we can charge into battle with our Bibles and our religious symbols, and our prayer chains, and swing the sword of faith across the path of an onrushing horde? Or are we perhaps—?"

Fahid Bashir turned, sighing, as he saw that the other man, ill-equipped for such complexities, had fled—truly no other word for the awkward speed of that impromptu exit—and Bashir was left there, onlookers peering inside, Dr. Abul al-Fahazi's body at his feet, a symbol of his dead, good friend's spiritual emasculation clutched so tightly in that one hand.

# =28=

Jassim Qaseer was shivering uncontrollably when his wife, Sari, returned home after getting a pail of water from their well.

*Soon this will end,* she told herself as she approached their little residence, smiling as she looked at the brand-new automobile parked in front. *We have gasoline trucked in every day, and yet I have been doing as women have for thousands of years, just to have water to drink, to use for bathing, for cooking.*

She nearly dropped the precious liquid over the dirt floor of their home as she entered and saw the condition of her beloved Jassim.

"What is it, husband?" she asked frantically as she knelt beside his shivering form.

He glanced at her, then turned his eyes away, saying nothing.

"Please, Jassim, let me help you," she begged. "What can I do? Please tell me!"

He held his trembling hands in front of a face from which all normal, healthy color had been drained.

"Something is happening here," he said.

"What are you saying?" she asked, having no idea what he meant.

"Dr. al-Fahazi was murdered today."

165

She fell back for a moment, the impact of his words like a physical blow against her. There had been no such violent death since the closing days of the Muslim domination of their village.

"By why?" she said, her mind spinning. "He was so kind, so good. What reason could there have been?"

"His money, his jewels, his gold," Jassim told her.

"Someone *here* then?" she remarked, with rising alarm. "Who could it have been?"

"Sari, Sari, it was not one of us!" he cried out. "It was an outsider, someone I have not seen before this morning."

"But how could they know? How could they—?"

He reached over to the little table at his left, and grabbed a pile of clippings and tossed it onto her lap.

"There!" he said. "The answer is there."

Newspaper articles about the oil find on the outskirts of the village. Magazine photo stories showing the surroundings and the ground-breaking ceremony months earlier. And shots of villagers showing off expensive adornments for the eager photo journalists: diamond rings, pearl necklaces, plus the automobiles and expensive clothes, and much more

"We are a sensation, Sari," he told her. "We are known all over the world."

Her eyes widened.

"And now the wrath of God descends upon us!" she exclaimed.

He slid off the chair and onto the floor, in front of her.

"You must never say that again," he said, angry and scared at the same time. "What have we done that is so wrong, that would cause God to judge us in that—?"

She studied the expression on his face, what his eyes were telling her more than what his words were saying.

"Look at you, Jassim," she said softly. "Your face is redder than a sunburned American. Your hands continue to tremble as though you have lost control of them. Your voice . . . it is filled with fear, my husband. There is something else. You must tell me. You must warn me so that I can be alert and—"

He threw his head back, closed his eyes, and let out a cry that chilled her through every bone, every nerve.

"What did you *see?*" she demanded, though it was unusual even for former Muslim woman to demand anything of their husbands.

"I saw evil, Sari, I saw evil," he finally said.

"You saw a demon?" she blurted out. "There was a demon in Dr. al-Fahazi's office."

He started laughing then, the laugh of someone who desperately needed release from an encounter such as he had experienced.

"No demon," he said after calming down a bit, "not in the way we always have thought of demons, though demons do exist in that form. This was not a creature spouting fire and smelling of decay. This was a man, Sari, an evil man, a man possessed, yes, but not by some supernatural force—a man controlled and dominated by his own sin. Satan didn't need to use a demon for this man."

He put his arms around his wife.

"I looked into his eyes, my dearest, and . . . I . . . I saw no emotion, nothing at all flickering inside them as he plunged the dagger into Dr. al-Fahazi's back again and again and again. Those eyes, they . . . they were so *dark!* And empty! I could not have expected remorse from such a man, or sudden fear, nothing like that, not from *his* type. But there was no pleasure there either, Sari, *not even that!*"

His arms dropped by his sides as his mind relived that sight, taking him through the trauma one more time. It was Sari's turn to reach out and hug him, and this she did as she whispered into his ear, "But we have seen evil men before. We have—"

She cut herself off for a second or two, abruptly realizing what Jassim had been trying to tell her.

"—yet not since the Holy Spirit entered this village," she continued, "and . . . and we submitted to Him."

"We submitted to Him, my wife, and to His control, we did that very thing, and now—"

They both had been living in the village when Wise One came that one afternoon. They both had stood among the crowd, and listened to him for a while.

*You want everything on the spot, and yet you claim to be unlike so many other villages and towns and cities in this world at present, untainted by many of the excesses of modern civilization.*

"Even then, Sari, the seeds were there," Jassim said. "Wise One was trying to warn us. Satan knew our weaknesses and let us feel comforted by our complacency and not the Comforter Himself. Then when he saw the opportunity, he—"

He buried his head in Sari's breasts, feeling their warmth pour over him.

"Jassim, let us go to bed," she told him. "Let us make love, and shut everything out for the night."

He was breathing heavily as he raised his head and looked into her eyes.

"He took that knife," Jassim said, "after he saw me, and he ran his tongue over it, drool dripping from the corners of his mouth as he wiped it clean of blood, and then cried, 'The curse of Allah on this village. May it be returned to the sand from which it came, *and all of you destroyed!*'"

# =29=

It once had been a garden, this hidden place, a magnificent garden. Derek Sparrowhawk didn't have to use much imagination to envision what the spot had looked like at that time.

Trees tall, with bark the color of cherry wood. Flowers of every possible color, each sending its separate, distinctive scent into the air, to mix with others in a kind of sensual bouquet, so sweet, so rich that you could stand there for hours and never tire of doing so.

And the animals!

Sparrowhawk could see their skeletons on the ground, bones white or grey-toned that would surely prove quite fragile to the touch. All manner of creatures once inhabited that place.

*And every bit of it surrounded by a very large and thick section of a huge mountain range that cut across several countries.*

Now acre after acre of dead things, the multitudinous skeletons of so many different animals, the petrified stumps of trees, of hanging flowers turned dry and brown and dead.

Of—

The shriveled, collapsed-in body of a large serpentine creature lying only a few feet away.

Sparrowhawk approached it cautiously, never having seen a snake of quite that length and thickness, if that was what it

169

once had been, not even the pythons and boas and anacondas he had encountered over the years of his travels through South America and Africa and elsewhere, often exotic places where such huge reptiles were hardly uncommon.

"It has been dead for a very long time," Wise One's voice penetrated the stillness of that place.

Sparrowhawk jumped, startled, not having seen where the old man had appeared.

Wise One stepped out from behind the thick trunk of a tree to one side of that astonishing carcass.

"What happened?" the Englishman asked.

"It was of no further use, and, therefore, it died naturally," Wise One replied as he looked about, and sighed deeply, before adding, "You know, it was so tranquil here that no animal attacked another."

"No birds having to fly to some safe haven from lurking predators of one sort or another?"

"That is correct. It was a joyous time. The weak had nothing to fear from the strong. The strong had nothing to fear from those that were stronger. There was no disease."

"How could that be? It doesn't look like a sterile environment to me," Sparrowhawk pointed out.

"Disease often brings death, and this place saw no—"

"Death, that's what you were going to say, isn't it?"

"Yes . . . oh, it was."

"But *everything* is dead now."

"It was a different world then, when flowers were in bloom here, when water ran in the streams, when—"

Wise One wore an expression of awe.

"When the animals talked . . ."

Sparrowhawk could react with nothing other than ridiculing laughter at that sudden revelation, which made him wonder whether Wise One was indeed wise at all or, rather, the victim of his own delusions.

"Old man, you must be fantasizing. That's fine, but how could you expect me to share in it with you, to *believe* that something like that was ever true?"

"It was."

"Nonsense!"

"No, not nonsense, my friend, *reality!*"

"Impossible. This *is* a game, isn't it? Fine again, and I am sure we could have some fun with it someday, but I am far from being in the mood for that sort of thing just now."

"Birds could talk with the fish."

"Stop it! I'm beginning to wonder if you have been misnamed, Wise One," Sparrowhawk said, voicing his doubts.

"And humans could talk with any of them."

"Are you insane?"

"To men, the wisdom of God is as foolishness."

"Don't try to retreat behind dogma, old man."

"Haven't you ever felt communion with an animal?"

"Depends upon what you mean by communion."

"A special link, a bond that is there but indefinable."

Sparrowhawk fell into silence for a moment. He hated admitting it but, yes, he had known times when he felt such communion.

"I periodically visited a home for the elderly," he said finally. "My father had had to be confined there during the last few years of his life. He took it all quite hard, you know, but one day when I arrived I saw a remarkable change come over him. You see, an organization had brought several cats to spend time with him and others like my father. He had one of the cats on his lap when I entered his room. Dad was alert, and happy, and, well, so different."

"That was what animals were meant to be, Derek," Wise One said. "They were to be helpers, friends, companions, never adversaries. But, today, creatures on land and fish in the sea attack and kill the unwary. While men in return shoot them down, club them to death, tear them apart through the ugliest of traps."

"And in laboratories, Wise One, don't forget that?" Sparrowhawk interjected, with some personal feeling this time.

"Yes, Derek, we must *not* forget that. It is one of mankind's crudest propensities, gaining profit from the misery of those they subject to experiments that often have no redeeming value whatsoever. God's creatures, meant to bring men and women warmth and love, are betrayed simply because a new lipstick color must be introduced or a new hair dye or some such useless product, the only purpose of which is to reinforce the vanity of—"

Wise One was trembling. And Sparrowhawk suddenly felt great empathy for the old man."

"The whole earth was meant to be like this place," Wise One went on. "Man was to have dominion over it from north to south and east to west."

"No crime? No pollution. No—"

"No pain. No sorrow. No death, Derek."

"What you're talking about sounds like a bit of heaven!"

"The personal creation of a holy God, that is what this corpse was supposed to be. A world designed to—"

"You're starting to sound like a certain TV preacher, you know, the guy who's always—"

Wise One held up his hand in a gesture that cut Sparrowhawk off immediately.

"You *don't* know where you are, do you?" he asked, a touch of pity in his voice. "You have no conception."

"That's right. I have no idea. Only legends like those about the Garden of Eden could be compared with what you are—"

"Follow me," Wise One interrupted.

"Whatever you say . . ."

They walked through that dried up place.

*No birds,* Sparrowhawk thought. *No insects. Nothing that lives and breathes is left here.*

He bent down for a moment, picked up a handful of what he thought was soil.

It turned to powder in his palm.

*And that odor . . .*

Sparrowhawk reached out and touched the drooping branch of a straggly looking tree.

It, too, became a pile of dust, trickling between his fingers and onto the ground at his feet.

*That odor, like the inside of a tomb.*

He turned and looked behind him.

A musty brownish cloud accompanied their footsteps, caused by the dusty soil at their feet.

172

Sparrowhawk started shivering.

"Where are we?" he asked.

But Wise One paid no attention.

Suddenly Sparrowhawk detected an odor that seemed especially out-of-place with the others.

Sweet.

The sweet odor of—

*Fruit!*

Something did live in that once-garden!

Sparrowhawk caught up with Wise One, then stopped short.

Wise One was standing in front of a tree that indeed was alive, a tree bearing an orange-red fruit.

"All that is left," the old man remarked wistfully.

"Great!" Sparrowhawk said. "I'm hungry."

He reached out toward one of the—

"Do not touch it!" Wise One declared firmly.

"But—"

"I said no."

"Hey, old man, who appointed you my boss? I don't take orders from those who have no authority to give them."

"It is the sweetest fruit ever grown," Wise One told him, his eyes sparkling with the very thought.

"But how do you know?"

Wise One smiled.

"I have been told by others."

"What others?"

"Those who *have* tasted it."

"Well, then, I must ask, why is it that you have never found out for yourself, Wise One?"

"The time for that will not occur again for—"

He cut off the words as though, by saying them, he would be violating some ancient code of secrecy.

"But I *want* to try such sweetness," Sparrowhawk insisted, more anxious than he cared to acknowledge.

He started to close one hand around—

Just then he heard a cry of torment unlike anything he had experienced in a lifetime.

*. . . all of creation groaneth and travaileth together.*

Those words heard in some long-forgotten church at
some time in his unenlightened past came back to him, so
stark and real that it was almost as though they had been spoken to him by someone who happened to be standing right by
his side, today, now, not decades earlier, when he was a child,
and unaware of what he could no longer believe.

Sparrowhawk quickly withdrew his hand.

"What on earth was that?"

Wise One walked up to the Englishman and spoke slowly
and with great solemnity.

"You have it wrong, Derek Sparrowhawk," the strange
old man said, his eyes narrowed.

"Wrong? What do you mean?"

"Not from here on earth, my English friend. That sound
isn't from this planet at all."

"Then where—?"

*Demon eyes, red, peering at him from the darkness . . .*

Suddenly Sparrowhawk found that he was covered with
cold perspiration as he looked around at what he could see of
that spot, the petrified remains of trees and bushes and shriveled flower petals, like those that had been pressed between
the covers of a sympathy card or one of those gargantuan family Bibles after it had been snatched from a funeral display,
forgotten for years, and then the card opened a decade later,
the contents as dead as the human being who was commemo-
rated . . . the dusty, crumbling earth, blackish, smelling of a
thousand centuries.

*And then this one living thing, this single tree, with its delec-
table-looking fruit . . .*

"O God!" Sparrowhawk said, his mind trying to grasp
the truth of where he was.

"Do not take God's name in vain," Wise One admonished.

"I didn't," the Englishman replied. "So help me, for the
first time in years, I didn't."

Sparrowhawk knew where he was.

He knew what this still so vibrant tree was.

He knew that he has seeing what countless others had yearned for over the ages.

"This really is what I think, isn't it?" Sparrowhawk asked, awe reducing his voice to a strained whisper.

Wise One nodded.

"All these years . . . ," Sparrowhawk mused.

"Isolated, dead," Wise One added. "An analogy for the spiritual condition of most of mankind, wouldn't you agree?"

"I'm not a Christian."

"Are you so sure you don't want to be?"

"Oh, yes, indeed I am. It is a barbarous religion, to be sure, a religion built on the abominable practice of blood sacrifice. I cannot tolerate, I cannot accept, anything of the sort."

"Are you so sure?"

"I already said so. Repetition is not the way to my soul."

"So there *is* a way, then, is that what you mean?"

"Don't make that assumption. I cannot be sure that I even have what you would call a soul, Wise One."

"Oh, you do, Derek Sparrowhawk."

"And if I don't accept this Jesus, I will spend it in hell?"

"I can answer only yes."

"But there is enough hell on this wounded planet of ours. That's the only hell I happen to believe in."

"Because your loved one died."

"No, all of us must die at some point. It was how she died. It was the uselessness of her death."

"Why did she die?"

"Because the most beautiful creature in my life had dared to fall in love with someone who wasn't a member of the Islam religion. She was counted as nothing more than a common harlot for doing so!"

"It wasn't *only* because of the relationship between the two of you," Wise One said, his voice tender.

"How can you *say* that? How could you possibly know?"

The old man went on as though he had never heard what the Englishman had just said.

"It was something more, my friend, something you could not have known, because that sweet, sweet woman did not have a chance to tell you, her beloved."

*My beloved! Oh, she was, a piece of beautiful porcelain, with a face sculpted by a master . . .*

Sparrowhawk was becoming annoyed, annoyed that Wise One seemed to be playing with his emotions.

*She was too precious, too kind, too good to be a topic of conversation between myself and this stranger . . .*

"Get to the point!" Sparrowhawk barked irritably. "Tell me what you're leading up to, please."

Wise One cupped his hands together, opened the palms upward, and reached them out in front of him.

"She would have had a gift, Derek Sparrowhawk," he said. "She would have had a most blessed gift and holy gift for you."

"And what was that?" the Englishman asked with obvious doubt that the old man knew what he was talking about.

"She was to be God's instrument in bringing you to a salvational acceptance of Christ as Savior and Lord."

Sparrowhawk burst out laughing.

"In your wildest dreams, I suspect," he said, "but nothing more than that."

Wise One kept his hands in the same position, without moving them so much as an inch.

"You might as well stop this . . . this evangelical nonsense," Sparrowhawk sneered. "It won't—"

Wise One's gaze and his own met, and locked. Sparrowhawk tried to turn away but somehow could not.

"Why are you doing this?" the Englishman asked. "Can't you see that I truly am not a candidate for—?"

"She died because she had become a Christian," Wise One said slowly. "The relationship between the two of you only speeded up the timetable, as far as those determined to destroy her were concerned. Without you in her life, she would still have been stoned to death by men who were possessed, if not by demons, then by the spiritual bankruptcy of the loathsome faith they professed."

Sparrowhawk was about to scoff at that latest revelation, and had started to speak again when Wise One cut him off.

"Yes, I know," the old man interrupted. "You regard Christianity as a collection of musty and rather silly myths."

176

He waved his hand in the musty air of that dead place in which the two of them stood.

"Is *this* perhaps one of those myths you have on some sort of list," Wise One asked him, "to be checked off as you analyze, research, and disprove every last one?"

Sparrowhawk was beginning to feel uncomfortable. He knew that Wise One was close to hitting the mark.

"It's just . . . just one of . . . of—," he tried to say.

"Just one of many? What about the others, isn't that correct, Derek Sparrowhawk?"

Wise One turned just then and as he did, he called over his shoulder, "Follow me, if you will, my stubborn English friend. I have another place to show you, the contents of which you will find perhaps even more interesting than what you see here."

Oddly enough, Sparrowhawk did so without question, though he couldn't imagine why.

# =30=

Jalil Arik-Arad had been waiting for a long time to taste the sweet fruit of vengeance, nearly twenty years since he had left that village, driven out by the appalling necessity to live in such close proximity to a growing number of infidels.

He thought of what the *Qur'ān* unequivocally demanded as punishment. It was enjoyable to him to serve as an instrument of Allah's wrath. The screams of the maimed were a kind of music; the more often he played that melody, the better he felt . . .

His palms were sweaty as he played over in his mind the scenes that he knew were waiting to be enacted directly from the words of Muhammad himself.

*Slay them wherever you come upon them . . .*

Indeed he anticipated that moment, taking a rifle or a knife or throwing a grenade or firing a piece of heavy artillery, using one or all of those weapons and killing dozens of the traitors himself.

*I hope I can hear their cries*, he thought. *I hope I can see many of them die before my eyes. I do not want to miss that!*

Arik-Arad had not always felt so strongly. He once even had been willing to tolerate their existence so long as they kept out of his way. But when they took over the community of his birth, he knew he had to strike back. And though he was far from alone, not everyone was as passionate as he had been. So, in time, he had to stop the mandated maiming, and he was forced eventually to leave along with many others.

*Allah was shamed then. We allowed the infidels to force us into retreat. And Allah has withheld blessing from us all these many years.*

*Now—*

"We will succeed," he said to the veiled old woman as they sat in the truck, waiting to give the signal that would send that force on its mission like bullets rapid-firing from a machine gun.

"You have been an inspiration to us," he went on. "You have been an example of all that is good about Islam."

She nodded slowly, solemnly, not as yet ready to participate in any exuberant celebration.

"Until the village is retaken, words remain words," she said, her voice thin, ancient-sounding.

"But they are mothers to action," Arik-Arad reminded her. "It is because of your words that we have never grown weak, that we have never forgotten what must be done."

"No one anticipates this more than I," she assured him. "No one feels the pain of what happened more."

Arik-Arad agreed.

"You have no need to convince me of that," he said. "Do you have the knife?"

She patted a pocket in the heavy garment that she was wearing.

"Good," he said. "It is time to start."

"But not before we ask the protection of Allah."

*Yes! We must do that,* he thought. *Else how could it be that we even hope for success?*

Arik-Arad climbed out of the truck and walked down the line of vehicles—other trucks, a few tanks more, plus the canvas-topped troop carriers—urging them to ask Allah's blessing on that upon which they were about to embark.

"Infidel blood running in the streets," he shouted. "Infidel hearts held high in our palms in praise to Allah!"

They all echoed their own commitment in strong words and loud voices.

"The oil is ours! It is on our land!"

"We will seize it from their very grip!"

"If they will not let go, we will cut off the infidel hand and feed it to the vultures!"

After seeing that the other Muslims had been sufficiently stirred up, Arik-Arad returned to his own truck.

"They are so eager," he said.

"As I," the old woman muttered. "As I."

# ꞊31꞊

Fahid Bashir leaned forward at the shortwave radio, and asked the individual who had sent the last transmission to repeat it, but more slowly this time.

Startled originally, he now listened to every word, committing them to memory. When he had signed off, he sat back in his rickety old chair, and swallowed with difficulty several times.

*O God . . .*

This was not in vain but a call for wisdom, a prayer, the beginning of a plea of desperation.

*O God, it starts. What Wise One tried to warn us about.*

He had to connect by radio to his country's central governmental headquarters. Trying desperately over the next half an hour, he finally got through to someone in the prime minister's office.

"We'll need troops," he said, panic in his voice.

"Yes, yes, of course," the man at the other end told him. "It will be done as you say. Thank you for calling."

Bashir knew he should have been relieved.

But he wasn't. There was something in the other man's voice, something that seemed almost—

*Mocking!*

Bashir sat up straight in the chair.

"He didn't mean a word of what he said!" the words shot out of his mouth.

*I don't know how I know that but, Lord, I do!*

He looked at the sheet of paper upon which he had scrawled that alarming message:

> *Shiite Muslim group intends to attack your village very soon, and take it over, especially the oil find. You must believe that they do not care at all about how many lives are sacrificed in the process.*
>
> *You are in grave danger!*
>
> *You must get help, Tahid. There could be a very bloody massacre. None of you can survive on your own. Please, please do something immediately.*
>
> *They consider that they will be rewarded in some royal manner by Allah for every Christian they are able to murder or torture, and they will do precisely that, given the slightest excuse or opportunity . . .*

"But how could they do anything like that without the government knowing and intervening?" he asked out loud.

*Because . . .*

The government did know!

Bashir comprehended, suddenly, what else there had been in that man's voice as it came over the shortwave radio or, rather, what had *not* been there!

Surprise.

None showed in the way he had spoken; he should have been as disturbed as Bashir had been, should have frantically indicated that the president himself would take care of it, should have asked him to remain calm and stay in constant communication, should have said all this and more.

No surprise whatever.

Nor had there been any trembling, any sense of outrage.

Just cold, hard words spoken as though memorized by a third-rate actor!

*The government knows, yes! But none of us did until now . . . because we're Christians, and, therefore, not only expendable but it's better for the sake of Islam that we all perish.*

182

*They really don't want any of us around any longer.*

*None of them ever stopped resenting what we did to them: cutting so many of their Muslim kin away from their Islamic moorings. That, in their eyes, was wholly unforgivable.*

He opened the center drawer in his desk and took out the British Bulldog, looking at it, realizing what a paltry weapon it would be to face even the minimum armaments that could be expected to be thrown against everyone in the village.

*I've got to get to Otto Kuhlmey! He has the advanced transmitter. He could contact Washington D.C. and get advice. The U.S. was instrumental in liberating Kuwait. Surely—!*

Not the same.

Kuwait had been taken over by another country.

*For us, none of that is involved. There is no question of foreign aggression. Our own government may be ready to sanction whatever is going to happen.*

He slipped on a jacket and hurried outside.

# =32=

Otto Kuhlmey respected Fahid Bashir, but he was finding it exceptionally hard to take him seriously as the man stood before him, talking about an impending Shiite takeover of the village, including the oil pumping facilities.

"Impossible!" he protested.

"What were the Kuwaitis saying twenty-four hours before Hussein ordered the invasion?" Bashir responded.

"That's a different matter altogether!"

"How so? The CIA had reports that it was going to happen, but those were viewed as so much propaganda, or whatever, a ploy by Hussein as a wild card to play in some forthcoming negotiations."

"But it's now kept us on the alert, Fahid. We've learned from experience. Besides, there's no one like Saddam Hussein on the scene now. There isn't a thing—"

"There will *always* be someone like him in this region, Otto. We give birth to monsters of that sort like a family of rabbits. It's a part of what has entangled our culture. Saladin was one example. So was Nasser. Not to mention the various ayatollahs over the years.

"Shall I go on? If they don't end up seizing power, then they become part of the suicide squads that serve the actual usurper, pledging their lives in the process!

"Arabs are born into some kind of ancestral persecution complex. The Israelis are always out to get us. And the Americans. Plus the British. They want to come in and take over. The Crusades failed, so the modern imperialists are waiting for just the right opportunity!"

"Do you believe any of that junk?" Kuhlmey asked pointedly.

"No, of course not. But then I made a conscious decision to jettison *everything* that was Moslem in any and all respects. That included a Pandora's box of stale old fears that nevertheless seem ripe enough to the average follower of Islam."

*Kuhlmey had to admit to himself the absolute truth of what Bashir was saying. Long before he rose to his present position with Americo, he nevertheless worked at the company in a lower echelon position, and he heard the horror stories of what life in Kuwait was like during the Iraqi invasion—the many instances of torture, some of which were covered through the media, many others remaining unreported since they were far too horrible for dissemination to the general public.*

Kuhlmey had been standing. He sat down at his deck and indicated a chair in front of it.

"You really do place credence in that one report, don't you?" he asked the other.

"I surely do, Otto. I wish I could say no, but that would be a lie," Bashir said honestly.

"A temple so recently erected . . . ," Kuhlmey said, his voice weary, with a touch of wistfulness.

Bashir felt a rush of empathy for the man.

"Wise One knew this was coming, didn't he?" Kuhlmey added.

Bashir bowed his head, keeping quiet for a moment.

"Are you feeling ill, Fahid?" Kuhlmey asked.

When Bashir raised his head, trickles of moisture were apparent on his cheeks.

"I think he did, Otto. I think, somehow, he knew."

"But that was a decade ago. How is it possible?"

"The Bible is full of examples of prophecy."

"Of course, Fahid! Don't you think I know that? I read my Bible every day. But I'm from a group that is convinced that prophecies will start up again in the—'

He fell back in his chair, his face suddenly going white.

"—end times," Bashir added the words that he knew would have been spoken by the other man.

"Could it be so, Fahid?" Kuhlmey said, a little uncertainly.

"And what does that make Wise One?"

"You must suspect the answer to that. Surely it seems logical now, surely it fits, wouldn't you say?"

*"Satan himself will try to destroy this village," he told not just the constable but the rest as well, speaking as though to every man, woman, and child. "He will attack most severely. The angels will protect you since they will be sent by God Himself, but this will happen only if you rededicate yourselves to the Savior."*

"A prophet?" Bashir said. "Is that what you and I are thinking?"

"What else could he be? How else could he possess that sort of wisdom? I don't think it was anything remotely as mundane as a lucky guess on his part."

# =33=

Stuart Brickley had followed Wise One, just as Derek Sparrowhawk did, across the stretch of desert between the village and that local section of the mammoth mountain range.

But the old man had got a considerable distance ahead of him and could no longer be seen as he disappeared, presumably into a pass in the wall of rock directly ahead.

*I'm far more out of shape than I ever thought I could be. At his age he should be in a rocking chair watching a sunset. But, no, he's outpaced me from the start.*

Brickley did not notice the scorpion that stood in his path. There was a quick burst of pain, and then it was as though entire his nervous system went to pieces.

His knees buckled, and he fell forward, tasting the sand in his mouth as he hit the ground.

So suddenly, so completely without warning, his body seemed to freeze in that one position, and he couldn't move though his mind kept urging the rest of him to do so.

He felt a chill, as though icicles were hanging from every nerve in his body.

*I'm going to die here!*

Some still conscious part of his being screamed those words.

*I'm going to die here, and they'll take my body back home, and in a week my family, my friends will be grouped around my coffin, saying or thinking words of farewell.*

He tried desperately to move, to do something as simple as open his eyes.

*It's made me blind. That's what—*

That was when he felt the gentlest touch he had ever known. Not on his eyes but under his left arm, lifting him up.

"Who's there?" he asked. "I need medical care. Please take me to Americo's—."

Then on his lips!

Soft, like the brush of a feather . . .

"I feel so weak," Brickley told whoever it was. "I may be dying. Something bit me. It must have been poisonous. You've got to hurry!"

A wave of weakness engulfed him quite suddenly, and he sensed that he was starting to fall until strong hands, the same hands presumably capable of such a tender touch, tightened their grip on him, and he felt himself steadying.

*My strength is made perfect in your weakness . . .*

"I can hear you speak, sir," Brickley said. "What is your name? I implore you, please, to take me back for treatment."

He was being picked up now, carried, though not roughly.

"Thank you, sir," he said, his emotions responding in a way he would never have thought possible under the circumstances, not with a burst of joy, noisy and extravagant, his heart pumping faster in anticipation of getting medication treatment before it was too late, but with a quiet, reassuring, unspeakably sublime peace.

He realized, then, that the pain was gone.

# ═**34**═

N<sub>ight.</sub>

The caravan of men and weapons was only a few miles from the village.

Jalil Arik-Arad had stopped his truck, pausing for a moment, uttering a silent prayer for Allah to continue by their side as they sought retribution in his name, as the *Qur'ān* directed, retribution that had been planned long ago to be as deliberately blasphemous and degrading to the infidels as possible, cutting to the very foundation of a faith that dishonored the Prophet, the great messenger of Allah.

*It is not enough this time to claim simply a hand or a foot,* Jalil Arik-Arad had decided years earlier. *Your crimes against Islam require the greatest sacrifice of all, on an altar that when used in the fashion I intend will stand around the world as a symbol of utmost offense to anyone who is a Christian.*

Crimes.

From Jalil Arik-Arad's perspective, that was the only word that sufficed. He had learned at his mother's knee how the *Qur'ān* dealt with *all* belief systems apart from Islam.

*. . . such is the recompense of unbelievers.*

There was more, another word embraced by Muslims because of the dictates contained in the *Qur'ān*.

*Retaliation.*

189

This was not something suggested, but ordered.

*Demand retaliation.*

But the most compelling verse of all, the one that named the greatest of the crimes against Islam was a verse that Jalil Arik-Arad had memorized when he was just four years old.

> *They will not cease to fight with you,*
> *till they turn you from your religion,*
> *if they are able; and whosoever of you*
> *turns from his religion, and dies disbelieving—*
> *his works have failed in this world and the next;*
> *those are the inhabitants of the Fire—therein*
> *they shall dwell forever.*

To turn away from the Messenger, the Prophet, to cast his words on the dung-head of their infidel heresies!

"You will have punishment in the next life, yes," Jalil Arik-Arad said out loud. "And that will be Allah's privilege. Right now mine shall be inflicting pain here, now!"

His hatred of Christians was both personal and religious. It was the latter because that was how the *Qur'ān* had spoken on the subject. It was the former because of what they did to the place of his birth. And it was for this that, even not so proclaimed in the *Qur'ān*, he would have hated Christians anyway, would have planned to mutilate, or, hopefully, kill as many as possible.

*I am a Muslim,* he proclaimed to himself. *I eat and sleep and live the quest for retribution against any who trample on the teachings of the Messenger, to be a "grievous trial" to every last one of the infidels.*

He seized momentarily upon that indelible phrase from the *Qur'ān:*

*Grievous trial . . .*

Jalil Arik-Arad had once written that phrase in the sand outside the village, just before he left with the other displaced Muslims, including the mother of Fahid Bashir, displaced because of their inability to coexist with those

190

whom they detested. Some vagrant wind blew across the desert moments later, and suddenly, the phrase was gone.

*But not in my mind, not in my heart, not in my very soul, for it will lodge there so long as I can think, so long as I can feel, so long as I . . . exist.*

How that recollection brought back memories of his childhood days, aided by the location in which he stood at that precise moment.

On the left was the local stretch of the mountain range that had figured so prominently in the history of several Middle Eastern countries. On the right was the village, once so inconsequential, now soon to become world-renowned for what would happen to it.

*The why of it will be a shock to the unwary,* he thought, anticipating the next few hours, *the long-festering reason, that when revealed, would be viewed from the vantage point of history as a singular turning point for the Islamic fundamentalist movement.*

Directly ahead he could see the faint outline of the pile of rocks at the entrance to the underground series of tunnels.

As a child, he had visited that place, had wondered where the tunnels led, had felt the oppressive atmosphere and had run from their confines when he thought he heard a strange and chilling voice calling, calling, calling to him.

*Where Evil Became Its March . . .*

"And here we are marching," he commented.

"What was that?" the veiled old woman asked.

"Nothing," he said. "An idle thought."

She grunted with annoyance at the one who had been responsible for reinforcing her own thirst for vengeance for more than a decade.

*It was only a short while now . . .*

# =35=

A cave, at the far end of the garden.

A cave so large that Derek Sparrowhawk imagined the village itself could have fit inside, the people if not the buildings.

Lit by row after row of candles.

"Looks like a Catholic church in here," he joked feebly.

"That wasn't the purpose," Wise One said, "I assure you, not *that* at all. It had to be ready for you. Everything had to be together. You are a disciplined man, and orderly."

"Surely not all for *me?*" Sparrowhawk repeated, mystified. "I mean, can I be expected to believe that you could have known?"

He saw the expression on the old man's face.

"How long has this been planned?" he asked.

"A long time," Wise One answered.

"Are you trying to brainwash me with that predestination malarkey now?"

There was no reply this time.

"It's big, but—," he started to say, entranced by the size.

Then a stunning thought hit him.

"Does this connect with that network of tunnels?" he asked.

"It did, once," Wise One said without elaboration.

Sparrowhawk stood in what was roughly the center of the cavern, cocking his head and gazing up at the ceiling.

"Unbelievable! It must reach halfway to the top of the mountain itself!" he exclaimed.

"That it does," Wise One assured him.

Wide ledges, enough to walk on, even to sit down on, began at the bottom, and worked their way in circular fashion up the somewhat rounded sides of the cavern. Someone with a good sense of balance could use them as steps to go as far as they were able to take him.

Sparrowhawk's neck was stiffening, and he pulled his gaze away from the upward reach of the cavern.

That was when he saw the objects on the hard rock floor. Each one had been placed in its own space, so that, despite the number, there was no impression of haphazardness.

"It looks like a museum in here," the Englishman observed, "or an archaeological dig."

"In some respects, it is a bit of both," Wise One told him.

"But why here?" Sparrowhawk started to ask. "Who could have brought them to this—?"

His mouth dropped open as his gaze fastened upon one of the objects directly in front of him.

A large cross.

He walked up to it, touched the dry old wood, took his hand away, saw the brittle little splinters on his fingertips.

"Hundreds of years," he mumbled. "I've never seen anything of wood as old as this."

"No, Derek Sparrowhawk, you haven't," Wise One interpolated. "But not hundreds. *Thousands!*"

Sparrowhawk felt the hairs on the back of his neck start to move, as though from the presence of static electricity.

"Two thousand years?" he asked slowly, deliberately, not wanting, really, to acknowledge even the remotest possibility that he had made the connection this eccentric old chap had intended.

The Englishman could see that Wise One seemed to be trying not to weep, at least openly.

"Yes, two thousand," the old man confirmed, sniffling, his eyes increasingly moist.

193

Sparrowhawk saw holes at either end of the crossbeam, and near the base as well.

He put his fingers in the indentations.

*And Thomas, who needed to see in order to believe, touched the nail-prints . . .*

Sparrowhawk shook his head, trying to clear his mind of those haunting old words.

"A Roman cross!" he exclaimed, not willing to take the connection any further.

"More than *a* cross," Wise One said, a note of offense in his voice at the fact that the Englishman had tried, for his own sake, to downgrade the significance of the large object in front of him. "Open your mind, Mr. Skeptic, as well as your heart, and you will *know!*"

Sparrowhawk's palms were sweaty as he saw something else a few feet to the left, by itself on the hard rock floor of the cavern

A red robe, part of it tattered.

He walked slowly over to it, bent down, and carefully picked it up.

Stains. On the back.

*The whips*, he thought. *The mocking words, the whips, the royal robe, and on His head, a crude, a cruel—*

*—crown of thorns. Underneath the red cloth!*

He folded the robe almost reverently and after placing it back on the ground, reached for the—

In an instant, a feeling of inexpressible sorrow gripped Sparrowhawk. It was as though he could hear a multitude shouting obscenities, along with "Crucify him! Crucify him!"

*He is an innocent Man! How can I stand by and do nothing?*

*A voice seems to be telling me, telling me something I don't, I don't, I don't want to hear.*

*Sin. It's about sin. I don't believe in rubbish like that. I don't, I don't, I don't, I DON'T, I DON'T, I DON'T, I—*

"Because your sin put Him there," the voice continues. "Because He died for you, and yet you have always turned your back on Him!"

"NO!" I shout. "It cannot be!"

Sparrowhawk had begun to hold the thorns more tightly in his hands, not noticing any pain as they cut into his flesh.

Wise One came up to him, and gently took the twisted old crown from his grasp.

Sparrowhawk looked at him, then at his hands which were crisscrossed with trickles of blood.

"No . . . Wise One," he stuttered. "This . . . this cannot be. Surely this cannot be. Tell me that, I beg you. Tell me or I shall not leave this place a sane man any longer."

"Is it from the cesspool of your unbelief that I hear you speak?" Wise One replied. "If so, then I shall consider only that you have given me mere silence and not something from the depths of your soul."

"But how could you ever expect me to react in any other manner, Wise One? I have scorned faith so much of my life. When I became an adult, I put away childish things, and a simplistic faith in any kind of divinity was part of all that, part of my maturation into being a man, not some foolish and superstitious boy."

"You *are* a man, yes. As a man, look around you, through a *man's* eyes. What do you see?"

"A cross and a robe and a crown of thorns. What are they supposed to tell me, Wise One?"

"*They* tell you nothing, Derek Sparrowhawk. I speak not of religious good luck charms, you know. Nor of relics stored in the catacombs of a pretentious Vatican. These are not to be used as objects of worship or in any way as conduits to God. They have no significance except in a historical perspective. There are no mystical powers to be gained from things physical."

"Then *what?*" Sparrowhawk pleaded, feeling very desperate, with a strange sense of rising panic.

"Your soul!" the old man replied. "What does that still small voice in your soul tell you?"

Sparrowhawk tried to laugh, tried to brush those intimidating words aside as meaningless, as gibberish from someone overwhelmed by rushing senility.

Tried, oh, yes, tried.

He turned away from Wise One and headed back toward the cavern's entrance.

"Do you not want to see what else is stored on the ground here, and then let me take you up on those ledges that so completely fascinated you a few moments ago?" Wise One asked. "I can promise you something most special up there, something on the other side of this mountain's wall of stone that I suspect will leave you quite speechless."

Sparrowhawk hesitated. After all, the discovery of ancient things had been an avocation of his for many years. And how could he justify ignoring all that the cavern promised, simply because he couldn't seem to cope with the implications of what they might be!

"All right . . . ," he said, turning around.

Wise One showed him scores of different items, including two broken tablets of engraved stone.

"**Are** you hoping that I will believe that *they* are the—?" Sparrowhawk asked. "Surely you don't think of me as so stupid!"

But he fell into silence when Wise One showed him an ornate silver goblet that appeared to have been handmade.

"So beautiful," he said, awed, "so perfect."

"Not as beautiful, nor as perfect as the first lips to touch it and drink of the contents," Wise One added.

*The silver chalice!*

*The legendary goblet from which Christ drank at the Last Supper and which was passed to each of the apostles, including Judas.*

A dark mood infected Sparrowhawk just then.

"Yes, but the one who was to betray Jesus also drank of the wine it held," he noted.

"You are correct, my friend," Wise One agreed, then suddenly held up a rope, an old, smelly piece of handwoven rope. "And Judas died at his own hand."

"There is more?" Sparrowhawk asked.

"Much more."

# =36=

It seemed like hours later that even Wise One had become exhausted, but finally he stopped before a hole in the rock wall, so far up that Sparrowhawk knew he dared not look down, dared not let his mind comprehend what his fast-beating heart had been trying to tell him.

"Look through here, Derek Sparrowhawk," Wise One said to him in a kindly manner.

"What is it?" the Englishman asked, not sure that what the old man wanted him to see could be any more impressive than what he had already encountered.

"See for yourself."

Sparrowhawk pressed his eye up against a small hole in the cold rock of that wall.

And then stepped back immediately!

"No, no," he said, "not this time. I cannot accept that. It's . . . it's not even supposed to be here. I heard that it was in Turkey, on Mount—"

"You heard incorrectly," Wise One interrupted.

"But there was such evidence! Take Montgomery, for example. He's hardly incompetent."

"You are right. But even geniuses see what they want to see when they want to see it badly enough."

"But there were others. That fellow was hardly alone. Christianity had for years claimed that finding—"

Sparrowhawk gulped several times as he cut himself off, turned back to that hole, and looked through it yet again.

The wood was soft, that much and more was obvious, soft, and blackened by rot, some planks turned to almost mush over the centuries.

*The centuries!*

How many?

It was a question Derek Sparrowhawk asked himself and then tried to reject since he thought he understood the very reason for it in the first place.

If he decided that what he saw, and see it he did, he knew he did, was thousands of years old, if it was, say, four thousand or greater, then the chronology of that answer necessarily would lead him to accept the reality of what that hulking shape indeed represented, not merely weakening yet another biblical story, which wouldn't have bothered him, but snatching it altogether from the realm of myth and legend and hypothesis and thrusting it into the province of fact.

"Look!" he said, as movement occurred from within the shape. "Something alive in there!"

"For generation upon generation!" Wise One said. "The most beautiful pure white—"

*Doves!*

There were scores of them, perhaps hundreds.

"They come for a season, then leave, and eventually return, then leave," Wise One remarked. "They seem unable to stay away."

The Englishman sensed that Wise One was trying out a little theology on him with that statement.

"I am not stupid," Sparrowhawk said. "They may be symbols for the Holy Spirit, and all that, but they're not Him."

"You are correct, Derek. Yet how can they be of any interest to you, the veteran journalist, since they represent Someone who, in your own view, is simply nonexistent?"

*There he is again!* Sparrowhawk thought with some irritation. *The old man's been toying with me!*

198

His shoulders slumped.

*But doing it successfully!*

*I've got to leave this place. If I stay, I will have to put these bits and pieces together and . . . and—*

"You are correct," Wise One suddenly announced.

"To what do you refer?" Sparrowhawk said, surprised.

"The Holy Spirit isn't there, amidst that rotting wreck. Those innocent, wonderful birds are *only* symbols."

"Then where *is* He? Still in heaven? As invisible as always?"

Wise One merely looked at him without speaking.

"I see!" Sparrowhawk said almost with a sneer. "Ah, yes, the Holy Spirit is here, now, among us as we speak. I suppose that's it, yes, indeed! Have I got this torturous theological matter right, Wise One?"

He had closed his eyes only for a second or two, marshaling his thoughts. When he opened them, Wise One was holding something out to him, a long, ruby-red dress, with a floral pattern on the front.

For a moment, Sparrowhawk couldn't cope, since he recognized the dress instantly.

*He had bought it for Talah as a gift. She had discarded her drab Muslim garb, veil and all, and slipped it on, filling out every inch of the dress exactly as he had thought she would.*

"My beloved's!" Sparrowhawk cried out. "I assumed it has been lost or destroyed altogether these many, many years."

He reached out for the dress, and Wise One let him have it willingly. He held it up to his nose, and sniffed in deeply.

"So hard to believe," he whispered. "After all this time, there is yet a hint of her odor, that delicate scent that was part of what captivated me. I could close my eyes and know that she was in the room without her ever having to say a word. Not a single word, Wise One, and yet I could tell, yet I would open my eyes and find that I was right, that she stood before me, smiling so sweetly."

He thrust the dress back into Wise One's hand.

"Where is she?" Sparrowhawk asked.

He inhaled, testing the air.

199

"Only the ancient, the dead, the still rotting bits and pieces of generations long, long gone!" he growled. "Why do you torment me this way, Wise One?"

He beat his fists against the rock wall.

"I can see the hulking presence of a vessel that is supposed to have saved a remnant of mankind and of the animals, keeping them from the waters of a universal flood. But what I cannot see is my beloved, Wise One. In my mind, yes! But she has always been there. She will never leave. Yet that is all I will ever have of her, all that remains."

He grabbed the dress back from the old man, and tore it to pieces, his screams echoing around the cavern below and whatever remained above, and then, realizing what he had done, fell to his knees, holding the shredded scraps, and in so doing, threw himself off balance and tumbled over the edge of that narrow ledge and into the abyss below.

Not far.

No, not far, a strong hand grabbing hold of his own, an old, bony hand, very old indeed, his more youthful flesh pressing against the hardness of the bones of a century of living, but a strength beyond explanation, a strength that held on, and pulled him up, pulled him back over the ledge until he and the aged figure named Wise One leaned against a wall of stone, their breath short, pain all over their bodies, but alive, but alive.

# =37=

People were being killed by the artillery shells or the tiny falling buildings they once had called home or, else, modest places of business.

Then the invisible invaders. The germs.

Some were standard strains of viruses that had been well known for decades, in some instances for centuries. Others were mutations based upon scientific hypothesis carried out through experiments in laboratories hidden in Europe.

Fahid Bashir saw friends suffocating out in the open air, their lungs constricted by fast-spreading disease.

Others ran through the dirt streets, screaming their pain under the star-punctuated night sky.

A handful had scrambled into their new cars and tried to leave the area, but in their panic and fear they had crashed into one another, igniting gasoline in seconds and lighting the night with flames.

After running until he had little energy left in him, Bashir approached the Americo compound.

It was in complete chaos.

The oil company had flown in two Apache helicopters and done the rebel forces some damage, buying the Americo staff enough time to board three company jets and flee, presumably beyond the borders of a friendly neighboring country.

Suddenly one of the helicopters caught a TOW missile broadside and crashed into the village itself.

Bashir could hear the sound of renewed screams from behind him.

*O Lord, you tried to warn us through Wise One. But foolish human beings have learned to be very adept at turning their backs on Thee.*

He remembered Jeremiah . . .

Inside the main building, he found Otto Kuhlmey in what may have been his office, partially buried under a pile of debris.

Dying.

"They left me," he muttered. "They took their *things*, they took whatever they could grab, and it was everyone for himself. I paid them well, Fahid, but I couldn't buy their decency."

"They had none to sell," Bashir told him, Kuhlmey's head resting on his lap.

"I *am* a Christian, you know."

Bashir nodded.

"I really hated so much of what we did. I have done so little to honor the Lord, you know."

"You and I don't believe in faith plus works as the way to salvation, do we, Otto?"

"No, no, thank you, Fahid. Bless you for that."

Kuhlmey's eyes rolled upward in their sockets.

"They want the oil wells, Fahid. Don't let those monsters have any of that wealth."

"What can I do? What—?"

"Set them ablaze. They won't know how to stop the fires. Red Adair won't accept their tainted money."

He reached up, grabbed Bashir's jacket.

"I'll tell you how to do this," he said, his voice getting weaker and weaker. "Don't let the rebels make a single cent from what they are doing. They're scum, Fahid, the worst scum imaginable. They mustn't be allowed to benefit in any way. I was going to flip the switches myself before . . . before—"

Bashir hesitated but only for a second or two before agreeing to do what the other man asked.

Kuhlmey then told him about some highly experimental explosives that already had been lowered into each well, then set to melt rock shelves that normally would have required constant drilling for a long period of time.

"That's how we were able to make such progress on the kind of accelerated schedule we've had. But it's all been shut down now that we've gotten through to the deposits. You see . . . this . . . this stuff works on a concentrated heat principle, Fahid, which changes the molecular structure of the rock itself, turns it into something that acts a little like runny butter.

"Since we hit pay dirt, we had to stop because the heat, which is concentrated and looks a bit like a laser beam, would have simply caused the oil to ignite, and . . . and explode, Fahid, probably the biggest nonnuclear explosion of all time!"

Kuhlmey closed his eyes, his strength ebbing rapidly.

"There's something else . . . the top layers of earth in this . . . this area are quite brittle, Fahid . . . it is only deep down that they get hard, very . . . very hard . . . that . . . that top layer when it collapses . . . Oh, the nightmare that will ensue . . . everything and everyone will be lost, Fahid, doomed."

He fell into silence, briefly, and Bashir thought that he might have died at just that moment. But Kuhlmey's eyes unexpectedly shot open, and seemed somehow to be sparkling in the moonlight.

"What is it supposed to be like when we die?" the man asked with perfect calmness.

"Angels lifting us from our old, tired, dead bodies and taking us to the very gates of heaven, Otto," Bashir told him. "That's one possibility. Another—"

He wiped his eyes as he spoke.

"—another is that we will simply be there, here one moment, there the next, instantaneously."

"And music? There's music, isn't that true, Fahid?"

"The music of angels, Otto."

Kuhlmey smiled, his eyes still closed.

"Give me your hand, Fahid."

Bashir extended his hand, the other man's fingers closing weakly around it.

"Light, Fahid. Not as the New Agers would have us believe, not as though from some demonic crystal. Not that, my brother. But light—glorious, beautiful."

Kuhlmey coughed three painful times, then: "It's from a pure white throne, you know. Light that is golden, light that—"

His eyes opened for only an instant, wide, sparkling.

"My name, Fahid! They're calling out my—."

The grip loosened, Otto Kuhlmey's hand fell to his side, his very large body shook once, and then it was still.

Bashir laid him back as gently as he could, reluctant to leave, thinking that such a man deserved to be buried properly, not among the wreckage of the company that obviously had been his life.

"Good-bye," he whispered.

Bashir turned and saw a young man standing in the doorway of the room.

"I tried to tell him something was going to happen," he said, "something quite wonderful."

"You call *this* wonderful?" Bashir replied angrily.

"Not this, sir, not this at all. It will be later, you know. I don't know when. The angels haven't told me."

The young man could see the expression on Bashir's face.

"I know that sounds crazy, yes, I know that it does. But this is the only beginning, you realize. When the leaves die and drop to the ground, we know that winter is not far—"

He grabbed his forehead with both hands.

*"The pain!"* he screamed.

The young man fell to the floor as blood started to drip from his nostrils, and onto his clothes.

"You're hemorrhaging!" Bashir said, hurrying to his side.

"It's . . . all . . . right," the other managed to say with apparent effort. "Please . . . don't worry . . . I have no pain *now*, I really don't . . . just this peace I tried to tell Mr. Kuhlmey about . . . just that, sir!"

The young man's eyes closed for a moment, his body shaking violently, then suddenly quite calm.

"About angels, sir," he said, opening his eyes, and looking at Bashir. "They're really extraordinarily beautiful, you know. Believe whatever the Bible says about them. They—"

He reached up one hand and Bashir held it gently.

"You don't have to do that, sir. I just wanted to touch one of them, that's all, just touch an—"

He let out a sigh, not of life escaping but of utter and total fulfillment.

"It's true about the music, sir," he added, his voice completely calm. "It's really true . . . very beautiful, very—"

He smiled then.

"Be prepared, sir. It's going to happen to you soon. Don't be afraid. There is nothing at all to—"

His body grew limp.

*. . . it's going to happen to you soon.*

Bashir rested the young man's body down against a clear section of the metal floor, then he stood and walked back out of the building.

*I hope I'm ready, Lord. I pray that I am.*

# =38=

Wise One and Derek Sparrowhawk sat for a very long time on the hard floor of the cavern after making their way down from where Derek Sparrowhawk had come close to dying.

There had been no conversation for hours.

At one point, Wise One had gone off by himself, leaving Sparrowhawk alone with the relics in that cavern.

The Englishman found pieces of the dress that Wise One had somehow managed to retrieve.

*Talah* . . .

As Sparrowhawk was lifting a handful of the pieces to his nose, ready to inhale that scent again, ready to let his mind roam back over the past, the ground began to rumble under him.

He jumped to his feet.

Explosions!

He was well familiar with these, having covered the violence of warfare many times over the years, whether in Panama or Lebanon or Kuwait or wherever. If he had not done so, he might have mistaken that jolt for an earthquake, but it was almost immediately followed by others, one after the other after—

"It begins," Wise One's voice filled the cavern.

Startled, Sparrowhawk spun around on his heels.

The old man had suddenly begun to look each and every one of the many years that he carried with him, his back no longer so straight, a pronounced slump to it, the lines on his face no longer looking simply weathered, but now deeper, wider, part of a face that had shed its previous robustness and turned forlorn to such an extent that Sparrowhawk was concerned about Wise One's health.

"What has happened?" he asked, alarmed.

At first Wise One did nothing but sigh, a sigh so loud that it was picked up by the echoing qualities of the cavern, and flung back at them, the recurring sound ghostlike.

He looked at Sparrowhawk.

"You have little time, my English friend," he said, "so little time, you know."

"Me? What does that rumbling have to do with me? That strikes me as the sound of artillery."

"I know. The village is being destroyed even as we speak."

Sparrowhawk knew he should have realized that, should have made the connection.

He hadn't.

"Fahid! Fahid's going to be—," he said, his blood pressure rising at the terrifying thought.

"Not by bombs or guns or anything of the sort. Not that way, but he will die soon, that is true."

"But what about me?" Sparrowhawk asked, tapping himself on the chest. "You said *I* have little time left."

"And me as well," Wise One added. "Dear brother, this aged man you think so wise, this frail human form you now see, there is precious little—"

Enormous sorrow fell upon the Englishman.

"But you have hurt no one," he interrupted, reaching out and grabbing the old man's sheepskin coat. "You have tried only to help, to warn them, to—"

Sparrowhawk's eyes widened as he added, "That moment you predicted! It's now, isn't it?"

Wise One did not answer directly.

"Whatever the case, Derek Sparrowhawk, they have done nothing but ignore me, otherwise they could have been better prepared. They have done nothing but plunge headlong into a trap set for them by the Arch Deceiver himself."

Sparrowhawk caught the expression on Wise One's face, an expression both accusatory and utterly sympathetic.

"Why do you look at me in that manner?" he asked. "Why—?"

Derek Sparrowhawk was an intelligent man, a journalist with a capacity for analyzing a given situation and arriving at a reasonable conclusion. In most matters, he could not be accused of being blind.

He knew the answer.

*Why do you look at me in that manner?*

He didn't want to know it, he tried, for a few hapless seconds, to pretend that he didn't know it at all, that Wise One had spoken in a deliberately obtuse fashion and, therefore, there was no reason why he *should* know it.

But he did.

"How can I be surprised at their rejection of your words," he started to say, "when . . . when—"

He fell forward, against Wise One's chest.

"Forgive me," Sparrowhawk pleaded. "I, too, have turned my back on you, not you exactly, but what you have been saying. I have scorned any of the wisdom you tried to—"

He could not continue.

Wise One put his arms around the other man.

"It is not this old lump of flesh, it is not these tired muscles and bones, nor this dulled and failing mind from which you need to seek forgiveness, Derek Sparrowhawk," he said with the greatest display of compassion that the Englishman had ever known in a lifetime, "it is not my words but the One who imparted them to me that you must reach out to, that you must offer your repentance to, and hold nothing, *nothing* back."

Sparrowhawk sensed all the years of denial rearing up from his subconscious to do battle with a tiny, tiny voice within him, all the professors in all the university courses with all

208

their own experiences mixing with his to form an impenetrable wall around him, a wall that was only heightened and deepened and strengthened when his beloved had been murdered by those she called family and friends and neighbors, and he had been robbed of the joy of fatherhood forever and ever, this battle not on fields of blood, with chemicals falling from the air, and germs—

*"Germs! No!"* he screamed abruptly, pulling away from Wise One. "Tell me they aren't going to do that, please *tell me!"*

"Tell you what, dear brother?" the old man asked. "What is it that you have need that I tell you?"

"That it's not true, that whoever is behind this couldn't be as monstrous as that. I don't *want* to hear anything else! I . . . I can't *imagine* hearing anything else. I don't want to see those good people, not Bashir, not any of them, I don't want to see a single one stumbling around, their blood streams clogged with . . . with—"

Wise One reached out for him again.

"I cannot tell you that it will *not* happen as you say," he said. "I cannot because to do so would be to lie, Derek. That *is* what has already begun. Those shells from those huge guns, so heavy that the ground is shaking where we stand, it is true what you say, those shells are carrying canisters of deadly germs developed in profit-making labs and shipped to the rebels.

"The rebels have taken over the government. They want the oil, Derek. But that is not all. They want revenge, too. And one old woman drives them on, a woman possessed of such hatred that she can scarcely control herself; it gives her life, it gives her strength."

"But who is she? What can be her reason?"

"Fahid Bashir's mother," Wise One spoke the words slowly. "His father died of a broken heart. She has never forgiven her son for his conversion to Christianity, and for the death of her husband.

"Since she now believes that he is no longer her son, she has claimed the sanctioning of Allah on his death. Indeed, she goes forward, convinced that she is to be Allah's instrument!"

"No, no, no, no!" Sparrowhawk repeated in a moronic manner. "Oh, God, no, no, no!"

"Don't," Wise One cautioned. "Don't use His name in that way, Derek. Please, don't!"

"Is that all that concerns you? A silly rule from a list of . . . of—"

He let forth with a stream of blasphemies then, seeming to delight in these, to draw strength from the freedom to say them.

"See!" he said, fairly dancing with delight. "I have said worse than 'Oh, God.' I *am* now damned, am I not? I am now hopelessly consigned to the pit of hell itself! *Go ahead and say something, old man!*"

He saw a spear resting on the ground a short distance from the cross, the robe, the crown of thorns.

He rushed over to it, picked it up, and held it at his side.

"I *cannot* go on, Wise One," he said. "God knows—"

Wise One nodded.

"He does, Derek. He does. God knows you cannot go on. God knows that this body of mine cannot go on, either. God knows Fahid Bashir cannot . . . go on. He will deal with us all in the same way."

"The same, you say?" Sparrowhawk repeated, hesitating. "By spear? By germs? By chemicals searing through our lungs and into our veins and . . . and—?"

He let out a cry of despair and started to plunge the spear into his side, but, in a move so quick that Sparrowhawk could scarcely believe that it was a century-old man doing so, Wise One had rushed up to him and grabbed the spear, tearing it from his grasp.

"Only one precious side has been pierced by this blade," he declared, his voice strong, deep. "It will never again draw blood, *never!*"

Wise One threw it to his left, and it landed at the foot of the cross.

"Where it belongs," he said knowingly. "Where it will remain, for a little while."

Another blast, stronger this time, shook the floor of the cavern, knocking loose some pieces of rock from the ceiling.

One of them hit a glancing blow at the back of Wise One's head.

He fell to his knees, dazed.

Sparrowhawk hurried to his side.

"Are you—?" he asked.

"I have pain, yes, and thank you for caring, but it is not yet that final time, Derek. And this is not the way."

"Are we coming to the end?" Sparrowhawk asked. "Is this Armageddon now? As we stand in the midst of Eden?"

"You know then, Derek?" Wise One said.

"Yes . . . ," the Englishman spoke softly. "I think I've known ever since seeing the ark, the instrument of a new beginning in the place where it all began. That sounds like something a Master Planner would put together."

Wise One smiled wanly as he said, "You asked if this was Armageddon. There is an event that must precede the Final Battle, and the Great Tribulation also. But, yes, Derek, we are entering—"

The rumbling increased in magnitude.

"Outside," Wise One said urgently. "Outside, Derek!"

Sparrowhawk helped him to his feet, and they hurried together to the mouth of the cavern and out into the garden.

They stopped suddenly as they saw someone both knew sitting beside a rose bush, not an ancient bush, it seemed, not one that had shriveled and died long before Luther and Calvin, before—.

A bush quite different from any of the others in that garden, a bush suddenly alive and vibrant and colorful, much changed from how it had been just a short while earlier.

"Ah, the English journalist!" Stuart Brickley said, looking up at him. "Yes, yes, you must witness this for yourself. There is an old legend, you know, myth or whatever, you know, that sort of thing. It says that the Garden of Eden will gradually return to its original and uncorrupted state just before the Millennium. Did you ever hear that one, Derek? Tell me, did you?"

He cocked one ear, listening to a sound that seemed, to him, quite nearby but barely discernible, and he could not be sure.

"I thought I heard a bird singing, Derek," he said, getting to his feet. "Isn't that wonderful? Please tell me that you—."

The sound of a rifle rang out in the otherwise funereal quietude of that secluded place.

Stuart Brickley's face contorted with pain, and he fell to the ground, stirring up a brown cloud of dry, dead earth.

Jalil Arik-Arad stood a few yards away, smiling, a gun pointed at the other two men.

"I hope I didn't kill him, you know," he told them. "This man does need to live. He really does. He can join the fun with the rest of us back at *our* village! We are destroying it only to raise it up again, you see. That sounds rather Christian, doesn't it? And, of course, the two of you also are invited. Is that not wonderful? None of you will miss a thing!"

"Run, Wise One!" Sparrowhawk said. "Don't let this—"

"Wise One?" Arik-Arad repeated. "What *are* you babbling about, Englishman? Too much ale perhaps. I remember your type well, when you dominated my people in this region."

Sparrowhawk turned quickly, knowing that Wise One had been by his side only seconds before.

"Hurry—!" he started to say but then realized why the rebel seemed so puzzled.

Gone.

Wise One was gone.

A sudden chill fell upon the garden, so intense that even Arik-Arad shivered from it.

"Don't you see what this means?" Sparrowhawk yelled.

"Oh, I do know what you will be raving about next," Arik-Arad told him, his teeth chattering. "I believe the word is, yes, Armageddon. Correct me if I'm wrong, but I doubt that I am. I knew some Baptist missionaries once. I had them over for dinner, you see!"

He seemed to think that that was uproariously funny.

Sparrowhawk started to lunge for him.

"I wouldn't," Arik-Arad said, raising the rifle and pointing it directly at the Englishman's chest.

Sparrowhawk, frustrated, wanted to get his hands around the other man's neck but wondered what Wise One would have done in that situation.

*Can I be sure whether you would show mercy to such swine as this, old man? Or would you strike back at them for whatever terrible crimes they are continuing to commit?*

In a few hours Derek Sparrowhawk would find out a great deal.

# $=39=$

$B$ashir had set a timer at each of the other wells. He was now at the last one, hesitating a moment.

"Oh, Lord, let it be as You want, and not as any of us would plan," he said.

The final timer had been activated. In less than two hours the explosives would begin their work.

And then—

He turned and looked back at the village.

*All my life! My home! My people! My—*

He missed his family. He missed being cradled on his mother's knee and seeing her face smiling assurance at him.

*Nothing is going to happen, my little Fahid. I'm here to protect you, dear, dear son. Rest easy.*

"Now nothing will be left for any of us to return to, all of it dirty, poisoned, diseased," he said aloud with almost palpable despair.

He turned from that last well and walked back toward the havoc-stricken village, then stopped.

Coming toward him was Jassim Qaseer, holding his wife's motionless body in his arms.

"She's dead, Fahid," the other man said, his face contorted with grief. "Some germs got into her system and ate away her stomach."

Bashir could see that the front of what looked like a brand-new, brightly colored, quite expensive-looking dress was soaked with blood, the hint of a strand of pearls around her neck. Dangling down was her arm—on the wrist, a diamond-studded watch; on her fingers, ruby and emerald rings.

"I'm dying, too," Qaseer said. "I feel as though my brain is going to explode, that it's been invaded by—"

He stumbled, and fell, the body dropping from his arms and landing on the sand beside him.

Bashir rushed to his friend.

"How could God judge us so harshly?" Qaseer asked plaintively as he looked up at Bashir. "We only bought a few things. We only spent some money."

He lifted up his wrist, showing Bashir the solid gold Rolex he had been wearing.

"Is this so . . . so wrong?" Qaseer said, his voice trembling, spittle dripping over his lips and down his chin. "Other people, vain, selfish people in this world, so opposed to any Christian values, don't think twice about having expensive cars or owning two homes or being waited on by a staff of servants."

"But isn't that the answer, Jassim? That is all they have. They get those things because they *need* them. They couldn't live without the evidence of their wealth around them, shouting its cold reassurance not only to them but to those who know them. They *define* their very existence by their bank accounts, my friend. Material acquisitions are the gods they worship daily."

"Yes . . . yes . . . but it isn't the same, it just isn't the same, Fahid. Their kind pay no allegiance to God, none whatever. Christ is nothing more than a curse word to them, to be uttered in anger, not in repentance. Is it so wrong that we—?"

"But how many in our village thought of Him as nothing more than a good luck charm of some sort and, later, as some sort of cornucopia of blessing after blessing after blessing?"

Bashir lowered his voice, an expression of tenderness on his face.

"Oh, Jassim, Jassim, how much went to the Lord? You spent all the riches on yourselves, isn't that right? Did a single denarius go to missionaries? Did you donate as much as a—?"

Qaseer was crying, his body shaking.

"God knows you are right, Fahid, you *are* right. But we cannot turn back now. It is too late for my dear one and me. We can never change what has happened. God's judgment is so relentless, so—."

Bashir wiped some perspiration off his brow.

"Yes, it may be His judgment, and His alone, mocking our people's new cars and our fur coats and so much else. But we are Christians, Jassim. We won't lose our salvation. God's promises aren't dealt out according to our bank accounts."

Qaseer turned to face his wife's still body.

"I just wanted her to have what she had been denied for so long. I got her dozens of catalogs, Fahid. She could order whatever she wanted. We had the money to buy anything she saw, *anything!*"

"God's judgment . . . or Satan's opportunity? They are hardly one and the same, Jassim."

Some greenish drool came slobbering out of the corners of Qaseer's twisted mouth.

"Praise God that Jesus died for our sins, Fahid. Where would we be if He had not? Where—?"

His eyes closed.

Jassim Qaseer was gone.

Bashir stood and looked at the village a few hundred yards in front of him. He could see shapes in the moonlight, moving frantically. He could hear cries of pain, of fear, of utter panic.

Fires had started. People were running about in flames.

He saw a teenager hop onto a motorcycle and start to speed out of the village. Part of his leather jacket had ignited. He tried to get it off himself but in doing so crashed into a nearby building, and the gas in the cycle's tank blew up, scattering him in a dozen directions.

"Let *me* join Thee *now*, O Lord," Bashir screamed, "so that I won't have to see my home, my world, my—"

216

Throwing his arms up in the consuming despair of that moment, he turned from the village, his limbs starting to ache, and proceeded to walk numbly toward the distant peaks, thinking that the place of his spiritual rebirth would be a good one in which to die.

He did not hear the old woman come up to him, nor had he any idea from which direction she came. The sudden pain of the knife entering his back spun him around, shaking him from the emotional numbness that had descended.

"I *wanted* to forgive you," a familiar voice spoke. "May Allah help me, I *tried*, oh, how desperately I tried. But you betrayed all of us. How *could* I ever pretend that that had never happened? How could I give up my faith for *you?*"

He reached out and tore the veil from her face just before she plunged the long blade into his chest this time, missing his heart by less than an inch, and as he started to stumble back, away from her, a single word tore past his lips, "*Yamma!*"

# =40=

Jalil Arik-Arad had had Derek Sparrowhawk and Stuart Brickley kept together just outside the narrow passageway into the garden area, leaving several men to guard them.

He remained behind, fascinated by what he saw.

"The fabled Eden."

So dead now. So—

Except for that one flower, as vibrant as he had ever seen.

He paused before it, bending over and taking in its scent, which was like perfume indeed.

And then he saw the husklike remains of the giant serpent, some fragments of verses from the Old Testament coming back to him.

*Satan! A name we use to scare and discipline our children, and to label our enemies!*

*But otherwise a Christian myth, a—*

*And yet—*

The chill intensified as vagrant breezes began to weave their way through the place.

Out of the corner of his eye Arik-Arad could see another flower spring suddenly to life, or so it seemed, a flower of dazzling color.

He stood amazed.

*The garden is coming alive again*, he thought. *One-by-one—!*

And so was the serpent!

He could not even scream as that body reanimated itself, as dust became flesh, could not scream as the gray remains assumed a writhing green, could not speak as it started to move, started to turn toward him, started to speak in a tone colder than the air.

"Ah, you *are* here," it said in a voice of venom. "I am truly more comfortable with one of my own. I think we should now join our fellow demons at the place where it all started. Why don't you follow me?"

The serpent reared up like a cobra and stood in front of him, its red, forked tongue darting out, darting in, darting out.

Jalil Arik-Arad screamed then, a scream so loud that it vibrated against several of the dead trees nearby, shaking them, stirring up the dust of the centuries.

He turned to run, then stopped, a strange breath on his neck, both hot and cold, and he could *feel* a presence **dark** and pervasive.

Then a *plopping* sound. Followed by a *rustling*, like fallen, dry autumn leaves being stepped upon.

He wanted to get out of the place as soon as he could manage it, to run away from that grotesque garden and never return to it again.

But that sound, that—

He turned, and saw the husk of the serpent as it had been, no hint of returned life arisen from the ashes of a remote time.

And more flowers, more plants alive now.

*We cannot stay*, a voice echoed in the corridors of his mind. *The garden will be reborn just before the rapture. That is not far off. It is no longer a place for your kind, for me, for any of us. Return to the outside world now, still in my grasp, but not here, not here, not here, not—*

Jalil Arik-Arad left on swift feet of the worst fear in the whole of his life.

Hours had passed.

The old woman had been found, cradling her son's dying, torn body. They pulled her gently away and took Fahid Bashir and threw him onto a canvas-topped army truck.

"Do you want to witness the execution?" a burly rebel asked her. "Or would you prefer to be elsewhere?"

She looked at him.

"My son's dying," she said.

"By *your* knife, yes!" the man reminded her.

She still held the weapon, its blade coated with blood.

"Let me take it," he said.

She handed it to him and started moaning.

"Are you hurt?" the rebel asked. "Was there a struggle?"

"None," she told him.

"Then what is wrong?"

"We have lost."

The man laughed.

"How can you say that?"

He waved his arm around at the scene before them.

"See for yourself!" he proclaimed.

Tanks surrounded the village. Rebels heavily armed filled in the spaces between the tanks. All of them, including the one with the old woman, wore germ-prevention masks.

"Please, take this," he told her, not without some warmth. "You shouldn't have left us, gone off by yourself."

She allowed him to slip on the mask, then looked at what was happening in the early light of dawn.

Villagers were periodically stumbling out into the desert, to be met by rifle or machine gun fire, their bodies falling instantly. In the village itself, fires yet burning, clouds of smoke rising at intervals, dim, phantom shapes moved about in a netherworld, some of them already showing the outward physical effects of experimental bacteria.

"The Christians talk of hell . . . ," she muttered.

"What was that?" the rebel asked, not understanding what she said, her speech muffled by the mask.

She shook her head, then fell silent, her mind filled with the barely glimpsed image of someone left behind in the village, standing upright, his diseased, twisted body frozen in its death throes, like a perverse statue, immobile, his head turned toward the disappearing stars, and beyond, yes, beyond.

# $=$**41**$=$

There was a wide ledge extending out from the base of the mountain. Each of three crosses had been stuck down in holes dug into it, the pieces that formed them taken from what remained of the barbed wire fence posts around the Americo headquarters.

Jalil Arik-Arad seemed unusually subdued.

"What is it?" one of his lieutenants asked.

"It is nothing. I have waited for a moment such as this, and now it is here before me."

"And you have to pinch yourself to see that you are fully awake!"

"As you say."

But it wasn't that of which Jalil Arik-Arad had been thinking.

His mind was focused on the garden, the beauty of that process of flowers blooming, more and more of them returning to life, but also that fearful encounter, real or otherwise.

"A resurrection," he said, hoping that no one heard him utter the unaccustomed word.

No one did.

As Arik-Arad had ordered, a contingent of rebels was intent on dragging the three men to the awaiting crosses, quickly hammering nails into their hands and through their feet, then stepping back at last and watching them, hoping to hear them scream in anguish, the death throes of the infidels in homage to Allah, whom they and their families had worshiped from generation to generation.

But the three on the crosses did not cooperate, did not scream in fear or whatever else. They were silent, incomprehensibly silent, only grimaces of pain on their faces showing that they felt anything.

"How *can* they do this?" one of the rebels said. "How can they resist screaming out into the air?"

*Sparrowhawk and Brickley exchanged glances, the two of them as amazed as that one rebel about how the pain seemed to be largely shut out. It was that way for Bashir as well, which was all the more curious, in view of the wounds he had sustained.*

*For the Englishman, it might have had something to do with the fact that he was thinking of someone very beautiful, in a stunning red dress, and remembering her special scent as he held her passionately in his arms . . .*

Jalil Arik-Arad was vaguely aware of a rumbling beneath his feet. Yet his mind was still fixed on the singular, loathsome image that would not loosen its hold on him.

*The serpent reared up like a cobra and stood in front of him, its red, forked tongue darting out, darting in, darting out.*

He saw in that creature centuries of hatred and a thirst for vengeance spewing forth in one monstrous outpouring.

*Hatred so like his own, the serpent a personification of all the rage that he had been feeling over the years.*

And yet it was more than that, as though by looking into the serpent's eyes, he had a glimpse of—

"Allah!" he screamed. "Why didn't you warn us about hell?"

The rebels buzzed among themselves, thinking that Jalil Arik-Arad was going mad.

The old woman looked down at the ground, then back at her son hanging on the metal cross.

She let out a cry of anguish and started to walk toward him.

And then the ground—

223

Fahid Bashir screamed at his *yamma*, but she could not hear him.

"Get away, run!" he begged her.

Even if she could listen, if she made sense of what he wanted, she would not have got far, the entire desert for miles in all directions having become a deathtrap for any within its boundaries.

The ground beneath their feet!

It had started to split open, jets of flame shooting up through the cracks. In seconds, huge chunks of it started to *sink!* The weak upper crust could not withstand the stresses being generated.

The rebels scattered in a hundred directions, cries of "Allah! Allah! Spare us!" going unheeded.

It seemed as though the jets of flame had become taloned hands grabbing at their feet, their legs, tripping them, holding on as their bodies caught fire.

*Yamma!*

She came stumbling forward, her clothes a curtain of fire, reaching out one hand for an instant, her eyes filled with agony, and then dropping to the desert sand a hundred feet away.

"I can't let her die like that," Bashir screamed, his head tilted upward, "not without another chance, Lord. I *need* another chance to proclaim the gift of salvation, *please!*"

Suddenly his mother stirred, ripping nearly all the burning clothes off her body and getting to her feet, barely able to move, body fluids from her seared flesh giving her a greased look.

"If only I could move," Bashir sobbed. "If only I could say something to her in time, Lord, I beg You, I beg You, Lord, help me to do that."

He groaned with the submerging pain that wracked his body as he used the tiny residue of strength that remained within him and pulled himself loose from the nails, first, agonizingly, at his left hand, then his right, then from his feet.

He fell to the hard rock ledge and crawled forward, trying to raise his head at the same time, and keeping *Yamma* in view. She had fallen a second time and was not able again to raise herself.

They were not far apart now, three feet, two, a foot separating them.

*Groans! Yamma is still alive. Yamma—!*

"Christ," he said, his voice hardly audible, "accept Christ, *my yamma*, accept Him, beloved one."

He was next to her.

He could see her mouth opening, closing, opening, closing as she tried to speak.

He pressed his ear to her lips.

"You cannot forgive me, Fahid. I . . . I have caused such evil here . . . this day."

"I can, *Yamma*," he told her, his mouth tasting the sand. "I can forgive you everything."

"No . . . there is no . . . no forgiveness as you say is so. It is only an illusion, a Christian deception, my son . . . there is no—"

Soon, Fahid Bashir was unable to tell her the rest of what he wanted to say, weakness robbing him even of that simple ability.

*He had often wondered what death itself actually would be like, a jolt from one existence to another, rather like a volcanic eruption perhaps, or a seamless blending, one life in cessation, the other taking over.*

*Or—*

*And then he was gone from her presence.*

*Truly so.*

*Yamma* reached out, took her son's hand, felt it go limp in her own.

*You can forgive like that, Fahid, as we die together like this? And you think that I, too, will be able to do the same, that I—?*

She saw someone strangely familiar then, a man, tall, with flowing white hair, a thin, almost gaunt face, and very, very old this man, but eyes filled with kindness she had never seen before.

*When other helpers fail and comforts flee, help of the helpless—*

The day long ago when she forsook the village, she had walked close to a group of Christians holding an outdoor worship service. She stopped for a moment, looked at them with an expression of utter venom, then passed on by.

She would spend the next decade trying to blot out those words, trying to do so by acts so cruel that even some of the rebels hesitated until she shamed them by doing herself what it was that she had asked of them.

And always she exhorted them to show no mercy, to drain any semblance of compassion from themselves.

Yet now it was mercy she sought, it was forgiveness of which her son had spoken, such a word this forgiveness, hardly in the Muslim vocabulary, a word that had been replaced by unrelenting retribution, every adherent a self-proclaimed instrument of Allah's anger.

But this old man was not a figure of anger in that moment when he looked at her.

Those eyes!

*Can I be forgiven?* she thought. *Can there be such a—?*

He smiled, and pure, cleansing light seemed to flood her soul.

She heard words then, not spoken, no voice as such but words just the same, sensed in her mind, bypassing her ears altogether, words that came from the old man without his ever moving his lips, words embodied in the beauty, the peace of that smile.

*What must I do?*

He swung his hand toward the three crosses on the mountain's ledge.

*Help them? How can I help them?*

He raised the other hand, stretching them both out in a sweeping gesture, and then, in a sudden moment, a moment that if she had lived she would have had fixed in memory, indelible as no other, in that moment she saw in her mind's eye a place called Golgotha, a place not unlike the one where her son had just hung on a cross between his two friends, and she heard words that told it all, that gave her what she needed, that filled the emptiness that had dominated her for so long.

*Father, forgive them . . .*

226

She struggled to a sitting position, pain over every inch of her body.

"As my son forgave me?" she asked, her voice uncertain, but her mind sharp and clear and very much aware.

*As I forgave him . . .*

In the seconds before she died, she remembered some of the moments over the years when her mother's heart overwhelmed her Muslim soul, and she wanted desperately to hold him again, to say that it was all right, that whatever he had done, whatever path he had chosen, it would no longer come between them, that she wanted him back, wanted him more than anything else in her life.

*I wanted to love my son . . . but my religion wouldn't allow it.*

Always there was Jalil Arik-Arad, his hatred reviving her own, never letting her love overcome the sense of blasphemy that she had felt that first day of confession on the part of the boy whose life entering the world nearly took away her own, and yet Allah had spared them both, spared them to enjoy a closeness that neither ever thought could be breached.

*Allah . . .*

She repeated that name just once in the midst of her dying agony.

*All those years thrown at the feet of a—*

She fell back then, and as she closed her eyes, the pain left, and she felt a hand take her own, with such tenderness as to be incomprehensible, lifting her up, another voice, familiar, joyous, calling in exultant welcome.

"Yamma, Yamma, I love you."

"Oh, my beloved son, my beloved son!"

"For eternity, Yamma, no more pain, no more hatred. God is good, dear, dear one."

"Praise the holy name of Jesus!"

Forgiven and cleansed, mother and son walked together down the golden streets toward a pure white throne as ten thousand upon ten thousand resplendent angels offered their hallelujahs in majestic chorus not in tribute to the dismal Allah of a bankrupt Islam but to the resurrected and ascended King of kings and Lord of lords.

# ═42═

Jalil Arik-Arad stood over the old, fragile, spent body, screamed a terrible blasphemy at her, spat in her face, despite the fact that she had died at least a minute earlier.

"How could you do this to us, to the whole purpose of our mission?" he spoke with contempt. "You were a symbol, someone we held high in our minds. We were willing to follow you unto death."

He cleared his throat, trying to get his emotions together.

"Praise the holy name of Jesus?" he repeated scornfully. "Is that what you were mumbling? How easily you fail Allah! How quickly you leave your heritage on the Christian dung heap, uttering blasphemy as you die."

*She is one of them now. She is an infidel, like the others "who fight against Allah and His Messenger, and hasten about the earth, to do corruption there . . ."*

Those words from the *Qur'ān*, unknown to most outsiders, rose in his mind where they had been memorized by rote over the years, from the age of a young child, seared into him, and becoming part of the foundation of hatred that was an intimate part of everything in his religious life, brought up as he was by Islamic fundamentalist parents.

*. . . they shall be slaughtered.*

He chuckled to himself.

228

*. . . slaughtered.*

What he lived for!

*What I myself would die to accomplish, if that were necessary to bring about the death of a single infidel!*

Contemplating such as this, searching the pages of the *Qur'ān* for other admonitions to visit violence, maiming, and bloodshed upon unbelievers brought to him great sublimity, as necessary to the conduct of life as eating, drinking, and breathing in the air around him.

*To have their red, polluted blood running through my fingers, to hear their screams, to—*

What *he* lived for, what any *good* Muslim lived for, to be convicted of the necessity of that slaughter, the providential *requirement* of it, as handed down to them directly from Allah through the Messenger.

*And so few in the infidel world, the foolish, unsuspecting infidel world realize that this is so,* Jalil Arik-Arad thought. *They have been blinded to the true essence of Islam, for there are those of us who seem so nice, so humble, so mild-mannered. Such a disguise, such a facade, hiding the compelling precepts.*

Again a page from the *Qur'ān* spewed forth its commands from the deep pits of his mind.

*They shall be slaughtered, or crucified, or their hands and feet shall alternately be cut off . . .*

His body always trembled with anticipation of the *reality* of such acts.

*We allow ourselves to be willing slaves to the dictates of Muhammad. We cannot be otherwise, we cannot do otherwise, for if we disobey what is written in the* Qur'ān, *then we become as infidels ourselves, lost in the barrenness that will descend upon us until another Muslim shows his true faith by slaying us as he has been commanded to do.*

Jail Arik-Arad was about to aim the barrel at her temple when a strong hand wrapped around it and tore the weapon from his grasp.

Jalil Arik-Arad spun around.

"Wise One!" he exclaimed.

"You have less than a minute," the old man told him.

Jalil Arik-Arad raised his fist in front of Wise One's face. In that instant he no longer confronted the figure of an old man. A transformation was taking place, like that of a moth shedding its cocoon.

A being of extraordinary radiance remained, a being with a countenance of shimmering pearl-white purity.

"Allah!" Jalil Arik-Arad gasped.

"Oh, no, no," the being said. "It is not Allah. The Allah you seek comes from a place very much like *that!*"

He pointed to the scarlet geysers of flames that had sprung up from every direction.

"Look at it! This holocaust is very much like where the Allah you worship will spend eternity."

The radiant figure moved about the charred corpses of the rebels who had joined together under the banner of Islam, pointing to those who were still alive, though barely so, moaning pitiably.

"*Your* Allah cares little about the suffering of those who follow him, for they are as scum to him, to be used up and spit out when they cease to serve his purposes but, even so, follow him they shall, into the very pit of hell.

"*Your* Allah is nothing more than a name, a phony and demonic name, a camouflaging mask over the countenance of Lucifer himself, the devil, the Prince of Darkness. And hell is where he awaits you now!"

Jalil Arik-Arad felt the most intense terror of his life, but he could not acknowledge, he could not *allow* himself to acknowledge, that anything of what was occurring was real, even slightly, negligibly real.

He turned toward the three crosses, the center one now empty.

*Crucify the infidels!* The *Qur'ān*'s command had shouted its vengeance to him even as early in his life as when he was five years old and did not know hatred, did not understand death, did not want to harm anyone. He had been a child of love in those days, approaching all foreigners with innocence. But his mother and his father could not let this be for very long, could not allow their son to cling to any shameful compassion, for such would never be honored by Allah, such was an abomination in the eyes of the messenger, and in contradiction of everything he demanded of his followers.

*The first time I shed the blood of another human being . . .*

*She was so young. She suspected little. She died so quickly . . .*

Crazed by that memory, confused by the guilt that suddenly asserted itself after being buried for decades, Jalil Arik-Arad took out a knife and stumbled toward the two remaining men hanging on their crosses as mandated by the brutal bloodbath called Islam, the gaze of someone maddened by his faith fixed first on Stuart Brickley.

Jail Arik-Arad knew that the man should have been delirious with pain, should have been moaning, his body seared with the agony of hanging as he was from nails pounded into the flesh of his palms and his feet. There had been cases, in the Philippines and elsewhere, where Easter rituals involved temporary "crucifixion," and the individuals thus pledging their faith would be taken down after five minutes, given medical care, and did not, as a consequence, experience any severe pain. There was no recitation of mere myth in these accounts but, rather, real stories of people driven in their ancient system of works to the belief that they were not fully accepted before Almighty God unless they *did* something quite apart from acceptance of Jesus Christ as their Savior and their Lord.

But there was nothing temporary in this scene of Islamic obsession for vengeance.

Not as long as the American had been hanging from a metal cross. Nor the Brit as well.

"You stupid American!" he yelled. "This is a trick, an illusion, the sham of carnival show magicians. And you there, Englishman, remnant of a ravaged empire, *we,* my kind and I, *will* get through this. We have the patience of centuries, you know. We *will* survive whatever has been concocted here. The village and the oil wells will remain in our hands. We have only to wait for Allah to give us yet another victory."

He reached the base of the cross on which Brickley was hanging and raised his knife, his expression wild, filled with hatred.

"I curse your damned and lost soul to the very hell that you seem to feel awaits all of us heathens!"

The knife entered the American's side, and a loud gasp escaped his thin, pale lips.

*I wanted so much to set things right, to get another chance to steer Americo in the right direction, to have more respect for how people lived, for the environment, for all that was decent and—*

*But there is no time any longer for any of that.*

*And soon the trumpets, Lord?*

He felt the world around him slipping away, his surroundings fading gradually, the crosses next to him becoming indistinct, the figure of Derek Sparrowhawk almost indistinguishable and the demented one of Jalil Arik-Arad little more than a grotesque blur, exaggerating his already overwrought features.

*Another world was coming into view, supplanting that of flesh and blood and cold metal against him, nails in his hands and—*

*He saw a man waiting for him, a man smiling.*

*An Indian from the village!*

*"My name is Soaring Eagle," he said.*

*"You were the one who—," Brickley started to remark as he recognized the other man.*

*"—was going to murder his family," the other interrupted. "But I did not. The Lord intervened in my life through a missionary couple who came to the village a day after you left. They wanted nothing from any of us. They wanted only to give to us.*

*"I told them how unworthy I was, how much I drank, the evil thoughts that possessed my mind, my intention to kill my loved ones. But they professed no shock, no rage, no fear. They just reached out to tell me of the sweet love of Jesus Christ, love given though undeserved, and all that He had sacrificed for the forgiveness of my sins.*

*"All the terrible acts, all the filth that had filled up my mind—it was as though these had never existed. As far as God was concerned, they were washed away by the cleansing blood of His Son, and if I just accepted Him into my life and laid all my sins, all my shame, all my guilt on His shoulders—for He was*

*willing to take my yoke upon Himself—if I did that, then salvation was a free gift bestowed upon me in return."*

*He was still smiling as he added, "My family and I were killed in an automobile accident a few months ago."*

*He reached out his hand.*

*"We have been waiting for you . . . to speak of the love we now have for you."*

*Stuart Brickley's tears were not of sorrow . . .*

The American's gasp of pain seemed to drive Jalil Arik-Arad on, in a kind of ravenous frenzy, as he scrambled over to Derek Sparrowhawk and looked up into his face.

The Englishman's eyes were open, fixed on him, but not with hatred, not with pain or dread.

Amazingly both dying men spoke, drawing from a source of strength neither could ever have known would be needed in such an instance but one remarkable for the courage it provided, the ability to ignore the agony that was preceding their deaths—the American behind him . . . a few seconds later, the Englishman directly in front . . . both very weak, Stuart Brickley nearly dead, but each able to say for one brief moment the same thing, their words wrapped in the sweetest peace any human being had ever manifested, a peace that also lit up their faces.

"How can you *sound* like that? How can you look at me as you do?" Jalil Arik-Arad yelled, his throat raw. "How can you both be *smiling*? You should be blind with—!"

Those words!

First from the American . . .

*I forgive you, even as Christ forgave me.*

Then from the Englishman . . .

*And I, too, forgive you even as Christ forgave me.*

"Stop it, bloody fools," he said. "Stop it now!"

Jalil Arik-Arad pulled a small pistol from a worn old holster under his left arm, aimed the short-barreled weapon at Brickley.

*I love you . . .*

"No!" the rebel shrieked like a man possessed. "You cannot be saying that. Some infidel trick is being played with my mind!"

He fired the pistol three times at the American who slumped forward on the withholding nails, his shoulders sagging slightly.

*"Here they are, my brother,"* Soaring Eagle told him.

*The man's wife and children were walking toward him, an angel accompanying each one.*

*But they were not alone. Other Sioux men, women, and children were coming forward, gathering around him.*

*"I reached most of my tribe for the Lord," Soaring Eagle said. "They all want to express how they feel."*

*Together the group broke into the most beautiful hymn of forgiveness that Stuart Brickley had ever heard, one that washed over him like a cleansing wave as he stepped forward into eternity . . .*

Bullets, also well aimed, hit Derek Sparrowhawk in the temple and in the chest, the Englishman jerking like a puppet entangled in its own strings, spasms ripping through him, and then he was still, but not before muttering just loud enough for Arik-Arad to hear what he had not wanted, ever, to hear, *I love you . . . in the name of the Savior!*

Jalil Arik-Arad clamped his hands to his ears, the pistol dropping, forgotten, onto the black rock, as he stumbled backward, tripping over the ledge, then scrambling to his feet and running, those words tearing like knives through his brain, until flames, leaping up through a large new fault under the sand at his feet, consumed him like the rest.

# Epilogue

Armageddon . . . ," Jerome Godesmith said ironically. "Every Christian in America probably thought that at first. I mean, prophecy books were a big seller for a while. But when no army of angels and molten fire came down from the heavens, well, that notion died along with the coverage."

He was in a helicopter with five other men, but so far he had done most of the talking, which was a commonplace experience as far as he was concerned.

"You think they were there all this time?" Jerome Godesmith remarked as the helicopter flew over the stricken area.

The three men in the back seat hesitated, then one of them told him that the geological survey suggested that, yes, the whole region was lined with faults, like a Middle Eastern version of California.

"The explosions started a chain reaction, Beebe?" Godesmith asked.

Beebe, who was hardly five feet tall, nodded in agreement.

"You three musketeers seemed uncharacteristically quiet. How come?" Godesmith remarked.

"The moment, Jerome, the moment," Beebe added, an edge of exasperation in his voice.

"Oh, yeh," Godesmith mumbled. "I see what you mean."

He didn't, really. On an emotional level, the sight of that devastated locale would have got to anyone, as Auschwitz had impacted Heinrich Himmler the first and only time he visited the camp. But that was as far as it went with him.

"Auschwitz, yes!" he commented.

"What was that?" another man, named Tompkins, asked, not hearing what Godesmith had just mentioned.

"Oh, I was thinking about how they turned Auschwitz into a tourist attraction of sorts. I wonder if something like that would work here."

None of the men cared to respond to Godesmith. The pilot, a thin, hawk-faced Saudi, grunted loudly.

The country had been liberated by Allied forces less than two months earlier. Nothing had been done to the area below the helicopter as yet except to clear away some bodies where feasible.

But it wasn't possible to continue doing this or anything else for very long because the ground had been severely weakened, and heavy vehicles could never safely approach the village or the oil wells.

Odors drifted up to the helicopters from the ground, the odors of decay, laced with sulfur and, even now, something akin to that of charcoal still burning a bit.

"The ground's still hot in places," the shortest, youngest man in the back seat remarked. "It may take months to cool down enough for *anyone* to be able to get into the village."

The village was a mosaic of the blackened husks of primitive buildings.

"What's that?" Godesmith asked, noticing a bright color amidst the lunar-like landscape.

The pilot swung the helicopter down lower.

The tangerine colored hood of a once-new car poked up through the debris.

"Funny . . . ," Godesmith remarked.

"Yeh, Jerome," Neustadt, the youngest man, added without conviction.

236

They could see other objects: washing machines; television sets; embroidered silk curtains, pieces of which had magically survived.

"They hardly had electricity here," the pilot added, speaking flawless English. "What were they doing with TVs?"

"Waiting for the day," Godesmith said, chuckling. "They could brag to friends and relatives in other countries that they owned fifty-inch projection sets. Never mind that they couldn't turn them on because there was no power!"

Something had caught the rays of the sun, sparkling forth red, green, crystalline colors.

"Get as close as you can," Godesmith told the pilot.

The helicopter soon hovered above a single human hand sticking out from a pile of rubble, the flesh nearly gone, but the rings on the fingers and the several bracelets on the wrist remaining.

"She tried to grab as much as she could," Neustadt observed.

"Well, it shows that nobody's got close," Godesmith added. "You can bet that stuff wouldn't still be there if that were the case."

"Robbing the dead?" Neustadt asked, shocked.

"So what else is new, my virginal friend?"

The young man blushed, and kept quiet.

"That's where the faults begin," the pilot told them, "at least it's what I have heard."

"There?" Godesmith said, suddenly excited. "Exactly there?"

"So it seems, sir."

The helicopter had approached the large pile of rocks that hid the entrance to the underground network of tunnels.

"The faults start under those very rocks and spread just a bit to the left but mostly to the right, under the village, and beyond," the pilot elaborated. "The main body of rebel forces was camped many miles away from here, but the resulting quakes still did significant enough damage, weakening them enough to make the Allied advance a piece of cake."

"How ironic!" Godesmith exclaimed.

"Enlighten us, Jerome," Tompkins remarked.

Godesmith told them the story of the place where evil began its march . . .

"But the tunnels themselves lead in the opposite direction, right?" Tompkins asked.

"Absolutely right."

"Where?"

"Over there."

He asked the pilot to swing around toward the distant peaks.

"Why there?" Beebe inquired.

"Well, according to a legend or two, that's where the Garden of Eden was located, dear buddy."

The three fell into silence.

"That got to you, didn't it? Well, I was hoping it would. Because now we're going to—"

The helicopter veered in a direction that gave them a full view of the three metal crosses.

At precisely that angle, at that time in the afternoon, the crosses reflected the overhead sun.

"*Dear Jesus!*" Neustadt said prayerfully.

The effect was nearly blinding, and they had to look away.

The pilot guided the helicopter to a side view.

Three crosses stood on a ledge of volcanic rock that extended out from a mountain range that traversed four countries and could have been millions of years old.

"Can we land anywhere nearby?" Godesmith asked, even he subdued by that sight.

"I think so," the pilot replied, "but we'll have to be very careful."

The desert had been badly ravaged by the holocaust, huge craters opening up in the solid floor that existed below the soil-turned-sand after countless centuries of drought, great masses of it having poured into each crater since the explosions that had ignited the underlying deposits of oil.

"I can't chance going anywhere but the ledge itself," the pilot said after a few minutes. "It's long, as you can see, and wide enough for us to land."

Five minutes later, they were standing in front of the crosses, the pilot joining them.

"My people did this, didn't they?" he asked, gazing at the long-dead bodies of Stuart Brickley and Derek Sparrowhawk.

"Not your countrymen, certainly," Godesmith told him.

"Muslims, though, fellow Muslims?"

"Yes, I have to say yes, al-Amiri."

He fell to his knees, and bowed his head, muttering a traditional prayer from the *Qur'ān*, then looked up at them.

"It no longer helps," he acknowledged. "It's supposed to drive away evil, evil thoughts, evil—"

Neustadt bent down beside him, placed his hand on the pilot's shoulder.

"That prayer comes from Muhammad," he said. "It is therefore taken from a source evil in itself."

"Don't, Neustadt!" Godesmith interjected. "Don't insult this man's faith."

Neustadt gulped a couple of times, and started to stand.

"No, no," al-Amiri told him, "it is right what you say. My people mocked a great prophet by killing these men in the way that He Himself died."

*These men . . .*

Two of the bodies still hanging from the crosses!

"We'd better be going," Godesmith said, but no one was listening, the four others all on their knees despite the stench from the bodies, despite the horror of whatever was left of them.

"Let's go now," he repeated, more firmly. "We need to be—"

Neustadt jumped to his feet.

"Doesn't this have any impact upon you, any at all?" he said, nose-to-nose with Godesmith. "Can't you stop thinking about products and . . . and—?"

"Yes! Yes! I can!" Godesmith growled. "I have emotions, too. I will experience nightmares for weeks from this. But we came here to survey what it all looked like and—"

"To see how you can exploit even this," Neustadt replied sadly, his voice lower. "To generate yet another profitable product, no matter how tragic the circumstances."

He waved his hand toward the rotting figures behind him.

"Got any ideas about *them?*" he said, his voice rising again. "Why don't you come out with three miniature crosses? Make them of the same kind of metal from which these three were fashioned. Leave the figures off—that would be too horrible, of course, even you would agree that this was the case. Oh, yeh, maybe you could come up with a catchy ad line that goes something like—"

He saw Godesmith's expression, no offense in it, no anger.

"Your face is as red as a beet, Jerry-baby," Neustadt observed. "Why is that, Mr. Showman?"

He saw the other man hesitating, perspiration breaking out on his forehead, and dripping down the sides of his cheeks.

"May God forgive you!" Neustadt said. "I guessed right, didn't I? You do intend to make something of this?"

The others gathered next to the younger man, staring at Godesmith, waiting for him to respond.

"This is a story of sacrifice," Godesmith finally said. "Everyone who buys a set of the crosses will learn what happened here because packaged with the product will be a little pamphlet detailing everything. It will encourage them to face whatever may be ahead in their lives."

"The product, Jerry, the product, of course," Neustadt retorted. "Listen to yourself. You've become capable of justifying anything. Do you think that's why the Lord enabled you to escape unharmed while *they* ended up *that* way?"

"Look," Godesmith protested, "we came here to see if there is any truth to what we've been hearing. Isn't that more important than any bickering between us? Commercialism aside, think of what it would mean to the Christian world to discover that the stories are true."

The other men looked at one another.

. . . *the stories are true.*

240

And what wonderful stories those indeed were, tales of the Garden of Eden being found, and fully in bloom after so many, many centuries!

"Can you deny that you're fascinated?" Godesmith persisted, realizing that he had hit a weak spot in their defiance. "And why now? After all these years? There have been other reports over the rest of this century and earlier about a dried-up, withered old place that could have been Eden, but there was never any substantiation. Long-dead gardens are a dime-a-dozen in the field of archaeology, you know that!"

He pointed to the helicopter.

"Let's fly around just a bit longer," he said. "Let's at least see if we can find any clues. What do you say?"

The others weren't pleased that Godesmith had a point, but they were honest enough to admit that he did, he did indeed.

"OK," Neustadt replied. "OK. We're here. We might as well see what happens."

"Good!" Godesmith told him. "Let's go."

"Not yet," al-Amiri spoke up.

They all turned to him.

"Forgive me for this but . . . but, to Muslims everywhere, as to the Romans, this kind of death is shameful. It is only criminals of the worst sort who are subjected to . . . to—"

"You don't suggest that we take them down and bury them, do you?" Godesmith remarked. "It's disgusting enough to look at what's become of their bodies, let alone take them down and—"

His face mirrored the emotions of the others.

"But don't you see why it *has* to be done?" al-Amiri went on. "Those factions in Islam who feel exactly like the men who murdered these two will go on pointing to those bodies as symbols . . . symbols, think of it . . . symbols of how each and every infidel should be treated, a direct and ugly rebuke to everything that your religion stands for. Only one Figure should be venerated by such an image. None should be subjected to ridicule or held up as inspiration for more of the same. Don't you see that? Don't *any* of you see that?"

None of them could talk for a few moments.

Neustadt finally walked over to al-Amiri.

"You speak almost as a Christian, my friend," he said, his voice kindly.

"Perhaps I am now closer than you may realize," the other man told him.

Neustadt turned to Jerome Godesmith.

"Are you ready?" he asked. "We are."

After burying the bodies of Derek Sparrowhawk and Stuart Brickley, they climbed into the helicopter and flew over that local section of the mountain range but could see nothing.

"Perhaps it's hidden," Godesmith suggested. "Perhaps it can't be seen from the air."

"Wait a minute," al-Amiri interrupted. "Look at that narrow pass down there."

They could just barely see what he was referring, to but once they did, the other men guessed what he had in mind.

"Let's see where it leads, right?" Neustadt asked.

"It leads nowhere, it leads somewhere," al-Amiri said. "We have—how do you say?—a fifty-fifty chance."

"Agreed!" Godesmith added. "Down we go."

The helicopter landed as close to the opening of the pass as possible, and then the five entered it, looking up in awe at the height of the sides of the mountain through which it cut.

A bird singing.

"There's life of some kind here," Godesmith observed rather obviously.

"I smell flowers," Neustadt said, breathing in deeply.

Ahead the pass widened considerably.

"Color! Look!" al-Amiri exclaimed.

He ran ahead.

"Hey, wait up!" Neustadt said, trying to catch up with him.

The others came along seconds later and stood with al-Amiri and Neustadt in the midst of the most beautiful scene they had ever experienced. No other word could there be to describe what it was like to be surrounded by a garden that made the most exotic greenhouse seem anemic in comparison.

"Praise God!" Neustadt said over and over, the scents filling his nostrils, the sights overwhelming his vision.

They decided, in unspoken agreement, to split up on their own, and explore the garden, each of them discovering a new wonder for himself, whether a large pond of the clearest, purest water in memory, which contained speckled koi, plump and healthy . . . or glorious hanging plants with blooms that shamed any tropical orchid . . . or a large plumed bird that showed no fear as it landed on someone's shoulder . . . or other encounters with vibrant living things all gathered together within the confines of that remarkable and unspoiled place . . . while directly outside the garden, in the world beyond, there were only the twisted, skeletal reminders of the destruction of which sinful humankind was capable.

Godesmith stumbled upon a cave at the opposite end from where they had entered.

"Oh, my!" he said though there was no one nearby to hear.

He found a cross. And a red robe. A spear. And a crown of—

"It cannot be," Godesmith said in wonderment as he held the twisted thorns in his hand. "How can it be after so long?"

There were other items, and he looked at each one in astonishment until he came to the hand-tooled silver goblet.

"The chalice!" he exclaimed. "This is the—"

He found a small leather-bounded book, written in Arabic. He wished he had studied more of that language while he attended a Bible college in the Midwest. But, even so, he managed to pick out just enough to realize that what he was holding was Wise One's diary.

Godesmith read through several of the passages. One of these quoted part of a verse of Scripture dealing with angels appearing in human form, and then went on to add:

*So many scoff at anything like the carnal appearance*
*of angels, especially in this so-called modern era. Even*
*among some of the evangelical churches in America and*
*elsewhere, there is a tendency to discard the idea. They say*
*it belongs to that crowd which dwells on the spectacular.*
 *But it does not, of course, . . .*
 *To think that the ethereal creations of Almighty God*
*can leave heaven and garb themselves temporarily in human*
*form, that they can know, for a moment, what mankind*
*was meant to be before Adam and Eve succumbed to the*
*temptation of Eden, that human beings were created to be a*
*blending of both flesh and blood and radiant spirit,*
*unspoiled by sin or disease or age, immortality with a body*
*that would never wear out because there was no way for it to*
*wear out, through sickness or anything else . . .*

And then Godesmith came to a passage that dealt with
what he had found in the cavern itself.

 *I have brought these objects here so that none could*
 *be used for the wrong purposes by any man. I pray that*
 *they will remain hidden from those who would seek to make*
 *commerce of them.*

Godesmith started to sweat.

 *They should not be destroyed, but they also should not be*
 *exploited . . .*

Feeling more and more uncomfortable, Godesmith
flipped through other pages until he came to the most revela-
tory portion of all.
 *And just before the rapture the garden will—*
He dropped the little volume upon reading the final part
of that sentence, missing the middle of it because of not being
able to translate the words.
 *. . . and the redeemed shall be caught up with Him in the—*
He bent down, picked up the book, and rushed back to
the cave's entrance, and outside into the wondrous garden.
 "Neustadt!" he yelled. "Tompkins . . . Beebe . . . al-
Amiri. Here! Look at what I found. Hurry!"
 No one came.

244

*I can't picture myself hanging on a cross.*
*That takes a special sort of man, Fahid,*
*and I just don't qualify.*
Derek Sparrowhawk, Journalist

Moody Press, a ministry of the Moody Bible Institute,
is designed for education, evangelization, and edification.
If we may assist you in knowing more about Christ
and the Christian life, please write us without obligation:
Moody Press, c/o MLM, Chicago, Illinois 60610.